FALLING FOR HER

Seasons in a Small Town
What Are Friends For? (Spring)
The Right Brother (Summer)
Falling for Her (Autumn)
Warm Front (Winter)

More romance by Patricia McLinn

The Wedding Series
Prelude to a Wedding
Wedding Party
Grady's Wedding
The Runaway Bride
The Christmas Princess
Hoops (prequel to The Surprise Princess)
The Surprise Princess
Not a Family Man (prequel to The Forgotten Prince)
The Forgotten Prince

Marry Me Series
Wedding of the Century
The Unexpected Wedding Guest
A Most Unlikely Wedding
Baby Blues and Wedding Bells

Wyoming Wildflowers Series
Wyoming Wildflowers: The Beginning (prequel)
Almost a Bride
Match Made in Wyoming
My Heart Remembers
A New World (prequel to Jack's Heart)
Jack's Heart
Rodeo Nights (prequel to Where Love Lives)
Where Love Lives
A Cowboy Wedding

Bardville, Wyoming Series
A Stranger in the Family
A Stranger to Love
The Rancher Meets His Match

FALLING FOR HER

Seasons in a Small Town
Book 3 (Autumn)

Patricia McLinn

Dear Readers: If you encounter typos or errors in this book, please send them to me at Patricia@patriciamclinn.com. Even with many layers of editing, mistakes can slip through, alas. But, together, we can eradicate the nasty nuisances. Thank you!
— Patricia McLinn

Dedication

For PVW, a friend like no "other"

CHAPTER ONE

"A WOMAN'S BEDROOM is the window to her soul."

Since women's bedrooms were not something Josh Kincannon let himself dwell on these days, he tried to ignore that statement from the man following him up this narrow stairway.

As a high school principal and single father of three, Josh was, as he ruefully reminded himself, essentially celibate back into misty memory and forward into the foreseeable future.

"It's a sitting room!" Mrs. Richards called from the foot of the stairs. "Don't you say I sent you to that young lady's bedroom, Malcolm Cottle. That's the sitting room. With a place to sit while you wait for her."

"We see it, Mrs. Richards. Thank you." Josh eyed a spindly-legged settee tucked under the attic room's sloping roof, and opted to stand for however long they had to wait for Vanessa Irish.

Needing to wait for her was a surprise.

He'd had the Chief Financial Officer of Zeke-Tech pegged as obsessively prompt. Especially for this first face-to-face meeting, which she'd set, here in the rooms she was renting while she was in town.

Add another notch on his Wrong About Women belt.

At least this one was minor.

Huffing after the steep climb, Malcolm called "Beg pardon" down the stairwell toward Mrs. Richards, then resumed his topic. "I read a study on the subject this past Wednesday. Or was it Tuesday?"

A study on women's bedrooms as windows to their souls? That stretched the limits of even Malcolm's odd studies.

"The study shows," Malcolm pursued, "that by observing an individual's bedroom, strangers more accurately assessed the individual than long-time associates did. Indeed, assessments by strangers—based solely on a brief observation of what was in plain sight in a bedroom—were more accurate than self-assessments. Truly, a study you would find invaluable."

Right.

Invaluable.

For all the women's bedrooms he encountered these days.

"I'm sure you'll be more comfortable in Miss Irish's sitting room," came Mrs. Richards' voice again, "what with everything in an uproar down here from the painting."

"We're fine, Mrs. Richards." A half step brought Josh to a dormer window overlooking the Drago River.

He needed to block out Malcolm, Mrs. R, and thoughts of women's bedrooms. He needed to focus on the coming meeting.

"Wednesday. Definitely Wednesday," Malcolm said from behind him. "It reminded me that Wednesday's child is loving and giving, which made me think of Zeke, in light of Darcie and the computer lab."

Loving and giving. Wouldn't Zeke-Tech's founder love that?

Darcie—Zeke's fiancée and a Drago cop—would tease, while Zeke would become as tongue-tied as he'd been when Josh tried to thank him for providing the site and funds to set up a community computer lab.

Considering all he was doing, Zeke's insistence that Zeke-Tech be represented on the project in the person of Chief Financial Officer Vanessa Irish had seemed inconsequential.

Until Josh tried working with the woman.

"…provide an uncannily accurate window into the subject's openness to experience, extroversion, emotional stability, conscientiousness, and agreeableness," Malcolm droned on.

After three months of phone calls and emails, Josh didn't need to see Ms. Irish's bedroom for a view through *that* window.

Conscientious? Oh, yeah.

Intelligent? Absolutely.

Agreeable? Not so much.

Not disagreeable, exactly. More like businesslike on steroids.

"Ah, and *here* is that very window to Ms. Irish's soul," said Malcolm.

Josh turned. Drago High School's senior guidance counselor was peering past a partially open door to the next room.

"Very interesting," Malcolm murmured.

Crossing to the door, Josh reached past the older man for the handle. Which presented him with a view of the entire room he could only miss by closing his eyes.

He didn't.

One dormer held an upholstered chair backed by a lamp, another a desk. A dresser and double bed completed the decor. But if Malcolm's study was right, they were a view into Mrs. R's soul.

On the other hand, the laptop computer precisely centered on the desk and not another personal possession in sight reflected Vanessa Irish's.

As Josh started to swing the door closed a beat slower than he should have, a flash of color pulled his head around to a swirl of blues and greens so rich and vibrant they left peacocks in the dust.

A robe.

Draped from the corner of the open bathroom door.

Josh Kincannon—high school principal, single father of three, and thus essentially celibate back into misty memory and forward into the foreseeable future—swallowed hard.

Celibacy suddenly didn't seem the least bit funny.

The robe wasn't filmy or see-through and, unless Vanessa Irish was seven feet tall, it would cover her from neck to toes. And yet—

"Josh. Your phone."

Malcolm's voice brought Josh to the abrupt realization that he'd stopped in mid-door-closing, staring at the robe, oblivious to his phone ringing.

"Mr. Kincannon," came the crisp voice when he answered. "I

scheduled our meeting for three-forty-five."

He yanked the doorknob, slicing his view into the bedroom in half, and turned his back on it for good measure.

"Yes, we did, Ms. Irish." Damn. Was she trying to back out? "If you're delayed, Mr. Cottle and I can wait for you here."

There was a slight pause. "Wait where?"

"At Mrs. Richards'." Without any input from his brain, his head turned back toward the robe. "In your rooms."

"My rooms."

The hairs on the back of Josh's neck came to full alert.

It was his personal early warning system and it came in very handy for tuning in to students' emotional issues rumbling under the surface. It also helped greatly in deciphering all the nuances of a teenager's "yeah," from guilt to ecstasy to uncertainty to grief.

But this…

Vanessa Irish's words conveyed no emotion at all. Yet those hairs were at full attention.

Odd.

"Yes." Carefully, he added, "Your sitting room at Mrs. Richards'."

"You were to come to the lab site. I'm there now."

He pulled out a crumpled pink "while you were out" note student aides still used because letting the kids on the school computer system was not happening.

The note clearly said 3:45 p.m., Mrs. Richards' house. On the other hand, the message-taker had been a sophomore girl he'd found sobbing over a boy who hadn't said hello.

"We'll be there in five minutes, Ms. Irish."

He ended the call, hustled Malcolm out—ignoring his and Mrs. Richards' questions—and reached the computer lab site in four minutes flat.

Not waiting for Malcolm, Josh jogged up concrete steps fronting a row of mostly boarded up storefronts and into what had once been the shoe-repair shop run by Zeke's late father.

A figure at the back of the long, narrow main room turned to face him.

Vanessa Irish.

The woman he'd failed to get a reading on during these three months.

The woman he needed to work with so this project happened fast and right for Drago.

The woman who wore that peacock's robe when she was alone in her room at night.

"Less than five minutes," she said, absolutely neutral.

She wore a suit the color of tree bark. Glasses hooked into the high neckline of a matching blouse. She had her hair up, smooth and contained.

If she had any peacock in her, every feather was carefully hidden.

Although even this boxy suit couldn't completely mask rich curves.

"Mr. Kincannon—" she started.

"Call me Josh." He extended his hand and smiled.

Some women connected with only their fingers. Not her. Her handshake was palm-to-palm and full wrap-around fingers. As businesslike as her voice.

He introduced Malcolm as the man who would organize programs at the lab once it was built.

"The contractor should be here shortly," she said. "Two Zeke-Tech employees are also coming,"

She hadn't invited him to call her Vanessa, hadn't unbent at all. No matter. He'd make this work.

He had to so the computer lab would meet Drago's deep and varied needs.

As for the hairs at the back of his neck indicating Vanessa Irish was hiding something—something he'd glimpsed in a robe, heard in a subtle tone—that was irrelevant.

Though it sure was interesting…

MORE THAN AN hour after the local contractor and Zeke-Tech's electrical and IT experts joined them, Vanessa adjusted her glasses and acknowledged that Josh Kincannon made her uncomfortable.

Recognizing and fully acknowledging her reactions to people was necessary, according to her executive coach.

He made her very uncomfortable.

She quelled a useless longing for her former state of complete unawareness of such matters.

Josh.

What kind of name was that for a high school principal? High school principals were Mr. Castro, Mrs. Albertson. Or Mr. Schmidt.

Not *Call-me-Josh.* And not—definitely not—accompanied by a smile rippling lines up his cheeks and revealing a triangle of white teeth.

Yet that couldn't be why he made her uncomfortable. She'd gotten over the nonsense of attractive men making her uncomfortable a long, long time ago.

He'd been in her rooms.

No. Absurd. That space at Mrs. Richards' house was no more hers than a hotel room was.

She straightened.

Recognizing and acknowledging was all well and good, but she had a job to do. She checked her list. "Next is accommodation for wiring."

"Looks good," said Larry, a Zeke-Tech IT representative she often worked with. He gave the local contractor an approving nod. "It's got one-hundred percent more space for the big pipe and the radius turns look good."

She fought the urge to cut them short as he, the electrical expert, and the contractor talked trench, conduit, and coaxial cabling. Larry had answered in his first two words. If she didn't trust his assessment, he wouldn't be here.

But her coach emphasized letting people expand beyond yes or no.

As inefficient as that was, employees did seem happier when she followed the practice.

To this point, Zeke-Tech's primary responsibility for the lab had been writing checks. Now that the local contractor had replaced doors and windows, added sprinkler, air conditioning, and heating systems, and created a bathroom from a storage area, the next step was melding space and technology.

She'd lined up these experts. They needed to be on-site. She didn't.

Except Zeke wanted her here, saying she needed a change of scenery. She'd told him she couldn't afford any distraction with the end of their fiscal year approaching. Zeke hadn't budged.

She swallowed a sigh. And encountered Josh Kincannon's gaze.

That was why he made her uncomfortable.

He kept looking at her.

Not brief, polite glances. Not the bored, uninterested looks of a certain class of male. But long, searching surveys. Like she was a puzzle.

"What about wall space for a blackboard?" the high school guidance counselor asked.

"No. Chalk dust and computers don't mix. A whiteboard. It will double as a screen for an overhead projector." Vanessa added that to her list.

Looking up she met Josh Kincannon's gaze again. She held it, lifting one eyebrow.

He didn't look away, instead returning her look with a shifting of his mouth she couldn't immediately translate.

"Excellent," the counselor said. "An overhead projector will be useful."

"That brings up how we'll control natural light." Josh gestured toward the original storefront window and a glass-topped door that together occupied nearly the entire front width.

"Remove the glass and make it a solid wall. Replace the door," she instructed the contractor.

"And block all that great natural light?" Josh objected. "Then— what? Put in fluorescent?"

His mouth shifted again.

A smile, maybe.

"Natural light causes screen glare," she said.

"Any light can cause glare," Larry said.

"Artificial light's easier to control," she said.

"Natural light's better. And—" Josh's eyes glinted with what might have been amusement or challenge or something else entirely. People's emotions were so … imprecise. "—it's free."

Larry coughed, the other Zeke-Tech employee shuffled his feet, and the guidance counselor cleared his throat.

Yes, she had brought them back to costs several times in this discussion. That was her job.

"I've been thinking about the entry," the contractor said. "You don't want the door opening directly into where the computers are because of temperature regulation."

"Good point," Larry said.

"And interrupting classes," the counselor added.

"I could build a wall, about here." The contractor gestured to a spot away from the door. "That would form an entryway, leave room for a desk for signups or business stuff without interrupting folks working on computers in the main area, like Malcolm said."

"Great idea, Todd," Josh said. "What about making the wall solid partway up, then the top part from glass blocks to let light in, but filter it."

The contractor nodded. "Sure."

"We'd have to check angles, but it could diffuse the light enough to leave very little glare," Larry added.

After a few minutes of their pacing off distances, discussing angles, and predicting effects of glass block at various levels, Vanessa said, "Fine. You—" She nodded at Larry, then the contractor. "—explore this, pull together comparative cost figures, and report back to me by—"

"And me," Josh inserted easily.

"—Tuesday," she concluded.

If the cost wasn't more than her solution, fine. And if Josh wanted an update, fine. She had the final authority.

Her mind zeroed in on another aspect. "There need to be privacy partitions between the stations. Cubicles, with a door to access each."

The five men—contractor, tech expert, electrical expert, guidance counselor, and principal—turned and looked at her. After half a dozen seconds, only Josh kept looking.

"Cubicles? Why?" he asked.

"For privacy when a user is at his or her computer."

"For classes everybody needs to see the instructor. And besides," he added, "who wants to be cut off from everybody else in a little cubicle?"

"Anyone who's sane." Vanessa couldn't believe she'd said that aloud.

But Josh smiled, quick and bright. "Nah. Everyone'll want it open, so people can kibbutz."

She saw two things: He thought she'd been kidding and he believed what he'd said.

Before she absorbed either observation, movement caught her attention. Three small figures stood outside the old storefront, the larger two with hands cupped to the window, the smallest pressing its entire face against it.

Josh released a low groan. "Excuse me." The next instant he was out the door. The three figures moved to him, the smallest hurtling itself at his legs.

"Josh's kids," the contractor murmured, and exchanged a look with the counselor, who said, "Josh has full custody. Nothing comes before his kids."

Admirable in theory. But her responsibility was to Zeke-Tech, and the two Zeke-Techers had a flight out of Chicago to catch.

"We have a tight schedule, and more to cover," she said.

More looks zipped around.

The counselor nodded at the contractor then walked to the door, holding a low-voiced conversation with Josh.

With the door open, she saw the smallest child as a genderless blob masked by an oversized jersey and dirt from the window smeared over its face. It had one hand wrapped around Josh's leg and the opposite thumb in its mouth.

The middle child, a boy, was thin and wore glasses, peering inside with curiosity.

The tallest, a girl, stared directly at Vanessa with the intensity of her father but without any of his apparent inclination toward amusement.

Detaching the smallest from his leg with a smile, Josh moved to the door while the counselor stepped out. Before the door closed, Josh said, "Be good, and I'll see you at dinner."

He remained watching as the children and the older man headed off. At last he returned to the group.

"Child-care emergency," he said. "Malcolm's pinch-hitting. Now, back to the spacing. Folks need room to put papers and books. And sometimes they'll want to use a computer together…"

The others picked up the discussion.

Uneasily, Vanessa recognized a deepening of an odd impression she'd had since arriving this morning.

If forced to define it, she'd say something was closing in on her. Which made no sense. Drago, Illinois sat in the middle of cornfields, with nothing but space around.

She straightened her shoulders and weighed into the discussion.

The sooner she wrapped up this project, the sooner she left Drago and returned to her office.

"THIS WILL BE great," Josh Kincannon said.

It was after six, and they were the only two left. For the past half-hour, they had thrashed out adjustments to a schedule that allowed just three months before the lab's scheduled opening in early December.

"The general contractor has done an admirable job," she said.

"Todd's more of an all-around guy. Did most of the work himself."

He slowly turned around the empty shell coated in construction dust. Then he faced her, as if expecting something.

"It's going to be great," he repeated.

His mouth slowly widened. His lips parted, revealing that triangle of straight, white teeth. Lines echoed up his cheeks like … like ripples in a pond overjoyed to have a rock thrown into it. His eyes, shining, narrowed slightly as his cheeks rose.

He was grinning.

At her.

With delight.

She couldn't begin to think of a response. But he didn't seem to need one. He began another circuit of the space, this one with a wider radius.

She'd had people smile at her, of course she had.

From polite to placating to pleased to distracted. And, back before she knew better, lasciviously. She'd also had people laugh around her, sometimes at her, occasionally with her.

But she counted the number of men who had grinned at her in delight on two fingers—Zeke Zeekowsky and Peter Quincy, the third original member of Zeke-Tech.

And their delight generally stemmed from her work, especially her ability to figure out how to make dimes stretch into dollars.

"This is what this town has sorely needed." Josh looked over his shoulder at her, then, slowly, turned the rest of his body without taking his eyes off her. "Don't get me wrong. Zeke moving a division of Zeke-Tech here is fantastic. It'll bring people and business in like Drago's never seen. But that's from the outside. This—this will let people pick up skills to help themselves. You know the saying about feeding people is nice, but teaching them to fish means they can eat forever. This will let the people of Drago fish. It will give them skills to stay here and still earn a good living."

She shook her head. "No. It will give them the skills they need to leave."

His grin died.

CHAPTER TWO

Vanessa began the next day, as she began every day, at her computer.

She frowned.

Not at the screen, which conveyed that all was as it should be in the financial world of Zeke-Tech, but at the window beyond it. The window was distracting.

Mrs. Richards had made such a point of what a perfect spot the desk would be for Vanessa to work that she'd felt obligated to put—and leave—the laptop there.

Since Vanessa's arrival yesterday, the landlady had repeated numerous times that if she needed anything to just call.

She hadn't called.

Yet the woman, who appeared to have some unsteadiness walking, had climbed the stairs—twice—to check that everything was in place.

It left Vanessa feeling as if her clothes were rubbing against her skin.

That made no sense. She hadn't worn clothes tight enough to produce that reaction for years.

Then there'd been dinner last night at the café with Zeke and his fiancée, Darcie Barrett.

"We're so glad you're here," each of them had said. More than once. Vanessa didn't share the sentiment, but, remembering Cathie's counsel, she had kept that to herself.

Even when Zeke and Darcie planned for future dinners.

"To get you acquainted with Drago," Darcie had said, as if offering a treat. Then she'd added, "We can start with Josh."

That was the closest Vanessa had come to voicing her objections. Not only did Josh Kincannon make her uncomfortable, but by the time they'd parted yesterday it appeared the feeling was mutual.

She didn't know why the light in his eyes disappeared when she'd said the computer lab would improve residents' opportunity to leave, but it had. Without needing to consult Cathie, she doubted that contributed to a good working relationship.

Movement outside caught Vanessa's eye. She peered over the top of her glasses and saw a flash of water between scattered tree trunks. Must be the Drago River she'd seen on the map.

Her focus sharpened. Some of the trees' leaves had a reddish cast and others were bright yellow.

Huh. Had the leaves in Virginia been changing when she left yesterday?

Her desk at Zeke-Tech faced away from the window and she kept the blinds closed to avoid glare. If she was out of the building during daylight, she had other things on her mind than leaves.

"Vanessa? Vanessa, dear?"

In the first fraction of a second she was thrown back, back to the last time she'd been called *dear.*

She caught herself.

This was Mrs. Richards, tapping on the open door to the bedroom.

"Todd left an envelope for you," she said, entering. "I'm so sorry I can't cook you a real breakfast with Marky painting the kitchen and everything at sixes and sevens. But I have a little something to tide you over—oatmeal and bananas. Real homemade oatmeal Anne Hooper grows out at Hooper Farm."

Vanessa ordinarily skipped breakfast. But the past twenty hours had taught her that going along with Mrs. Richards required less time than resisting. Under the same theory, she did not ask who Todd was.

"Thank you, Mrs. Richards." She spotted the business return address on the envelope. Ah, Todd was the contractor. "I'll be down in ten minutes."

Her landlady didn't leave.

"I wasn't at all sure about having anyone stay here with Marky painting and such, but Zeke—such a nice young man—said you wouldn't mind. And the kitchen truly needed freshening up."

The older woman detailed all the kitchen improvements ahead, and how they would be followed by new paint for the rest of the first floor.

Thinking her landlady had finished, Vanessa slid a nail under the flap of the large envelope. Likely the schedule she'd requested yesterday, though why he hadn't emailed it—

"That must be to do with the computer place Todd's building." Mrs. Richards nodded toward the envelope.

"The computer lab."

"Did you know that's where Zeke's father had his shoe repair store?" Before Vanessa could say yes, the woman continued, "What a fine man Mischar Zeekowsky was. He died when Zeke was a senior in high school, you know. I expect that's why Zeke didn't come back for all these years—too painful after his father's death. Such a shame Mischar's not here to see how well his boy is doing."

Vanessa lowered the envelope. "Zeke's accomplished a great deal with Zeke-Tech."

"Oh, yes, the business." Mrs. Richards dismissed a top tech company with half a shrug. "But I meant Zeke and Darcie. Mischar would be so happy to see his boy happy. And pleased at Zeke bringing jobs here, and this computer lab. So you and Josh are working together on the computer lab."

Vanessa blinked at the shift, and raised the envelope again. "Mr. Kincannon is providing local input on the project."

"Mr. Kincannon? So formal. Josh is such a nice young man." That seemed to be Mrs. Richards' standard praise. "Poor soul hasn't had the easiest time of it. Three children to raise, and all alone."

Vanessa said nothing, which generally kept Zeke-Tech employees' conversations to a minimum.

Not Mrs. Richards'.

"His wife up and left two years ago. Melissa Kincannon never was content. Always saying she had ambitions. Like other folks don't. One day, with Josh at work and the kids at school and day care, she packed up and took off. No warning. Didn't tell Josh, didn't tell those babies. All she left was a note. Hasn't been back since."

She shook her head. "Melissa barely sends her children birthday and Christmas cards. Only contact with Josh has been through lawyers getting divorced and giving him custody. Well, it's not as if he hadn't been doing most of the raising already. But still. Some said good riddance, but no matter what, it's hard on those babies. And Josh … he certainly has his hands full."

Vanessa remained silent. The older woman sighed.

"Well, I'll let you read whatever's in that envelope. I need to have a word with Marky about the trim. Come have your breakfast soon."

Vanessa shifted her shoulders, aware she'd sat motionless for a full minute after Mrs. Richards left, her mind uncharacteristically blank.

She moved her shoulders a second time and it turned into a little shiver.

Ignoring that, she opened the envelope and began reading.

"MR. KINCANNON."

Uh-oh.

He didn't know Vanessa Irish well, but that tone couldn't be good.

This is what he got for bringing the kids into town to patronize Drago's shops. If he'd gone to the discount stores off the Interstate, his Saturday errands couldn't be interrupted by being accosted on Main Street by tech CFOs who managed to look both coolly distant and irritated.

And yet … at the sight of her, his bloodstream kicked up, like a gas pedal being tapped.

Had to be his memory of that robe.

It sure wasn't the unsmiling expression he faced now.

He shifted Livvy to one side so he had a hand free to stop Topher from crossing the street without them. As usual, his son had been so lost in his own world he was unaware the rest of them had stopped.

Xena needed no such direction. She was assessing Vanessa from head to toe.

"Mr. Kincannon, I would like to speak to you."

He'd admit that her certainty yesterday about Drago's citizens viewing the computer lab the way prison inmates would the key to the main gate had got his goat. That didn't mean he intended to let her keep it.

"Hi, Vanessa. Nice morning, isn't it?" Nothing like friendliness to throw off someone who expected a tussle. He'd learned that his first year teaching. "I'd like you to meet my kids. This is Xena, Topher, and Livvy. Kids, this is Ms. Irish. She works with Zeke, and we're working together on the computer lab."

Xena and Topher said dutiful hellos.

Vanessa froze an instant. "Hello," she said stiffly. "Xena. Tougher. Libby."

"To-fer," Xena corrected. "It's from the end of Christopher. And it's Livvy. Short for Olivia."

"My kids don't stick with the names they're born with," Josh said. "Xena's birth certificate says Alexis."

"Priblonny!" Livvy proclaimed, beaming at Vanessa.

The woman's expression didn't change, but he saw confusion in her eyes, swirling like the colors on her robe.

"I beg your pardon?" Vanessa said to his smiling youngest.

"Priblonny," Livvy said.

"I'm sorry, will you repeat—?"

"Xena, how about taking Livvy down to the corner to look in Warinke's window." Josh swung his youngest from his hip to the sidewalk.

"It's a hardware store," Xena complained.

"I'll be there in a minute."

He had interrupted, not because Livvy's failure to communicate would upset her, but because many adults, in an effort to show concern, fussed so much that *that* upset her.

Xena took Livvy by the hand. Topher trailed after, not quite connected to the girls.

Josh turned to find Vanessa watching him with that expressionless expression that gave him nothing to grab onto. Maybe he'd fooled himself about swirls in her eyes. Maybe the robe meant nothing. Maybe she was as humorless and buttoned-down and number-numbed as she appeared.

"You're probably curious, but thanks for not saying anything in front of the kids."

"Saying anything about what?"

"About Livvy's talking—not talking."

Her brows dipped. "She talked," she contradicted him.

"Sounds. Not talking. No need to be polite. At her age she should be speaking in complete sentences—paragraphs, even. She's been tested—God knows she's been tested." He ran a hand down the back of his head. "Every expert says the same thing. Her brain's fine, her understanding's fine, her ability to speak's fine. For whatever reason, she's decided not to communicate."

Vanessa's gaze went to the three children standing in front of the hardware store.

"I wasn't being polite. I'm generally told I'm too blunt," she said, almost absent-mindedly. "She does communicate."

It took a second to recognize the import of those last three words.

She had a point—part of a point.

"Yeah, she conveys emotions and desires. What she doesn't do is speak English. The experts say she hasn't formed a specific language of her own. They're nonsense syllables."

Vanessa's *huh* was an acknowledgment of his words, yet richly edged with doubt. "She spoke as if the syllables have meaning to her."

He nodded. "Not everyone gets that. Her intonation and cadence indicate Livvy's speaking complete thoughts as much as any child her age. Sentences. Questions. Exclamations. It's like someone's typing sentences and paragraphs, but with their fingers a couple letters off on the keyboard. The structure and rhythm are there, but the words aren't."

Why on earth was he pouring this out to her?

"She has the structure, she comprehends, and responds to what you're saying, so she understands the language." She was matter of fact. "The probability, then, is that she's decided not to use it."

"Decided? I don't think that's—"

"I went a year without speaking."

To this point his attention had been divided between his kids and her. Now he swung around to face Vanessa squarely.

"Why on earth did you do that?"

He shouldn't have phrased his surprise so directly.

Especially not when he was staring at her.

This woman didn't like to be the focus of attention. He'd concluded that after mulling her reactions yesterday. She went into possum-playing-dead mode, as if bland clothes and no eye contact made her disappear, leaving only a CFO's numbers, like the Cheshire Cat and his smile.

If someone looked at her directly and let her know it hadn't worked, it threw her for a loop.

But after saying that she didn't speak for a year, he wasn't about to have her withdraw into silence now.

"Please. Tell me," he said. "You might help me understand Livvy."

Her tension eased by a tenth. "It won't help."

He waited.

"I was older," she added at last, clearly reluctant. "I knew how to talk, I chose not to."

"Maybe Livvy can talk, but decided not to, too. If I knew why you made that choice, maybe I can figure out if she has. Then I could fix it."

She flipped one hand in dismissal. "I didn't have anything to say."

And that was all she'd say now. He got that message loud and clear.

With her face impassive, she edged past him.

He made the mistake of drawing in a breath. He'd thought it would ease the urge to pin her to the wall until she told him everything about a year of silence. Instead, it pulled in some essence of her that didn't ease a thing.

Abruptly, he asked, "What did you want to talk to me about, Vanessa?"

She stilled for half a beat.

Didn't matter. He had a pretty clear idea of what was going on behind the façade. She'd lost sight of her goal, distracted by Livvy's situation. That lapse surprised her—the line of her mouth thinned—and displeased her. But it didn't slow her long.

"You told the contractor—uh, *Todd*—" Producing the name seemed to represent a victory to her. He'd noticed yesterday she hadn't called Todd by name, yet knew what he'd been paid, down to the thirty-six cents after the decimal point. "—not to factor construction of cubicles into his schedule."

"Right."

"Your interference means the schedule he gave me this morning is useless for establishing a delivery timeline for furniture and equipment as well as training instructors or—"

"Dad!" Xena called. "You have to be at the high school in an hour and we still have to go to the grocery store."

"Okay. Just a minute." He told Vanessa, "The schedule's fine. Nobody wants cubicles. Why would you think they'd want to be shut up that way?"

"Why would you think they'd want no privacy?"

"Because I know the people who'll use the lab."

"I know computer users."

"In general, sure. But most of the folks using the lab won't be your kind of computer user. They won't be doing programming or spread-sheets or building websites. Not at first, and maybe not ever. Some folks have had basic computer training but new technology has run right past them. Some have never had any. They'll need a lot of instruction."

"Classes, certainly. But—"

"Not only formal classes. They'll want to lean over to a friend at the next terminal and ask which button to push without making a big deal of it."

"Training material will be available in each cubicle."

He shook his head. She didn't get that building the lab would be a great success if it drew people together—from planning to building to using it. She didn't get that operating the lab would be a failure if it locked users into isolation.

He checked the kids again. Livvy was restless. Topher had wandered two storefronts down, and if they didn't corral him soon he'd be blocks away before he came out of his haze.

Josh didn't have time, standing here on Main Street, to explain his town. Especially since the chances she'd accept his word were slim and none.

"Look, instead of us arguing, how about if we call a meeting of potential users and get their input."

"Organizing a meeting that would draw sufficient attendance under the time constraints—"

"Will be a breeze. As long as we don't go up against bingo night. Xena! What's on for tomorrow, say six o'clock? Am I free?"

"Repairs at the Congregational Church. Better make it seven-thirty."

"Oh, right. Okay, seven-thirty. At… The lab's too rough and my house is too small. Let's say the Congregational Church basement. They'll already have coffee and food set up for the repair crew. It'll be easy."

"But your church might not—"

"It's not my church. We rotate fixing up all the churches. So, unless you hear from me, we'll see you tomorrow at seven-thirty. Ask Mrs. Richards where the Congregational Church is."

"If residents don't have computers, you can't email them. To reach enough—"

"Don't worry. Everyone will know."

And everyone would show up, he thought as he said good-bye, retrieved his meandering son, and headed for the grocery store—

damn, barely fifty minutes until kickoff.

Everyone would show up because they wanted to see the important newcomer in town, Ms. Vanessa Irish.

And wouldn't she just hate that.

CHAPTER THREE

"You're early."

Vanessa was fairly certain Josh Kincannon's tone meant he was pleased. But why?

"I wanted to be sure to find the church," she said.

That was partly true. The other part was to offset his advantage of familiarity with the setting.

He chuckled and shifted the little girl he held. His younger daughter. She saw the older girl talking with a woman at a doorway. The son sat twisted around in a plush chair, bending his knee to put a sneaker-clad foot on the seat, his cheek to the back's upholstery, a book tucked in the cave created by his body.

"If you'd come a little earlier you could have followed the sound of swearing. We were repairing rotted-out window sills and for a while there we hit more thumbs than nails." He wore battered jeans and a paint-spattered shirt, but his hands appeared freshly scrubbed.

"I hope no one was seriously hurt," she said.

"Nah. All appendages accounted for."

The little girl—Livvy, short for Olivia, she remembered—appeared half asleep, and utterly relaxed as she hung over his one arm in fear-defying trust that her father's hold would withstand gravity.

Vanessa looked away from the child's limp abandon. "Where should I set up?"

The walls were masked by children's drawings. Old couches and easy chairs formed roughly concentric circles. Tables stood along a wall, with huge coffee urns at either end and a scattering of plates with brownies, cookies, and cupcakes. In the middle, one tray held fried chicken and another stacks of sandwich halves.

"Set up?"

"My presentation." She hefted her laptop. "If you point out the screen I'll know where to set up."

"Uh, sorry, no screen. I wasn't planning on presentations." He looked around and gestured. "Maybe the chalkboard?"

"Mr. Kincannon?" A teenage girl materialized at his side. "Can I talk to you?"

"Sure, Fay. Do you know Ms. Irish? Vanessa, this is Fay O'Hearn."

They exchanged hellos. Initially the girl with the wavy brown hair had appeared driven by urgency. Now she hesitated.

"I'll..." Vanessa tipped her head toward the chalkboard.

"No! I mean, please." Fay O'Hearn wore jeans and a sweater, had on little makeup, and what might have been worry clouded her brown eyes. "What I want to ask about has to do with you, with both of you."

"The computer lab," Vanessa said. No one in this town could have any other reason to talk to her.

"Yes. I want—I mean, you'll need people to work there, right?" She hurried on, "I don't know much about computers, but I can do a lot of other things. Answer phones, keep track of appointments."

"A receptionist position hasn't been discussed."

"I'll run errands or clean or—or anything."

Switching his daughter's weight, Josh rested a hand on the girl's shoulder. "Fay, we don't know if we'll have positions like that. If we do, it'll be December at the earliest. Besides, you're babysitting."

"I need a real job, Mr. Kincannon. The new jobs in town are going to adults. I know they've been out of work, but... No place is hiring kids."

"Things okay living with your aunt and uncle?"

"They're great. I couldn't ask for—" She swallowed. "I ... I just need a job."

"I know Al was out of work a long time—if your aunt is sick or it's the mortgage...?"

She shook her head. "Uncle Al's back at work and that's okay. But

I need a job—a full-time job."

Josh's mouth thinned, but in a breath he had his reaction—displeasure?—mastered. "You don't want to let your grades slip."

"I know." It faded almost to a whisper.

Josh shifted his daughter again. "I can give you some hours babysitting, spelling Mrs. Mudge, but you have to promise we'll talk about this—"

"Thank you, Mr. Kincannon. I'll take every hour you can give me. And in December—" She looked to Vanessa then back to Josh. "—you'd consider hiring me at the computer lab?"

"Sure," he promised easily. "But first we have to get the thing built. And everybody's here, so let's get started."

Vanessa looked around at the filled chairs and couches.

She'd never set up.

HE HAD TO give Vanessa Irish credit. She rolled with the punches.

After more than two hours of discussion, Josh flopped into the chair beside hers and reconsidered that thought.

No, Zeke-Tech's CFO was not a roll-with-the-punches type.

More like she took her lumps and refused to go down.

"Okay, so we're agreed," she said, sitting upright and alert. "We'll meet tomorrow after we've each gone over what we gathered tonight."

They were alone, everyone else having finally left.

It had been quite a turnout. Even more than he'd expected, with a number of surprises, including his neighbor and babysitter, Mrs. Mudge, and her best friend, Mrs. Richards.

For the past several years, with a freeze on hiring at the schools, there hadn't been new teachers to rent Mrs. R's attic and supplement her income. Josh had heard Zeke persuaded the widow to take Vanessa's rent in advance, to pay for badly needed maintenance. The income also meant her friends wouldn't worry this winter about Mrs. Richards' heat being turned off.

But he had to wonder how she and her tenant were fairing.

No doubt he'd hear all about that from Mrs. Mudge.

She'd taken the kids home to put them to bed, though he expected Xena would wait up for him as usual.

He shifted and winced where a two-by-four dropped by two fellow workers had hit his shoulder. He not only felt like he'd been run over by a Mack truck, but the truck had been outfitted with tire chains.

"Yeah, we're agreed," he said. "But only because I'm too tired to battle with you tonight. Let me get some sleep first."

She almost smiled. That was a victory, wasn't it?

"You know very well that the attendees backed your position, as you knew they would."

He suspected her equanimity over everyone favoring an open plan stemmed from pragmatism.

"True. If only they'd agreed in fewer words."

Another hint of a smile. She pulled out her phone. "I have a five o'clock flight out of O'Hare, so it will have to be morning or early afternoon. We'll meet at the lab site. Not, uh, anywhere else."

In other words, not her rooms.

"It'll have to be somewhere else." He'd deliberately yanked her chain. Possibly dangerous, but he did it anyway.

She stiffened. "Mr. Kincannon, I do not hold meetings where I'm staying, and certainly not … well, where I'm staying."

"Sorry about that mix-up Friday. As for going up to your sitting room, you don't know Mrs. R. if you think we had a choice. Theoretically, I could have insisted Malcolm and I camp out in her front parlor, which was the only spot on the first floor not crammed with stuff from the kitchen. But I've been told nobody's been in that parlor since Mr. Richards died some forty years ago, and you're braver than I am if you would have suggested it. Besides, it was interesting." He saw the warning signals not to venture there. He did anyway. "You're very neat."

"Mr. Kincannon—"

"But tomorrow, we'll have to meet at the high school. The vice principal's on maternity leave so I need to be on site."

"At the café during your lunch hour."

He shook his head. "I eat in the cafeteria. Keeps up morale. For the cafeteria workers, I mean. Seeing me deal with the ravening hordes, too."

Not even close to a smile, although some of the stiffness in her spine eased. "Very well. Ten-forty-five at the high school."

"Great." He gave directions to the school, and his office once inside.

As if it had been waiting for them to settle that matter, another wave of weariness washed over him. He liked to think he was pretty darned good at keeping all the plates in his life spinning. But nights like this, it felt like one more plate would bring the whole thing crashing down.

He dropped his head so the top edge of the chair's back pressed against the tightness at the base of his skull. It was almost as good as a neck rub. Almost. "Sometimes people are a pain in the butt," he muttered.

"Most times." Her agreement was quick and crisp. "Numbers are much easier. They're—" She searched for a word. "Reliable. They don't lie."

His comment had stemmed from momentary overload.

Hers seemed to flow from something deeper.

He tugged at the conversational thread. "Numbers can be fudged."

"Not by people who are honest."

"So, you're back to dealing with people."

"That's the problem."

He rolled his head on the chair again. "You don't mean that. You're a natural."

"Anything but," she said in her usual measured response. Then a run of words followed. "You must get tired of taking care of everybody else."

He looked up, surprised. "That's my job."

Her mouth tightened—from disapproval, to hold in words she didn't want to let loose, or both?

"And I like it. Because that's what community is about," he added. "Individuals helping other individuals."

"Community is the antithesis of individuals."

"Community's a bunch of individuals cooperating," he shot back. "The individuals have to decide they want to be part of it before there can be a community. It's all up to the individuals."

"Not always."

The edge to those two words sounded personal. Like a glimpse of that robe showing up in her otherwise tailored-suits conversation.

Before he could dig deeper, she said, "Look at this program. You've said your goal is to keep people here, instead of giving them the skills to let them go where they want."

"Whoa. It's not like I'm chaining people to Drago against their will."

"What about that girl?"

"Fay? She's a kid, and she's not looking to get out of town."

"A desire to leave this town is the reasonable explanation for her adamant desire for money."

"Not necessarily," he said. "But, yeah, if Fay wanted to leave, I'd do my best to keep her here and in school full-time, certainly until she's old enough to make reasoned choices."

"Chronological age doesn't necessarily bestow good decision-making."

"Something we agree on." He grinned.

She looked wary.

Not the response he'd been going for.

"Anyway," he picked up, "about the computer lab—I hope it does keep people here. But believe me, I know you can't make someone stay when they don't want to." Her gaze sharpened, and it was his turn to slide past the moment. "The idea is to give people who want to stay a chance to do that. To have the choice. The individual choice."

"If you believe in individual choice you won't try to sway that girl."

He angled his head to see her better.

She turned away far enough so he couldn't see her expression.

That irked him.

"So you see everything in black and white? No, wait, not black and white. Plus and minus. Everything has to go on one side or other of the ledger—plus or minus."

It came out harsher than he would have liked. Certainly sharper than he would have allowed himself to be with staff or a student or his kids. That was the problem with being tired, things got under your skin, and then you said things. Things that might be true, but didn't need to be said.

But Vanessa Irish didn't shrink from his accusation. Instead, she turned toward him, her expression calm, certain.

"That's my job," she said.

VANESSA ENTERED DRAGO High School through an institutional entry the same the world over.

Two sets of mostly glass doors with a buffer of space between, and ribbed rubber underfoot.

Beyond the doors came a tunnel of tiled floors and ceilings with gray locker-lined walls on either side, occasionally punctuated by recessed doors, presumably leading to classrooms.

Not identical, yet similar enough to spark the memory.

Standing alone in a long-ago corridor. Excited. Frightened. Lost. Hopeful.

Completely ignorant of the world she was entering with only one tool. Intelligent ignorance, Mr. Schmidt had called it. "We whittle away at the ignorance and what we have left is intelligence."

Closing off the memory, she turned left into a slightly wider corridor.

Two-thirds of the way down its length, she glimpsed a stairway on one side and a glass wall on the other. Josh pushed open a door by the glass wall and raised a hand in greeting.

At that moment, a shrill sound burst over her head. Almost simultaneously, doors banged open all around her. Flashfloods of teenagers swept out, sending her first this way, then the other. Eddies of them—talking as fast and loud as possible—swirled her around until she didn't know which way to go, even if she'd had the strength to swim against their cross-currents.

"—Then she told me that he said that she said that she likes Jason—"

"—I toldya there'd be a quiz—"

"—Like I'd really wear what my mother bought when—"

"—so I got stuck with Dondrik for my project partner—"

"After practice I'm working at the dealership. How 'bout tomorrow?—"

"—she's so totally hot—"

"—every answer. Why's he even in school if he's so smart? What a geek!"

"Told you he was weird. Like he's from another planet or—"

"—new song? They must say the f-word a hundred times."

Amid the raucous voices and physical turmoil of their hurrying bodies, Vanessa felt her old self grabbing onto her, pulling her. Down. Down. Down to where she couldn't breathe.

A hand wrapped around her arm.

"Pretty wild, huh, Vanessa?"

She forced herself to see the man in front of her. Josh was smiling, yet concern narrowed his eyes, intensified their focus on her.

"These hordes would send Genghis Khan running. But don't worry, they're not really dangerous."

She should reclaim her arm from him, but she wasn't sure she wouldn't slip back under if she did. "I'm fine."

"Sure you are," he said cheerfully.

He guided her toward the glass wall as the flood thinned. But, along with thinning, the flood sped up with urgency.

"No running in the hall, Brian!" Josh commanded.

"I'll be late," protested a young voice.

"You'll be later if you fall and you'll be dead if you bleed on Mr. Studivant's clean floor."

Several voices chuckled.

The bell rang again. A brief surge of dismay rose, then only hurrying feet and closing doors, until silence reclaimed the academic tunnels.

They stood alone, his hand still around her arm.

"Want to get some air outside or a soft drink or——?"

"I'm fine." She would be. One more deep breath. "It makes no sense to delay our meeting. Neither of us has time to waste."

"In that case, here we are." He pushed open a door in the middle of the glass wall with his free hand.

She used the motion of going in to detach her arm from his hold.

THE MAYHEM THAT descended on Drago High School between periods jolted any sane adult.

Vanessa had looked more than jolted.

Not only had she known exactly what was happening, Josh decided as he settled at his desk and let her open the discussion in her brisk manner, but she'd felt it constituted an express trip to her personal hell.

Interesting.

Not his first reaction, of course.

No, his first reaction had in no way resembled the emotional equivalent of his current posture—rocked back in his chair with his hands linked behind his head. His first reaction had been to plow through the maelstrom of kids to get to her.

Not exactly coming to the aid of a damsel in distress, but, yeah, his first reaction had been to rescue her.

Which he'd be sure to tell her next time he wanted her to freeze up.

Only after she packed away a vulnerability that held as many colors and patterns swirling through it as that robe of hers, did his me-Tarzan-you-Jane protective instincts recede and *interesting* emerge.

Why had being caught in the hallway thrown her for such a loop? And what did it have to do with a woman who tried to pretend she was all numbers and just-the-facts-Mister when, in private, she wore a robe of many colors?

"Although the townspeople who attended the meeting last night indicated their preference for an open plan," she was saying, "my experience with computer users persuades me that is not the right format."

Hoo boy, he better be careful about letting contemplation of her robe make him forget her status as a tough-minded CFO, or he'd have a terrific computer lab that was all wrong for Drago.

"You heard what they said—"

"Yes, however, people who attend such a meeting are those most predisposed to an open plan. The non-attendees are most likely to be those who prefer privacy."

And then they really started wrangling.

THE DAYS BACK in her office at Zeke-Tech headquarters had been a welcomed return to routine.

Now, driving from the urban intensity of O'Hare airport toward Drago, Vanessa again had an impression of things closing in on her.

She deliberately looked out in each direction, seeing only horizon-sweeping expanses of cornfields. She kept that image firmly in mind as she drove in to town.

Nothing closing in.

Space. Lots of space.

The moment she swung the rental car's door open, Mrs. Richards was there. "You're back at last."

Mrs. Richards hurried Vanessa toward the kitchen, barely giving her time to release the handle of her roll-aboard suitcase at the bottom of the stairs.

Darcie Barrett called out, "Finally! We've been waiting and waiting for you."

From the threshold, Vanessa blinked at Zeke's fiancée, who sat at Mrs. Richards' kitchen table with Jennifer Truesdale.

She'd met Jennifer, a high school classmate of Darcie and Zeke's, and her significant other, Trent Stenner, the night before she'd left Drago. That dinner had been surprisingly pleasant. Largely because Jennifer and Trent were easy-going. Perhaps also because Josh had not attended.

"Why have you been waiting for me?" she asked the two women.

Darcie sidestepped the question. "We've been admiring Mrs. Richards' kitchen, but now that you're here, we're ready to go."

"Go where?"

"You'll see. We're kidnapping you for a Sunday afternoon off."

"I have work—"

"No work!" Darcie commanded. "It's a gorgeous day and we won't get many this warm again until next summer."

"I have reports to read and—"

"No use arguing, Vanessa," advised Jennifer in her husky voice. "Not when Darcie's in her forceful law enforcement mode."

"I'll play the Zeke card if I have to, Vanessa. Get him to order you not to work."

"And did I mention she can be ruthless?" Jennifer murmured.

CHAPTER FOUR

"**T**HIS IS WHERE you're taking me?" They had pulled into a parking space under big trees.

"Yup," Darcie announced. "Come on, we're getting out."

"Lilac Commons," Jennifer filled in.

"But lilacs bloom in the spring. That's when your festival is." Vanessa regretted the words immediately. As if Darcie and Jennifer didn't know lilacs bloomed in the spring. As if they didn't know the timing of the festival that had drawn Zeke back to his hometown last spring.

"True. But it's a park all year round. C'mon."

Darcie, carrying a square white box in both hands, led the way up a path under arching tree branches, while Jennifer, who slung a blanket over one arm and hooked a six-pack of water with the other, waved Vanessa ahead.

They stopped on a gentle slope with a view of a fountain splashing in front of a grass-covered raised platform. Vanessa helped Jennifer spread the blanket in dappled sunlight under a tree mixing green with yellow, orange, and red. Darcie placed the box in the middle of the blanket, and flipped it open with a flourish.

"Have a seat, Vanessa. And take your pick," she invited.

The box held pastries—doughnuts, small tarts, Danish, and more she couldn't identify amid their ruffs of white bakery paper.

"No, thank you. I had lunch on the—"

"Forget lunch. That's mere nutrition. This is sanity in an insane world."

"Besides," added Jennifer, "you're our guest. We can't have any until you do, and I'm salivating so much the park will flood if you don't pick one fast."

Vanessa smiled, and reached into the box for a raspberry-topped tart. Jennifer took what looked like pecan pie in bar form. Darcie selected a Danish with lots of icing. For a moment the only sounds were *Mmms*.

Then Darcie announced: "I have run away from home."

The ominous words were at variance with Darcie's tone, both women's expressions, and certainly with the gusto with which they were eating their pastries. But surely they called for some response. "You and Zeke—?"

"Oh, no," Darcie said easily. "It's not Zeke. It's my mother."

"And Zeke's mom," added Jennifer.

"They are non-stop wedding machines, and I needed an afternoon off. This time it was ribbons for the bouquets. I didn't even know bouquets had ribbons. When they asked what color I wanted, I said white, figuring that would be easy. This morning, they show up with enough white ribbon to wrap the entire county three times over. I called Jennifer for reinforcement."

"Without mentioning what the *emergency* was," Jennifer told Vanessa.

"I'm not stupid. You wouldn't have come," Darcie said. "I told them to pick whatever they wanted."

"Yeah, that went over well."

Darcie rolled her eyes, and said to Vanessa: "They kept saying it's my wedding and they don't want to intrude or—heaven forbid—take over. When they went upstairs to settle whether my dress is ivory, cream, antique white, or plain old white, I got Corine—she's the police dispatcher—to call and pretend I was needed at the station. I grabbed Jennifer on the way out, and we decided to come get you, because we all deserve an afternoon off. This—" Darcie's eyes closed as she licked a drip of red filling, having moved on to a doughnut. "—is worth every extra mile I'll have to run."

Vanessa nodded. She should have said something—keeping a

conversation going was one of the points Cathie emphasized—but she couldn't think of a thing.

"It's sinful," Jennifer agreed.

"Right." Darcie rolled her eyes and gave Vanessa a conspirator's look. "This from the one who doesn't run and never gains weight."

Jennifer sighed. "That could change. The waist of my pants are tighter lately."

Darcie nodded, with an expression probably meant to look wise.

It made Vanessa want to giggle. She never giggled.

"Because you and Trent are together, huh? Because you're off the worry-to-death diet?" Darcie said.

"You make it sound like he's some knight in shining armor who rescued me. I can take care of myself—and of Ashley."

Ashley, that was Jennifer's daughter. Vanessa was sure of that.

There'd been something else about Jennifer. Something Mrs. Richards had said—

"I know, I know," Darcie said. "Okay, how about because you've got Stenner Autos on firm financial ground."

"Not firm. Better, but nowhere near firm."

"Firm's a sliding scale," Vanessa said.

Jennifer turned to her. "Exactly. When I left real estate and started with the dealership, a regular paycheck was marvelous. When Stenner Autos opened and money came in instead of only going out, it was nirvana. Then we had a week when we actually made a *profit*... Now, I want more."

"With Zeke-Tech, one of our milestones was Zeke, Quince, and me having enough money to buy fast food after living on noodles for months. A burger has never tasted so good."

Darcie chuckled, but Jennifer's eyes widened. "Really? I knew in theory you must have struggled, but I never considered how much."

"I'm not complaining. I knew what I was getting into when Zeke recruited me."

"It sounded less like a complaint and more like you missing the bad old days," Darcie said.

Vanessa considered. "Not missing them. That would deny all the company has done. It's—"

"Including all *you've* done," Darcie interposed.

"—more remembering how simple things were. The more successful a company becomes the less you see all the moving parts that make it come alive, and the more factors you weigh with each decision."

Jennifer sighed. "Don't tell me this. Here I've been thinking you have the perfect job, and now you make it sound all too much like raising a teenager."

Vanessa had no idea what raising a teenager entailed, but if it was anything like the growing pains Zeke-Tech had gone through, she felt for the other woman.

Darcie asked Jennifer, "How *is* Ashley doing?"

That was it. Mrs. Richards had said Ashley was in a car accident at the start of the school year.

There had been more to it, judging by the time her landlady had devoted to the topic.

Now Vanessa wished she hadn't tuned out the details.

Jennifer lifted her shoulder. "She's making progress, but it feels like two steps forward, one step back, and about seven steps sideways."

"Her injuries are healing?" Vanessa offered tentatively.

"Oh, yes, physically she's doing great. Thank you. It's the growing up part where it gets complicated."

"Are you letting her come to the final fitting of the dresses?" Darcie asked, then added as an aside to Vanessa, "Jennifer's my matron of honor, and Ashley's fashion mad, but she's under restrictions."

"I don't know. I'll see how she's doing when the appointment comes up. How are the arrangements? I mean, besides the bouquet ribbon—everything else going smoothly?"

"Nothing would dare not go smoothly with my mother and Mrs. Z doing the planning. I'm thinking of renting them out."

"As wedding planners?" Vanessa ventured.

"As take-over-your-lifers. I'd make a fortune. Retire and be a lady of leisure."

"Right," Jennifer scoffed. "Like they'd do this for anyone other than you and Zeke. And like you'd be a lady of leisure. You're only getting married, consulting with Zeke about Zeke-Tech's move here, renovating your house, and working full-time as a police officer."

"Speaking of renovating the house," Darcie said. "Quince is adamant about leaving when we're ready to move back into the house. So keep your ears open for a place for him in January."

Zeke and Darcie occupied an apartment over the garage while they remodeled Darcie's family home, which Zeke had bought for her last spring.

When Quince was in Drago, he used a bedroom in the house unaffected by renovations.

"Why don't you swap, and have him live in the apartment?"

"That's exactly what I said, Jen. Zeke'll make it his home office eventually, but we can delay that while there's this housing crunch in town. Quince says he's too smart to stand between Zeke and his office ever again. But he won't explain and Zeke just looks blank."

The women turned to Vanessa, with *Do you know?* clear in their faces.

"When we started out, we lived and worked in one room. A delivery of equipment came the same day Quince received a box of his clothes. Zeke unpacked the equipment, saw this other box didn't have equipment in it, and threw it out with the empties."

Darcie chuckled. "That's my one-track-mind guy."

Vanessa had never before told anyone that story. When she talked to people outside the company it was about facts, figures, projections. Come to think of it, that's what she talked to people inside the company about, too.

But these were friends—of Zeke's, she meant. More than friends, in the case of Darcie.

Even though she didn't share the connections, it was surprisingly pleasant sharing the memories.

"Quince wore a sign on his back for days that said 'I am not garbage. Do not throw me out.'"

Both women chuckled.

"He gave up when Zeke asked what on earth the sign was about—he was so lost in his next breakthrough he'd already forgotten."

Now they were laughing, and she joined in.

"That is so Zeke!" Darcie said.

Vanessa stopped laughing first. She had an idea. "Quince could have my room at Mrs. Richards'. He needs to be in Drago more than I do and—"

Darcie and Jennifer laughed harder.

"Sorry, sorry, Vanessa," Jennifer said after a bit. "It's the idea of Quince living at Mrs. Richards' house."

"Men hardly cross the threshold, much less live there," Darcie added. "It took Josh and me talking for weeks to persuade her it would be perfectly proper for Marky to paint inside her house, even if no one else was around."

"But then why did she send Josh up to my rooms? I mean, Mrs. Richards' rooms." Vanessa faltered, then added, "To wait when he mistook our meeting place. With Mr. Cottle."

She was acutely aware of Jennifer's searching look.

"Two men?" Darcie said. "And Marky painting the kitchen? She probably couldn't face three men all on the same floor—needed to spread out the testosterone. And if there's one thing Quince has plenty of, it's testosterone. No, she's much more comfortable with the wide-eyed young student teachers she used to rent to, or better yet the veteran schoolmarmish types. She loves them."

"Besides," Jennifer said quickly, as if afraid Vanessa would take offense by applying Darcie's final comment to her. "Where would you stay?"

"Darcie can persuade Zeke that I can look out for Zeke-Tech's interests sufficiently from Virginia."

"Why would I do that? We all want you here."

"Some believe the project can run smoothly without me here."

"How *are* you getting along with Josh?" Darcie asked.

Jennifer rolled her eyes. "Tactful, as always."

Ignoring that, Darcie looked at Vanessa, awaiting an answer.

"We have different approaches and priorities," she said carefully.

Darcie nodded. "Makes you a strong team. And—"

"Hey, there are the guys," Jennifer said. She stood, called out, and waved. Coming across the grass were Zeke, Josh, Quince, and Trent.

Josh said something that made the others laugh, and Vanessa's gaze naturally went to him.

He walked with relaxed assurance. Sun glinting on his hair highlighted that it was even more disordered than usual. He wore jeans—the pair he'd worn to repair the church unless he had an assortment of jeans worn to faded softness—and an orange t-shirt with a growling bear on it.

They were close now. His gaze was on her, and he was smiling.

She looked away, taking in the others. They all wore jeans and t-shirts bearing signs of ill-usage, they all were wind-rumpled and smiling. She had noticed Josh only because she'd seen him first.

Amid general hellos, Quince gave Darcie a casual salute. "Reporting in, ma'am. Zeke has breathed fresh air as ordered."

"Thanks, Quince. He'd breathe only computer fumes if I let him." Zeke dropped onto the blanket as she spoke, his arm going across her back and his lips touching her hair. Darcie leaned into him. "What were you guys doing in all that fresh air?"

"Playing touch football," Trent said.

He shifted a football to under his left elbow. Vanessa knew from Mrs. Richards that he coached the high school football team, while Jennifer ran the auto dealership Trent had bought earlier in the year. With his right arm free, he hooked it around Jennifer. They came together as easily, as rightly, as Zeke and Darcie.

"You were?" Darcie looked at Zeke.

He grinned, something Vanessa wasn't quite used to, though no one else appeared to consider it unusual.

"Yeah, I'm surprised, too," he told his fiancée as he took a brownie from the box. Darcie gestured for the others to help themselves. "Though they didn't let me get the ball much."

"Me, either," said Quince. He and Josh bent for their pastry, then remained standing. "It was Josh and Zeke against Trent and me, so each team had a jock and a geek."

"You're not a bona fide geek," Zeke scoffed. "You're too good an athlete to be a true geek. You're one of those nerd wanna-bes."

"Hey, you've got surprisingly good hands, Zeke," said Josh, taking a bite from a chocolate-covered doughnut with sprinkles.

"Surprising for a nerd, you mean?" Zeke smiled.

"You made a great catch to tie the game."

Josh finished the doughnut on his third bite. A sprinkle caught at the corner of his mouth, as if it wanted to stick around that grin longer.

Zeke said, "I stuck my hands up in surrender because Quince was whacking the heck out of me in this so-called touch football game, and the ball dropped into them. Nobody was more stunned than I was."

But also pleased, Vanessa realized.

That surprised her—that catching a ball pleased Zeke and that she recognized it.

"We could play touch football at Zeke's bachelor party," Quince said.

Darcie glared. "I will not have my bridegroom pulverized the week before the wedding. I have plans for that body. Any bruises, and you'll answer to me."

"Yeah," said Trent, "and if Darcie doesn't get us, Mrs. Z. will."

"And Mrs. Barrett," added Jennifer. "You should have heard them."

As Jennifer and Darcie recounted the tale of the bouquet ribbons, with detours to the bridal party's attire, Vanessa's mind followed a different track.

In the years working with Zeke she'd come to know the rhythm of his creativity, the meanings behind his silences, and when to demand his attention. Yet in these few moments, he'd surprised her, and not just once.

Had he been changed by coming back to his hometown last spring, by restoring ties—especially with Darcie? Or had Zeke displayed similar reactions and emotions all along and she'd never before noticed?

"What are you thinking about so deeply, Vanessa?" Quince asked.

She looked up to find everyone watching her, though they kept talking.

"Security," she blurted out. "Security needs for the computer lab."

The other voices silenced.

She knew why. They had been on a social plane, as Cathie called it. She'd jerked them back to the professional plane.

The jerk from one plane to the other causes discomfort, Cathie had told her. Like an elevator suddenly lurching.

She knew exactly how that felt, because right now she felt as if the elevator had dropped a dozen floors.

"Good point, Vanessa," Josh said. "We'll have to address that. Though not with the level of security you're used to."

He spoke with his usual ease. For some fraction of a second she wanted to scream at him, at his comfort, his assurance. In the next fraction practicality rose up and grabbed the opening he offered.

"Not the level of security we use for Zeke-Tech, of course," she said, "but there are dangers."

"Yeah," Zeke said. "I have an idea—"

"Not today, you don't," interrupted Quince. "You promised Darcie a whole day of breathing fresh air."

"I can breathe and talk at the same time."

"Not when you're talking Zeke-Tech," Darcie said. "Thank you, Quince. Another second and he'd have whipped out a laptop from under his shirt."

Everyone laughed, and Vanessa took the opportunity to stand. As she did, Zeke tightened his arm around Darcie's shoulders, she leaned back against it, and they looked at each other.

Vanessa had known, of course, how they felt about each other. They were getting married, after all. Besides, she'd seen them together any number of times. Yet, this was different. She could nearly hear a sizzle.

It staggered her, the realness of it. The trueness of it. The power of it.

And the total alienness in her universe.

Yet Zeke was part of her world, so how could it be totally alien?

"I'm glad I only compete with a team of thirty-some teenage boys for Trent's attention," Jennifer said.

Trent objected, followed by more laughing, more teasing, more easy conversation.

"Vanessa? Where are you going?" Zeke asked.

If she hadn't been irked at his calling attention to her withdrawal, she would have marveled that Zeke—*Zeke*—had noticed at all.

"I was just…" She looked over her right shoulder, as if something urgent called her.

"Oh," said Jennifer, "it's in the library. The main door's around the corner, past those tall trees."

Vanessa blinked.

"What's in the library?" Zeke asked.

"Books," muttered Quince, with a faint smile.

"The bathroom, of course," said Darcie.

"Oh," Zeke said. "Why didn't you say so?"

Darcie and Jennifer rolled their eyes, Quince's smile grew, and Josh… Josh frowned as if he knew her departure had nothing to do with the bathroom.

Vanessa muttered a farewell and headed in the direction Jennifer indicated, resisting the urge to run.

"Meet you at the car!" Darcie called.

ROUNDING TREES THAT screened her from those she'd left behind, Vanessa let out a breath and slowed her pace. The path ended at stone steps leading to a patio. A building tucked partly into the hill was to the right—the library, she assumed.

"Hi."

On a bench in the patio sat Xena and Topher Kincannon, each holding a stack of books.

She deduced Topher had greeted her, since Xena was popping him in the arm in apparent reproach.

"Hello." Perhaps perversity prodded Vanessa to walk toward their bench, considering Xena's nose wrinkled in displeasure. Or perhaps it was the tentative smile from the boy, sitting with his knees at the bench's front edge, his feet not reaching the patio.

In the unseasonable warmth, he wore shorts that revealed thin legs. Beyond white socks, his high-top gym shoes appeared so big that dangling there above the ground, it looked as if his feet weighed enough to pull his legs even longer and skinnier, like a cartoon.

"How are you today, Xena and Topher?" She pronounced the name the way Josh's family did.

"Fine," Xena mumbled.

"Good. We were at the library." Topher held up a book that looked thick for a child his size. "We're supposed to meet Dad for a ride home. He was playing touch football."

That last sentence had some meaning Vanessa didn't understand. Subtext, Cathie called it. "He and the other men are talking with Darcie and Jennifer. He should be here before too long."

"Why aren't you with the other grown-ups?" Xena demanded.

Despite Vanessa's bent toward bluntness, she wasn't pathological. She certainly wasn't going to tell this girl why she'd left the group. "They were talking about Darcie's wedding dress, and I'm not interested in clothes."

"You're not?" Topher seemed surprised.

Xena clucked her tongue. Definitely disapproval. "Our mother designs clothes. She's *wildly* talented and she designs clothes in New York City." She named the city with a flourish that stopped just short of *nyah-nyah-nyah-nah-nah-nyah*. Xena looked over Vanessa dismissively. "*She* wears fabulous clothes. All the time. Our mother is beautiful. Everybody says so."

"She'd have to be."

"Why would she have to be?" Topher asked.

Xena turned smug. "Oh, she means because Mom was with Dad. Women are always saying how handsome he is. What a catch he'd be."

"I'm sure they do, but I meant because you both are attractive."

The girl stared. Searching for mockery, perhaps. "No, I'm not."

"Yes, you are."

"You're—" Xena snapped her mouth shut.

The word *stupid* hung in the air. Apparently the girl had been taught saying it was not acceptable. Xena huffed her disgust—possibly at such limiting conventions, more likely at Vanessa—hopped up and stalked off.

Vanessa half expected Topher to follow, but he watched his sister's departure with observant eyes, then turned to her.

"I'm not attractive. I'm a geek," he said solemnly.

An odd tightness below her collarbone gripped Vanessa.

"I'm a geek, too. So is Zeke. Do you know Zeke Zeekowsky? I'm told he was called Zeke the Geek when he was growing up here."

"But he's famous," he said, as if that offset geekiness. The boy's expression turned thoughtful. "Are you ... different? From other people, I mean. Do they tell you you're different?"

"Yes."

He studied her, pushed up his slipping glasses and studied her more, as if he could look through the lenses and right into her, just as his father did. Geek or not, someday this boy would set hearts fluttering.

Hearts fluttering... That tightness was her heart. Not fluttering, but responding to the child nevertheless.

Vanessa quelled a frown. She didn't want Topher to think she was frowning at him.

His survey completed, he nodded. "Dad likes being around people lots. Xena and Livvy, too." She refrained from pointing out his sister had shown no sign of enjoying being around her. "Don't you?"

Vanessa looked at him. And saw ... was that hope?

"It's not that I don't like being around people. Exactly. I don't like the process of getting to know them."

Or the point when they disappointed her or let her know she had disappointed them. With very few exceptions.

"Mrs. Teramori said if I make more effort I might find I like people. She—" He looked at her over the top of his glasses, gauging her reaction. "—wants me to be in a play. Don't tell Dad," he added quickly. "Please."

"I won't."

"He'd want me to say yes, and I don't know…" He sighed. "He gets bummed when I'm not good at sports and things. Football."

So that's what had been behind the way he'd said tag football earlier.

She knew other people would reassure the boy that he was an excellent football player. But she had no idea if he was.

She'd been on the receiving end of similar words—though not about football—and they had only made her more uncomfortable.

"Your teacher must think you'd be good in the play."

He shrugged. "I'd rather read."

"Some people say you should do whatever's hardest for you to do."

Zeke had said that when he'd recruited her. He'd sat across from her and said he couldn't guarantee anything except that she'd be in on building a great company. She'd asked how much autonomy she'd have.

"Rather work alone? Me, too. Quince will handle people mostly, but you'll have to deal with some, plus me, and Quince. But it's good for all of us to do whatever's hardest, because then we get better at things." He'd smiled that rare Zeke smile. "Come on, it'll be great."

Passing up lucrative offers for an iffy start-up, she'd said yes. She, Zeke, and Quince had been unified by a goal. Working toward it they'd come to respect one another.

Last spring, though, Zeke had nearly imploded—potentially taking the company with him—until he'd asked Darcie to marry him.

Yet Vanessa hadn't settled back into her own groove. Zeke-Tech had the capital it needed. She had systems in place. She even had people capable of carrying on without her.

Had Zeke sensed her unsettledness? Was that behind his talk about her needing a break? But how could he have, when she didn't even know—

"Why?"

At the echo of the question that would have completed her thought, Vanessa blinked back to the little boy asking a different question of *why*—why was it good for you to do what was hardest for you?

"Because it makes you grow. It, uh, stretches unused muscles."

"I don't have any muscles." He was absolutely matter-of-fact.

"Not physical muscles. The ones in here." She tapped her head. Then dropped her hand lower and tapped over her heart. "And here."

She considered a second, then dropped her hand lower still, to her belly, "And here. It's about becoming a stronger person. Not physically stronger, but more able to do things. Out in the world."

What on earth was she doing talking to a child about this sort of thing?

His magnified eyes, wise and uncertain looked up at her. "Did you like to read a lot as a kid, too?"

"Yes. But I liked numbers even better."

"I like numbers. But…" He stared at the sky. "Maybe I'll be in that play."

A feeling—no, a sound, even if she was unaware of hearing it— pulled her focus to the steps. Josh was coming down them, his gaze on Topher.

The boy stood, and the oversized black high tops no longer looked so out of proportion to his body. He picked up his books, but paused to look up at Vanessa, a smile so like his father's spreading across his thin face.

"We're kind of friends, aren't we?"

She hesitated. Not enough for him to notice, but enough to feel it in that spot under her collarbone, before she said, "Yes, we are."

He walked away in the direction Xena had gone.

CHAPTER FIVE

Age was relative. Josh Kincannon had recognized that early in his tenure as Drago High School's principal.

Not that it *seemed* relative. It truly was.

Sometimes, dealing with the kids at school, years clicked past like seconds as he aged. Other times, a switch flipped and the process reversed—the kids were keeping him young.

And it wasn't only kids.

Malcolm would be waxing enthusiastic, and Josh would feel as if their birthdates had swapped and he was the one nearing retirement. Then someone—say, Mrs. Mudge—would look over her half-glasses at him, and he could swear he'd slipped back to single digits.

But the certainty that age was relative never came stronger than when he observed his unaware son—as now, with Topher talking so solemnly with Vanessa. In these moments he could almost believe Topher was an ancient who'd gotten into the wrong skin.

Topher had never been voluble, but since his mother left, he'd closed down. Especially when it came to his father.

It worried Josh.

Hell, he worried about all of them, first on general principle, and then about the impact of Melissa's leaving. Livvy's response had been to adopt this non-language language. Xena's had been to become boss of the world. But Topher's lack of response bothered Josh the most. Because a lack of response could indicate a wound so deep it couldn't be bared at all.

What did it say that Topher connected with a woman so unlike his mother? A woman with a calculator for a brain and a business plan for a heart ... and a robe that contradicted both characterizations.

And—Josh's mouth twisted—what did it say that the woman who avoided his company appeared to enjoy talking with his seven-year-old son?

Or was his Wrong-About-Women penchant once more at work in thinking he was the reason she'd skedaddled?

With no answers to those questions, Josh started down the steps.

Simultaneously, Topher and Vanessa looked up. For an instant he saw a similarity there, though they shared no physical resemblance.

He blinked, and that reflex hazed over a momentary insight he'd almost grasped. Another blink and both faces had turned away.

His son stood, gathered his books, exchanged a few more words with Vanessa, then walked away.

"Topher!" Josh called, but the boy was gone. Vanessa also stood. Doggedly, he kept it light, "Don't go on my account."

"I wasn't. I'm going to the car to meet Darcie."

"I'll walk you."

"No need."

"I want to." He took her elbow. "Of course, you could try shaking me off by using the bathroom excuse again. Although twice in such a short time might start rumors of a medical condition, when it's really an apparent aversion to—" She stopped, and with his hand still holding her elbow, he stopped, too. At arm's length, they faced each other. "Never mind. Forget I said anything, Vanessa. Let's—"

She stared at him, the frown deeper, and all the intelligence in her hazel eyes focused on him. "Say what you were thinking."

He felt both amused and nettled. "You want me to be as blunt as you are, huh?"

Her response was clear and certain. "Yes."

"Okay," he said slowly. "We were a fair way to an easier working relationship before you left town, Vanessa. I won't go so far as saying a rapport, but some understanding. And it's clear Darcie and Jennifer are trying to be your friends. Zeke and Quince already are, and Trent's a great guy. But you couldn't get away from us fast enough."

She said nothing, and he couldn't read her expression.

He tried again. "You shut things down when they get too close."

"This is like your saying I see everything in black and white," she said dismissively.

"I corrected myself, remember? To saying that you see life as a series of pluses or minuses. And the negatives, the ones that drive your numbers into the red, oh, how you hate those."

"Of course I do. What sane person doesn't prefer pluses to minuses?"

"Life can't be quantified, Vanessa. It can't be counted up like a column of figures."

"I know that." She said it with a peculiar flatness. She tugged her elbow free of his unresisting hand, and calmly walked toward the parking area.

Only when she was out of sight did he realize how she had turned the topic away from her shutting people out.

ZEKE'S SOLUTION TO security for the computer lab was eighth-grader Warren Wellton.

That didn't surprise Josh. Warren had become Zeke's protégé, thanks to Darcie's machinations last spring.

Darcie had figured out Warren tried to steal important information from Zeke, and put the fear of God into the boy. Then she'd wrangled Zeke into overseeing Warren's restitution work on the police department's computer system. According to Darcie, Zeke remained aloof for two minutes, until he recognized Warren's talent.

Vanessa had set this afternoon's meeting at the lab for two-thirty. Before Josh had gotten out more than two words to suggest a later time, she'd insisted.

He'd shrugged and said it was her call.

Most people who knew him might have been suspicious. Then again, most people would have let him explain.

In their three phone calls since that day at Lilac Commons,

Vanessa's conversational style had barely allowed him to get out complete sentences. As for anything more personal, she might as well wear a neon sign flashing *Do Not Enter.*

It irked him. All their progress toward an easier relationship, gone. Worse than square one, because now he was irritated and she was on guard.

Why?

He got so sick of the question, he swore at it and did punishing workouts with the football team three days in a row. He was stiff as all get-out, forcibly reminded he wasn't a kid anymore, and still that damn word hounded him.

Why?

At first, he'd intended to arrive with Warren and Malcolm, letting her stew while she waited past her two-thirty edict.

He'd reconsidered.

He might have time alone with her. And, apparently, if he wanted to punish Vanessa for high-handedness, inflicting his presence on her was the way to go.

Petty, maybe, but what the heck.

Josh stopped by the computer lab nearly every day. Officially to check in with Todd for any hitches. Really for the punch of pleasure each time he saw progress.

Today, Todd was framing the front entry wall. He nodded at Josh, then tipped his head toward the rear of the building, saying, "They're in back," punctuated with a loud *th-wack* of his nail gun.

They. So, Vanessa wasn't alone.

Beyond the open rear door, in the alley, a young woman he recognized as a Zeke-Tech employee wore an earpiece and appeared to be talking on the phone.

Vanessa looked up from placing notepads and pens around a piece of plywood atop two sawhorses in an area yet to receive much of Todd's attention. Folding chairs surrounded the impromptu conference table.

"As soon as Warren and Mr. Cottle get here we'll start."

As an enthusiastic greeting, it stunk. "Won't be for a while. Malcolm can't drive them here until the middle school lets out at two-forty-five."

"You didn't tell me the school day doesn't end until after two-thirty."

"You didn't let me."

Her frown deepened. "That was wrong of me. I should be open to information from any source."

Here he'd been thinking she'd avoided him, but her apology, along with dropping him into the "any source" category, disabused him of the notion of being that important.

That stung.

He split open the plastic wrapping on a flat of chilled water bottles and began putting them around the table. That brought Vanessa back into his line of sight. She was watching him. When she demanded "What?" he knew she'd been assessing his grimace.

"Just thinking this isn't what you're used to at Zeke-Tech."

"No. But it hasn't been arduous. The contra—Todd insisted on helping set up the table and chairs."

"Good."

"He should have kept working."

"You shouldn't be hauling lumber and chairs," he retorted.

With the water distributed there was nothing left to do. Vanessa took a seat at the head of the table. He sat on her right, leaving a chair between.

Odd how the *th-whacks* from the main room and the woman's voice from outside could leave a silence in between. Vanessa was so carefully not looking at him that his neck muscles strained in sympathy. When she checked her watch the fourth time, he couldn't take any more.

"Have you decided on a present?" he asked.

Her eyes had a protective veneer, but she did look at him. "Present?"

"For Darcie and Zeke's wedding. Did you think I was angling for a present?"

"I have no reason to give you a present."

"Could be my birthday." Yeah, he was baiting her. The adult version of pigtails in the inkwell—if you can't get the reaction you want, go for any reaction.

He wished to hell he'd never seen that damned robe. Then he could just take her at face value and get on with it.

"Even if it were I would not give you a present."

"Is it just me or don't you do birthday presents?"

"I don't do birthday presents." She took off her glasses and began to polish them. "But even if I did, I wouldn't—There would be no reason to—"

"Uh-huh, I get it. No presents for me, regardless. But if you do do wedding presents, we're back to my first question."

"It's taken care of."

"What did you get them?"

"I don't know."

"Then how can it be taken care of?" Her answer sounded illogical, but he'd bet the farm—if he had one—there was faultless logic behind it, and the contradiction tugged at him. As her other contradictions did.

"Janine, my assistant, takes care of that."

"Ah."

"Why do you say it that way?"

"What way?"

"Like a balloon deflating."

He chuckled at the observation. "Maybe I was jealous of you having such an efficient assistant. My office help can't be trusted to take phone messages."

She regarded him with a slightly puzzled but curious expression he'd noted before. Then it was gone.

"I believe that's Warren and Mr. Cottle arriving." She went to the back door and called, "Mavis. We're starting now."

Now proved overly optimistic, but after Malcolm's chit-chat,

Vanessa said to Warren, "I'm told you have suggestions about security."

The boy's peers, some of whom had previously ridiculed Warren's braininess, had been awed when Zeke-Tech licensed a program from him. The attitudes had evened out since the school year started, helped greatly by Zeke and other Zeke-Techers treating Warren with matter-of-fact regard.

"Yes, ma'am." Warren's manners had improved hugely from rubbing shoulders with the Zeke-Tech professionals. "You could use off-the-shelf software to lock down each computer's configuration to prevent students from fooling around with system settings."

"That would prevent hacking?" Malcolm asked.

"Not by someone outside—that's what secure servers, firewalls, passwords, and a few other ideas I have will be for. But I can write a program that'll keep users from wiping the files on the hard drive and installing their own programs. It'll have the configuration locked down, too."

"Make it so spares can be hot-swapped if necessary," Vanessa said.

Josh settled back, jotting phrases he'd ask Warren to explain later.

The meeting broke up when Mavis, who worked in Zeke-Tech's security section, had to leave for the West Coast. Malcolm had promised to get Warren to the police station for a computer tune-up there, so they left on Mavis' heels. Vanessa invited Josh to leave, too—more than once.

He stayed.

He tossed the last empty water bottle into the bag he'd recycle at home, and ventured into the silence. "You dealt with him very well."

Vanessa looked up.

"I mean, for someone not used to kids." He'd gotten that impression when she'd interacted with his three, but basically, he was fishing. Shamelessly.

She made a noncommittal sound and resumed gathering pens.

"So you must be a natural," he said.

"You said that before. You're wrong. I'm not. I take lessons."

"Lessons?"

"In dealing with people. Though nothing regarding children."

He considered her, intrigued by her matter-of-factness as much as the idea of lessons. "Do you like the lessons?"

She looked up again. "Liking isn't the issue. The issue is if they are effective, which depends on Cathie being on-target with what she teaches and me being a satisfactory student."

"Is she and are you?"

"That has not yet been determined."

He wasn't going to let her close off this conversation. "But you're not used to being around kids, right?"

"I didn't say."

How could he simultaneously want to grin and growl. "Have you ever been around kids?"

"Yes."

He raised his brows and looked at her.

She tried to hand him the pens. He kept looking at her.

She put the pens down in front of him. He kept looking at her.

She slid papers into her briefcase, closed it, clasped it, and stood. He kept looking at her.

For one instant he thought she would walk out. And he'd stake a month's worth of hall duty she thought so, too.

Instead, she placed her hands on the table and spoke.

"When I was very young there were other children in the commu—community where I was raised. Although fewer and fewer as I grew up and the—" She barely hesitated this time. "—community struggled."

He never knew a pair of eyes could hold expressions as intricate as the design of that robe. Surprise at herself, wariness, calm, determination, unpleasant memories, a desire to escape, expectation. They all dipped and swirled and re-formed.

"The commune struggled, huh?" he said.

He watched her lips part, and prepared for her to back away.

"Have you heard of many that thrived?"

He forced himself to keep it light. "Can't say that I have. Did you like it?"

A commune.

A community tightly wound within itself.

One that had failed.

Did this explain her expectation that people wanted to get out of Drago?

"You're the first to ask that." She compressed her lips, grabbed the first chair, folded it, and took the next one.

"I'll carry the chairs," he said.

"There's no need, I—"

"I'm carrying the chairs."

She handed over the chair, but didn't look up. Those chairs sure must be complicated because they were absorbing all her attention.

"We need to finalize the security arrangements. I'm leaving the day after tomorrow and I won't return for some time. Not until the wedding."

Now, why did he have the feeling she'd just made that decision to stay away for the better part of a month?

"If I didn't know you, I'd think you were telling me to butt out." He collected the chairs as she folded them, leaning them against his side. "But I know you'd say *butt out* if that's what you meant."

"You don't know me."

The same words Melissa had thrown at him in tearful accusation so unlike Vanessa's flat certainty.

As it turned out, he *hadn't* known Melissa. The proof of that came when she walked out.

And the few women since then? Nope.

So what made him think he *did* know this closed-off woman?

His gut.

And a reaction somewhat south of his gut.

"I know you better than you think." According to Malcolm's study, anyway. "In fact, I might know you better than you know yourself."

She looked up. "That's absurd."

"Did you know strangers who see a subject's bedroom draw more accurate assessments of the person than their friends do? More accurate than the subject himself. Or herself."

He held her gaze. Held it, even as he knew she didn't want it held.

Then she rallied, and snapped the connection like a brittle twig.

"That's absurd." She folded the last chair.

"Neat. Orderly. Contained," he said. "Who wears a robe that looks like a peacock. A swirl of rich color and passion that would take anyone's breath away if she'd unfurl her feathers."

Her breathing had sped up, but he wouldn't have noticed if he hadn't been watching carefully. She masked any other reaction well. "Absurd."

She handed him the last chair, keeping her eyes on it. She walked to her briefcase and picked it up, then she turned to him.

His heart stuttered.

"It's male peacocks who have the colorful feathers. The females are quite drab. Besides, it's just a robe."

JOSH WAS IN no mood to cooperate with Vanessa's let's-get-this-over-with approach.

Two days after that afternoon at the lab when he'd outed her robe, she'd emailed, requesting this meeting at his office.

Email, not phone, so he couldn't change the subject.

His office, not the lab, so they'd be sure to be surrounded.

And another of her boring suits, not the robe, so she could keep hiding.

Just a robe? No way.

He wanted to put his hands on her shoulders and shake her out of her hiding place.

Or maybe he just wanted to put his hands on her.

"Since I won't be back to check on progress until after the wedding," she was saying when he forced himself to tune back in to her words, "you are responsible for ensuring construction stays on schedule. The plumbing—"

"Todd will stay on schedule."

"You are responsible for seeing he does. The plumbing and me-chanicals will be installed the last two weeks of October. It's essential the structure is adequately cool and dry before the computers arrive."

"By late October, cool won't be a problem."

"At the correct temperature, whether it requires heating or cool-ing," she elaborated, unruffled. "Construction dust must be eradicated, Not only the entry area and main room, but the back office, restroom, and—"

"We've been over this, Vanessa." He rubbed his eyes, wishing he'd gotten more sleep. Too many dreams about robes. On and off.

"—storage areas must be completed. Since we need to work around Warren's other commitments—"

"Like Language Arts," he muttered.

"—security measures will take considerably longer than I would normally allow."

"As I said, we've been over this. Several times."

She looked up, her eyebrows rising. "Re-checks are necessary to make sure everything is done correctly and in the proper sequence to open on schedule in early December."

"All right, all right," he grumbled.

"You seem…" Her brows dropped. "Peevish."

"Peevish?" Despite himself, his irritation lifted some. "Only you would call somebody peevish."

"It's accurate."

"Maybe. Look, skip the details, take my word for it—everything will get done on time."

"That's not reasonable when you have been explicit about the importance of this project to the people here."

"It is important. That doesn't mean—"

But he didn't get to say that she treated him like a kindergartner who would forget his mittens if he didn't have them hooked to his sleeves—okay, maybe he *was* a little peevish—because she talked over him.

"I met Fay in the hallway on my way here and she commented on how much she's looking forward to the computer lab being open before she completes her senior year and leaves Dra—"

Josh slapped his palms on his desk. Vanessa's widened gaze snapped to his face.

"Will you please stop trying to nudge, push, and pull every living soul out of Drago?" He forced himself to dial down the volume. "If you're only building the computer lab in the expectation that this place becomes a ghost town, then pack it in, Vanessa. People like it here. It's our home. Yes, we want the computer lab. Yes, it will let people add skills. Yes, it will help them communicate with the wider world. And because of all that, the computer lab will allow people who otherwise might have had to leave Drago to find opportunities to stay right here."

He saw in her still wide eyes that she was assessing his words.

"Would having the opportunities offered by the computer lab have made a difference with your wife?" she asked.

She was blunt all right. Like a blunt instrument. And it had landed a solid blow.

He knew this feeling.

He'd felt it when he'd been blindsided by a three-hundred-pound defender in his first varsity football game.

It was physical: the explosive expulsion of every atom of oxygen in his lungs, as if his ribs collapsed and crashed together somewhere in the middle of his chest.

It was mental: the acute observation that disconnected from himself.

What he'd seen then was the inside rim of his helmet, the muddied shoes of his teammates, the brush-cut surface of the grass.

What he saw now was Vanessa. The slight delay between her words and her recognition of their impact on him. Her flash of consternation, her intention to apologize.

"Josh, I—"

He couldn't take her apologizing. "You're very blunt."

"I know. I'm sor—"

"So I'll be equally blunt. You ran away from something. What?"

"Wha—?" That's all that came out. It was plenty to signal he'd hit a sore spot.

And that, he recognized, was why he hadn't let her apologize.

He'd wanted this opening to probe her past. "The commune?"

"That has nothing to do with—"

"My ex-wife leaving Drago? Looking back I can see she was leaving bit by bit even when she was here. All her promises to be there for the kids, then phone calls saying something had come up, she'd be late, she couldn't make it, another time—all the damned phone calls … She was all about the superficial. But—since we're being blunt—are you any better if you won't let anyone see what's beneath your clothes." He shook his head, a sharp jerk. "I don't mean that. Not that way." Although … no, better not go there. "I mean what you have inside. Who you are. What made you the individual you are. One way or another, you ran away from the commune, yet it helped form who Vanessa Irish became."

"No, it didn't."

He forged ahead. "Your parents. How did they raise you? What sort of relationship do you have with them now? What about siblings? How do you fit into the wider Irish family—?"

"I'm not part of any family named Irish."

He held his questions, using his expectation and his silence to draw out an answer. It came in jerks of uneasy words.

"I never had a last name. My mother was Starlight and my father— the man I believe was my father—was Sol, short for Solstice. They would never tell me other names, not theirs, not mine. After they died, the authorities tried. But they had no information to track, no clues. I knew they wouldn't succeed. When I was younger, I'd searched everywhere. There was nothing. By the time Starlight and Sol died, I didn't care where I'd come from, only where I was going."

"So you created your own name."

"Yes." She sounded untouched. But he knew better than that ... didn't he?

"Why did you pick Irish?"

"It was Saint Patrick's Day."

"And Vanessa? Where did that come from?"

"From a signup sheet at the courthouse when I acquired my legal identity. I needed a name. Vanessa was the most legible one."

He had daily practice at not reacting to what teenagers told him about their lives. Outrageous, wild, pathetic, funny, sickening, inane— he heard it all. He heard it with a steadiness that let them keep telling him things. Yet at this moment he had a major fight going on with muscles twitching to stand, circle his desk, pull her up, and wrap her in his arms.

Without parents, without family, she'd taken control of her life— given herself a new name, new identity, new life. What incredible strength she must have had—what incredible strength she had now. And how alone she'd been.

A thousand questions tumbled through his head. How old had she been? What happened to her parents? Did anyone help her?

What came out was: "What did your parents call you?"

Her hand tightened around her phone and she straightened in her chair. "Why?"

He was pushing her limits of self-revelation to the breaking point. If he pushed too far, he might never learn another thing about her.

"I'd like to know how they saw you."

"That's not relevant to our working rela—"

"Humor me."

Silence.

Damn. She was going to let it hang there, long and hollow. She was—

She raised her head, looked at him with fathomless eyes and spoke without inflection. "Breeze."

He slowly nodded. "I can see that."

She was shaking her head before he'd finished. "It's not my legal name—certainly not now and possibly it never was because if I have a birth certificate no one knows about it. Vanessa Irish is my name. Officially and legally."

"Did someone want to call you Breeze instead of Vanessa?"

She blinked twice. He'd gotten that right. "It wouldn't matter, because officially and—"

"Legally, I know." He grinned. She didn't smile back, but some of her tension eased. "I wouldn't ever call you by any other name than Vanessa."

He saw her struggle. Counted it as a victory when she asked, "Why?"

"Because Breeze was what someone else named you. Vanessa is who you've made yourself. How can any name fit you better?"

CHAPTER SIX

I WOULDN'T EVER *call you by any other name than Vanessa.*

She stood in her Zeke-Tech office, turning her back on the computer cursor blinking a reminder that she hadn't started the memo on the upcoming fiscal year-end closing of the books.

Beyond the immediate area of the desk, her office was dim. It kept her focus where it should be, on work.

Vanessa is who you've made yourself.

Mr. Schmidt hadn't seen that when he'd tried to persuade her to continue being Breeze. As generous as he and Mrs. Schmidt had been, they hadn't understood that she'd never truly been Breeze. That somewhere underneath she had always been Vanessa.

Sunlight angled in at the edge of the blinds.

How can any name fit you better?

How about *idiot?*

Telling him things.

Letting him into her past.

Getting goose-bumps at the way he'd said those words. At the way he'd looked at her.

She turned the wand to pivot the blinds and blinked at the dazzling afternoon light.

Idiot also described her blundering into Josh Kincannon's past.

Would having the opportunities offered by the computer lab have made a difference with your wife?

Her words had hurt him.

The knowledge brought an echo now of the odd reaction she'd had at the time. A sort of… Yes, admit it. *Triumph.*

It wasn't attractive, but it was the closest she could come.

A triumph that her words mattered enough to hurt. At the very same time she'd experienced pain at the injury she'd inflicted on him.

She hadn't intended to hurt him—or to feel his hurt herself. She'd honestly wanted to know.

Words often tripped her up. They had so much impact beyond their bare meanings. Cathie emphasized that she needed to consider how words might be received.

But she was not going to ask Cathie for coaching on—

She yanked up the cord, clearing the blinds from the window.

She *should* go to her coach. Because her dealings with Josh were business. *Had* to be business.

"Vanessa, I—Oh!"

Her assistant, Janine, stood motionless, halfway across the office.

Janine had been acting strangely since Vanessa's return from Illinois.

When she'd arrived directly from the airport, the two of them had worked smoothly through her checklist. Until they reached the item she'd added during the flight from Chicago.

"Janine, what have you purchased as my present for Zeke and Darcie?"

"Nothing."

"I know there's time. However, shipping to Illinois—"

"Time's not the issue. Etiquette experts allow a year after the wedding to give a gift."

"You're waiting a *year* to send a gift?" Janine did everything on time, if not early.

"I'm not sending a gift at all—not from you. My gift for them is already sent."

"But you always buy a present for weddings I'm invited to."

"For employees or business associates. Those are business gifts. This is a personal gift. It needs to come from you."

Vanessa had been speechless. It felt as if the world had just tipped.

"Couples getting married usually register for what they'd particularly like to get. I'll give you store names and websites, so you can get ideas," Janine had said, almost gently.

It had occurred to Vanessa that her assistant might feel sorry for her.

"If there's a list, select a few options, I'll okay one and—"

"No." So Janine wasn't feeling sorry enough. "This is a personal gift, and my employment agreement says I do not select personal gifts. It hasn't—"

Janine swallowed the end of that sentence, but Vanessa was confident it would have been the accurate observation that the situation hadn't come up before.

"Besides," her assistant had gone on, "some etiquette experts don't approve of gift registries. They insist the gift should come from the giver's thoughtful observation of the recipient's likes and needs."

She'd left the office then, probably thinking Vanessa would get on with work.

Instead, she'd been lost in useless remembering.

"You opened the blinds," Janine said now.

"It's a sunny afternoon." Vanessa waited, but her assistant stared wordlessly out the window. Or was she staring at Vanessa? She walked back to her desk. "What is it, Janine?"

"Oh. Yes. I printed the registries. If you pick something, check the website again to be sure it hasn't already been purchased. Then let the store know when you buy, so other guests don't duplicate your gift."

"Thank you, Janine."

"You're welcome. I know this is new for you, but it is for Zeke."

"Yes."

"Okay." She placed papers on Vanessa's desk. "Well, let me know when the memo's ready…"

"I will."

She waited for Janine to close the door before she picked up her glasses and the pages. Thumbnail pictures accompanied each item on the modest list. She would select one, order it, have it delivered, and that would be that.

But the more she looked at the printout, the less she had any idea of which to select.

The gift should come from the giver's thoughtful observation of the recipient's likes and needs.

Presumably this list indicated Zeke and Darcie's likes and needs, so any observation on her part would be redundant.

An effort wasted—she dropped the list to the desk—and almost certainly futile.

"YOU LOOK TIRED, Vanessa."

She rubbed her neck without looking up from the screen.

Even if she hadn't recognized Quince's voice, she would have suspected it was him. Few people entered her office uninvited.

"I am. All this time in Illinois is putting me behind with my real work."

She'd kept the blinds closed all day today. It hadn't helped as much as she would have expected. And it didn't matter now, because it must be after eight at night. She looked at the clock. Make that after ten.

"The computer lab isn't real?" Quince dropped into a chair across from her desk.

"You know what I mean. When you go back and forth to Illinois you're accomplishing something important—laying the groundwork for moving the division. For reasons known only to him, Zeke has saddled me with this busy-work project, and it's interfering with what I need to do—closing the books, consolidating, the annual report, all of it."

She sounded uncharacteristically irritable, and made no effort to hide it. For one thing, she *was* uncharacteristically irritable.

More important, this was Quince.

Quince, whom she trusted.

Oh, not at first. Not the way she'd trusted Zeke. At the start, Quince had made her uncomfortable.

Like Josh.

It had been the way Quince looked at her.

Not the way males had looked at her before she'd learned to ward off their attention, but with a similar sort of *seeing* as Josh did. And yet ... not similar at all.

Somewhere along the line, she'd come to know that while Quince saw, he would never probe.

Totally unlike Josh, who asked questions. Worse, he asked questions she heard herself answering, to her utter bafflement.

"Tell Zeke you want to hand off duties," Quince said.

"I have. He insists I handle the computer lab on-site."

"I meant hand off duties here."

"Why on earth would I do that?"

"That's where we started—because you look tired. Zeke is set on having us spend time in Drago. And, since he's the genius, our choices are to go gracefully or to go kicking and screaming."

She had no pretensions to grace, but kicking and screaming did not befit Zeke-Tech's CFO. She wanted a third option.

"You don't seem to mind." It sounded like an accusation.

Quince stared at the closed blinds. "I think I might have been getting a little bored." His mouth quirked up. "It's not much of a challenge promoting products that people are drooling to get their hands on. Takes all the fun out of it. Drago has the advantage of being something new and different."

She snorted. "Glad you're having a good time. I have work to do. Go away."

He chuckled. "Maybe Zeke wants you to spend more time in Drago to hone your people skills."

That cut close to the bone.

"Of course," he continued, "since it's just me, there's no need for people skills."

She looked up, absorbing a sudden insight.

He'd added those words because he'd noticed her discomfort.

In fact, she realized, Quince did that a lot.

Not Josh.

He asked his nosy questions and made statements and huge assumptions.

I know you better than you think. In fact, I might know you better than you know yourself.

And he didn't back off.

With a start she realized Quince was talking. "…more relaxed. Every question is not the start of an IRS audit."

Was he talking about Josh's questions? But how could he know? "What are you talking about?"

He sighed, then clearly began repeating himself. "The other day at Lilac Commons, when I asked about your day. You acted like I'd re-opened the Spanish Inquisition with you as the first customer."

"I don't know what you mean."

He turned his head, but kept his eyes on her, with the look he got when he was going to—

"You're a lousy liar, Vanessa. A good trait to have in the person handling Zeke-Tech's money, but it can't be comfortable for you."

—be wry. And she'd been right.

"It's not." She said it absently, occupied with the fact that she had known, at least in general, what Quince would say.

From his expression.

"Want to know why I asked you what you'd been up to that day at the park?"

"No," she lied.

He grinned. "Because I don't remember ever seeing you looking that relaxed and … un-concentrated."

"You see me at work. I concentrate at work."

"I've seen you outside work, but never like that. I might not have noticed, though, not right away, if I hadn't seen Josh watching you."

She couldn't begin to think of how to respond.

"How's that going? You and Josh."

She cleared her throat. "We're establishing a beneficial work relationship.

Quince's eyes held a glint she didn't understand. He set his hands on the chair's arms. "All right, all right I'm going. I can take a hint. But let me give *you* a hint—no charge. Open up. Talk. Ask questions. Let the people of Drago get to know you. No—don't make that face."

"I wasn't making a face."

"Yup, that's the one. It's great for across the negotiating table, but not so great for a lazy afternoon at a park." He stood. "I wish you knew what a great person you are, Vanessa."

She found nothing to say.

He sounded his usual relaxed self when he added, "Just remember my hint about opening up. You can start Saturday."

"Saturday I'll be here, catching up."

"Nope. You'll be in Drago. Zeke had Janine get you a flight back Friday. To go to the high school's football game."

"Football!"

"Yup. Zeke has a contingent of Zeke-Techers going to show we're part of the community. Including you and me."

"Zeke didn't say a word about this when we talked today."

"Haven't you noticed our resident genius is a chicken when it comes to having you do things he knows you won't want to do?"

"It doesn't stop him. He just has you—Oh. So that's what this visit is about."

"You got it. My duty's to tell you that you're ordered to attend the football game Saturday, eat hot dogs and popcorn, yell for the home team, and generally have a good time. I know," he said in mock sympathy, "having fun is a tough job—but somebody's got to do it."

Fun, her foot. "It means I have even less time to get through this work. So go away—and I mean it this time."

He walked to the door. But there he stopped.

"What?" she demanded.

"Who would be your picks to fill in if you had to let go of some of your work?"

"That's a useless hypothetical."

"Humor me. I know you, so I know you have contingency plans. Give me names."

"Beth and Rajeed."

He nodded, then smiled, with what might have been mischief. She considered. Yes, mischief. "It might be time to get them up to scratch."

Ridiculous.

He was past the doorframe when she called, "Quince, what are you giving Zeke and Darcie for their wedding? Something from the registry?"

He stepped back in. "Nah. I got Mrs. Z to dig out pictures of Zeke and Darcie together in high school. I've had them blown up and framed. Same wood as the bookcases in their family room."

"Oh." She couldn't even select something *on* the list, much less think beyond it.

"Don't like my idea, huh?"

"Oh, no, it's great, Quince. Original and personal. I have no ideas at all. That's why I sounded so, uh, bummed," she finished, using one of Topher's words experimentally.

Quince chuckled as he left.

"THIS IS A pleasant surprise," Josh said as he sat on the step next to the bleacher seat occupied by Vanessa Irish. "Since you said you weren't returning until the wedding."

He'd been following his pre-game routine for a football Saturday at Drago High School. Roving the stands, glad-handing school board members, noting this week's pairing ups among the kids, welcoming alumni, soothing a parent here and there, swooping unexpectedly under the bleachers to shoo out lurkers looking for a place to make out or occasionally less savory activities.

Then the motion of a hand trying to tame sun-sparkled hair caught his eye.

Vanessa, battling the spurting wind for control of her hairdo.

From just beyond Vanessa, Darcie waved and Zeke nodded, then returned to their conversation with a Zeke-Techer on Zeke's far side.

"A surprise, all right," Vanessa said with a twist somewhere between bitterness and resignation.

He laughed out loud. Several heads turned, smiling even without knowing what he was laughing about. You had to love that about people.

Or maybe you had to love everything on a day like this.

It was the sort of day that earned Midwestern autumns their reputation. Everything about it was crisp and brilliant. The dazzling blue sky, the air so pure that breathing it should cure any ill, the pristine grass, the scent of popcorn and coffee from the concession stand, the beat-keeping drums as the band marched in.

And Vanessa Irish sitting a couple feet away.

Yeah, crisp and brilliant worked for her, too.

"Well, it's definitely pleasant from this vantage point," he said.

He met her gaze, letting her see he was enjoying everything he saw, along with liking the surprise of her being here.

He caught a flash of sizzle in her eyes—he was sure he did, even if she covered it completely, and even faster than it had come.

No, it wasn't so much that she covered it as she jumped back from it. Like someone who'd been rubbing sticks together without any hope for ages, and then, when a spark flared, it shocked them so much they let go.

Although he suspected Vanessa had had no intention of rubbing sticks together.

Josh felt a tap on his shoulder. He looked up into Malcolm's face.

"Mr. Kincannon, you are obstructing the aisle," the older man announced, leaning on the walking stick he used to climb around the bleachers. Josh had offered to relieve him of football duty because of his bad knee, but Malcolm wouldn't hear of it. "If you read the study on spectator safety that I put in your inbox last month, you know very well that obstructing an aisle constitutes a fire hazard."

Aw, damn. He would have liked a couple more minutes.

"You're right. I shouldn't—"

But as he stood, Malcolm pointed his walking stick down the aisle, nearly clipping Josh in the nose.

"You there," Malcolm commanded, gesturing to Darcie and Zeke, "move in closer so there are seats for everyone."

Vanessa closed the gap between her and Darcie, but the others paid no attention, apparently absorbed in conversation.

At the same time, Josh felt Malcolm's free hand on his back, displaying unexpected strength. Caught off balance, Josh half stumbled, catching himself only by taking a sudden seat on the end of the bleacher Vanessa hadn't quite vacated.

"That's better," Malcolm said severely, as he marched smartly past.

But Josh had caught a glint in the counselor's eyes that had nothing to do with preventing fire hazards. More like provoking them, considering the celebration Josh's body was throwing at being packed in like this against Vanessa.

Malcolm, you old goat...

"Ow." Vanessa's complaint definitely didn't match his reaction to sitting hip to hip. "What are you poking me with?"

A barely stifled splutter of laughter came from Darcie, proving she hadn't been as deaf to what was going on as she'd pretended.

"Sorry. Must be my keys." He emphasized the last word for the benefit of Darcie and her fellow eavesdroppers trying to tune their ears to this conversation as carefully as true believers searching the skies for messages from extraterrestrials.

He dug in his jacket pocket, pulling out the offending metal.

"Good heavens." Vanessa eyed the wad.

He rarely gave the keys a thought, other than their being a familiar weight. But he supposed it was impressive.

"It looks like you have a key to every house in Drago."

He shrugged, liking the way his arm slid against hers. "My house, a few friends' and neighbors'. Most of the keys are for other stuff."

"The school," she ventured.

"Yeah, and the computer lab, library, community center, city hall, and a couple churches."

"Why?"

He supposed at some childish level he'd hoped she was at least mildly impressed he was trusted by so many. On the other hand, her bafflement gave him an excuse to shrug again. Yeah, he definitely liked that friction.

"Guess I'm the designated backup guy."

A shallow crease tucked between her brows deepened.

He should have known it wouldn't impress her.

You must get tired of taking care of everybody else ... Community is the antithesis of individuals.

Her experiences growing up clearly soured her on community. Not that he knew specifics, since she'd run back to Virginia as soon as he'd asked a few questions.

"What are they doing?"

It took him a beat to realize her puzzlement had turned to the field, where captains from each team gathered around the officials.

"The coin toss." The official peered at the coin, then gestured with extended arm in the direction the Drago Dragons would be trying to move the ball. "Good. Trent's been working hard with the kids on offense. If they can move on this first series it'll give them a lot of confidence."

Along with the rest of the home crowd, Josh cheered when a senior running back broke free for a long gain, groaned when an opponent got through the line and sacked the quarterback, rocketed to his feet yelling when a short pass became a twenty-five-yard touchdown play.

Then fans from both sides of the field moaned.

"What happened?" Vanessa demanded.

"The scoreboard clock's stopped. It happens a couple times a game. Unless it's raining and then the outages multiply like rabbits."

While officials conferred on the field, Josh mentally acknowledged he'd have to get money from somewhere to replace the damned thing. But that was a worry for another day. One when the sun wasn't shining and he wasn't sitting next to Vanessa.

"Does this bring back memories of your high school days?" he asked, though he had strong suspicions, considering her reactions. She resembled a first-time attendee at an unfamiliar church, trying to keep up with the service.

"No." Her look ordered him not to tread near the commune.

That was fine with him. This was no place to try to discover her secrets. "Me, either," he said.

"But you know all the rules."

"I played. Quarterback—the guy who gets the ball from the center—for a nearby town."

"Oh." She looked at the field, then at him. "You liked playing football."

"Loved it."

"But you don't love watching it as much."

That took him aback. No one had spotted that before.

"Maybe I loved playing so much that it's hard being up here. I played against Trent when he was at Drago High. You know, he's made a huge difference with these kids. It's hard for them to accuse Coach Brookenheimer of being out of touch when a former NFL player like Trent respects him. Some folks in town weren't happy when the top player was put off the team because he got himself in trouble. But Trent's been great there, too. Listening to people, but not budging, and most everyone's come around. You know community makes a big—What? Why are you giving me that look?"

"I am not aware of giving you any particular look. But I was thinking that while you say I view everything as a plus or a minus, you have quirks, too. You turn talk about yourself to talk about the community."

He chuckled. "Nonsense."

"You hide behind community."

Her flat statement coincided with eruption of applause around them for the resurrection of the scoreboard clock and resumption of play.

The noise covered her statement from any eavesdroppers and gave him a reason to look away from the certainty in her eyes.

CHAPTER SEVEN

J OSH LEFT SOON after, saying he needed to make his rounds.

When the game resumed after the break called halftime, Vanessa volunteered to get snacks.

It wasn't that she disliked the game. It had a certain appeal, being based, as it was, on numbers, with the yardage and downs and time allowances. She appreciated the weighted scoring of touchdowns, field goals, and extra points, which added nicely complex calculations to the strategy.

It was the desire to escape Darcie's not-quite-questions that prompted her offer. Ever since Josh left, Darcie had been drawing her closer and closer to revelations that Vanessa simply didn't make. Certainly not to two people within such a short amount of time.

Vanessa was considering that as she waited for the woman inside the concession stand to gather her order, when a voice interrupted.

"Ms. Irish? Hi, I'm Fay, remember? Fay O'Hearn."

"Yes. Hello, Fay."

"That's quite an order. Would you like a hand carrying it?"

"That would be helpful. Thank you." Remembering her lessons with Cathie, she added. "Are you enjoying the game?"

"Oh, it's okay. I used to love the games, but…"

The concession worker brought the last box of popcorn, Vanessa paid, and she and Fay consolidated items to two trays.

As they moved away from the stand, Vanessa said, "You used to love the games, but…"

"I have, uh, other things on my mind." Fay shot her a look. "It's hard to have fun when I don't know… I mean—you went to college didn't you? Of course you did, what am I saying? You're so successful, you must have gone to a great college and had help from your parents and … and everything."

"I attended a state university," Vanessa said. "I learned then, and have had it reconfirmed while hiring staff at Zeke-Tech that a student's attitude and desire have far more impact on his or her education than the name of the university does. As for parents, no, mine didn't support me. They—"

She half stumbled, cola slopping over the rim of one cup. Good heavens, had she been on the verge *again* of revealing her background?

"You didn't get along with your parents?"

There was sympathy, perhaps hope in Fay's question. Vanessa ignored it. "If you don't feel that your parents support your goal to attend college, Fay, that might make daily life difficult?"

She didn't know if her voice had risen to make that a question because she was heeding Cathie's instructions to keep conversations open-ended or because she wasn't sure why on earth she'd ventured into this territory.

"It's not daily life. I don't live with them—her. My father hasn't ever been part of the equation. And … well, I live with my aunt and uncle."

"I see."

"No, you don't see," Fay said in a tone that seemed to Vanessa a cocktail of emotions. The only flavor she recognized for sure was bitterness, yet that didn't seem to be a primary ingredient. "My aunt and uncle—they're good people, they really are. But they have these *ideas*. They keep saying I have to go to college somehow. But it's—it's all so messed up."

Vanessa waited.

The girl gave a short, unamused laugh. "I know, I should be a good girl and listen to the grownups."

"Not necessarily."

Fay looked at her, looked away just as quickly, then slowly turned back. "You don't think I should go to college?"

"I have no opinion. And my opinion shouldn't matter to you if I did."

The girl's eyes widened. Vanessa wasn't sure if she was more surprised at the idea that Vanessa didn't have an opinion or the idea that the girl shouldn't care about outside opinions.

"If you want to go to college there are scholarships and grants and financial aid. What matters," Vanessa continued, "is what you think."

"I... I want to go to college more than anything."

Vanessa nodded. "Then you have your answer."

"YOU'RE PILING UP evidence that proves me right."

Vanessa pivoted toward the unexpected words from the familiar voice.

She had been heading toward the parking lot ahead of Darcie and Zeke, but with their progress once more stalled while they talked with people, she had stepped out of the stream of departing spectators.

Josh stood close, his face even closer as he must have leaned forward to pitch his voice so only she could hear. So close that he was out of focus.

Except his mouth.

That she could see clearly. His lips on the verge of opening for one of those grins. But not there yet, so if she leaned forward even half as much as he was, it would bring their mouths together. Touching...

She jerked back.

"I don't know what you mean."

His eyes held a peculiar glint.

Even before Cathie's lessons, she'd read about maintaining eye contact. But it had never before caused burning in her lungs.

She looked away.

People skills could be over-rated.

"Evidence," Josh said, "that proves what I said before. You deal well with kids."

"I don't know what you mean."

"You know, Vanessa, I'm getting suspicious of that sentence—*I don't know what you mean.* I think you use it when you *do* know what I mean, but don't want to acknowledge it."

She considered that, welcoming the rational process of assessing his words. "Perhaps I suspect what you mean, but don't want to accuse you without being certain."

"Giving me a second chance? Or enough rope to hang myself?"

She felt the corners of her mouth twitch. "That depends on how you respond. Although in this case I truly don't know what you meant."

His gaze dropped from her eyes to her mouth. A dent tucked in between his brows. Not frowning, she thought. Concentrating.

"Oh, yeah? I mean about you dealing well with kids. I saw you and Fay O'Hearn earlier."

"She helped me carry snacks to the stands."

"Looked liked more than that. You both looked pretty intent."

"That has nothing to do with my dealing well with children. She seems more grown up than many adults."

Any trace of smile vanished. "She's had to be. She's had a rough time."

She considered that. "She confides in you?"

"Yes."

"So you wouldn't break the confidence she bestowed on you by telling anyone what she's talked to you about."

"Pretty neat, Vanessa. Make it sound like you're being understanding and thoughtful, while blocking me from asking about your conversation with Fay, which you clearly don't want to discuss. Just don't get her a bus ticket out of town without telling me, okay?"

"There is no bus line through Drago."

"Figure of speech, Vanessa. This time you do know what I mean, and we both know it."

She said nothing. He was right.

He looked to his left, and she followed his gaze to where Darcie was bearing down on them. He spoke in a low voice. "I will tell you one thing, as strong as Fay's been, she's vulnerable in a lot of ways. And she's still a kid."

ZEKE'S SCHEDULED ACTIVITIES for her did not end with the football game.

He and Darcie had the Zeke-Tech employees, along with a number of Drago residents, to their house dinner.

"Casual," he said. "The kitchen's not done yet."

"Wouldn't have mattered if it was," Darcie said cheerfully, "I can't cook. But don't worry, we had this brought in, so it's really good."

Crates were covered with red and white checked cloths, with folding chairs around the large open area that would become the family room.

When Vanessa emerged from the buffet line, her gaze met Josh's. He tipped his head to an empty chair next to him. She saw another at the other end of the room, among Zeke-Techers. She shook her head, declining his invitation and headed for that one.

Josh was among the first to leave.

She stayed late to help clean up, along with Quince, Jennifer, and Trent. She felt nearly as relaxed as with Zeke and Quince alone.

Perhaps that sociability then prompted Vanessa to linger at the doorway to Mrs. Richards' TV room instead of saying a quick goodnight.

The older woman muted the volume. "Did you have a good time, dear?"

"Yes, thank you." Rather to her surprise, Vanessa recognized that as the truth. Good thing, considering her lying appeared to be as bad as her people skills.

"You must have enjoyed having dinner with all your friends."

Vanessa blinked at *friends*, but didn't contradict her. "It was enjoyable."

"I hear the Barrett house will be something to behold when it's finished."

"Yes—but how did you know we were there?"

"Molly Harkin's youngest delivered the food—Molly cooks for folks, you know—and her youngest told her boyfriend's mother about it. That's Karen Osterhauge. Karen was talking with her mother, Beverly Mudge. Do you know Beverly? No? I thought you might, since she sits with Josh's kids regular. Beverly happened to mention Molly doing Darcie and Zeke's dinner when she called tonight."

Vanessa's head swam with the names, connections, and rapid-fire delivery. "It was interesting to see the ongoing renovations. And the food was delicious. I hope you'll tell, uh, your friend how enjoyable it was."

"Oh, I don't see Molly much—she's that busy—but I'll see her mother-in-law at bingo come Monday and I'll be sure to mention it."

"Thank you."

Mrs. Richards gave her an encouraging smile. "And the game?"

"It was … interesting."

"I used to go to the games, but I don't get around the way I used to, and those bleachers are hard to climb. I'm glad you enjoyed it."

"Yes. I, uh, met a number of people, as well as talked to some I'd met before. Including a student, Fay … uh, Fay—"

"O'Hearn," Mrs. Richards supplied, then sighed. "It's such a shame."

With no more encouragement, her landlady launched into the tale of Fay O'Hearn.

Fay's mother was wild growing up, but nothing folks didn't think would straighten out when Ellie joined the Army. Then she came home after her stint, more unhappy than ever. The good thing was it seemed she'd shaken the drinking habit she'd gotten into in high school.

Soon it became clear she was pregnant. Six months later, Fay was born. Ellie juggled the baby and a job at the grocery store, helped by her older sister, Rose.

Fay was a year old when Ellie fell off the wagon the first time.

That set a pattern. She'd be okay, then she'd fall in with folks she shouldn't—"most often a man," Mrs. Richards said with significance. Soon Ellie would be drinking. Because the man had left or because he hadn't. Things would go downhill. Fay's Aunt Rose would come to the rescue, taking care of the little girl until Ellie dried out, and the cycle started all over.

"As Fay got older, it's been her taking care of her mama more than the other way around. I don't know where that girl would be if it wasn't for Rose and Al—Rose's husband. They're good people. Rose doesn't ever touch a drop, you know. Says it's in the family, and she's not taking chances. I suppose that might be part of why Ellie resents her. Not a word of kindness to her sister for all she's done, not a word."

"Fay lives with her aunt and uncle now?"

"Ever since Ellie's latest moved into her place. She's picked some losers but this one's a doozy. Police have been out there a dozen times." Her voice lowered. "From what I hear, Ellie is giving as good—or as bad—as she gets."

Mrs. Richards shook her head. "Josh wanted to get Fay out of there when she started coming in with bruises. That man moving in pushed it over the edge, and Fay went to Rose and Al. Official reason is the bus route changed, so this makes it so she's not on the bus three hours a day. But I'm here to tell you, Josh changed that route so there'd be the excuse.

"Fay's a smart one. Always at the library, studying things you wouldn't believe a slip of a thing like her would. Be a real shame if she can't get to college. But Al's just back to work after three years without a job, and they've been squeezed near dry, what with three little ones of their own. Heaven knows Fay won't get money from Ellie."

"A good student can obtain scholarships, grants, loans. She can put herself through college." Vanessa knew that first-hand.

"I sure hope so. It would be a shame for her to lose out like that."

"Yes, it would." The computer lab could help the girl. Not only ensuring she had skills she'd need for college, but also as a resource. Vanessa made a mental note to talk to Malcolm Cottle about a class on using the Internet to apply to colleges and for aid.

"Josh will do his best for her. He's such a good young man." Mrs. Richards exhaled. "It's a shame he hasn't found the right woman. He's dated since Melissa, but nothing's come of it."

"I have an early morning, so—"

"Of course, with those children it's to his credit that he's careful not to let them get attached to someone who's not right. But a young man that age, it has to be hard. Men have urges you know. Why even my dear Charlie—"

"Good night!"

Vanessa didn't realize how loudly she'd spoken until the woman blinked.

"Oh, yes. I don't want to keep you. I—"

"See you in the morning," Vanessa added to soften her departure. Her landlady's voice followed her.

"Good night, dear. Sleep well. It so nice you and Josh are hitting it off. He's a fine man. He deserves happiness."

Vanessa decided she was far enough down the hall to let those comments fade away to nothingness.

"CONSTRUCTION COSTS ARE on track," Vanessa concluded, making a notation. "We'll tackle the schedule next."

Josh laced his hands behind his head and stretched, watching her.

It was Monday night, the two of them back at the computer lab's sawhorses-and-plywood table, now in the main room, since Todd was tearing apart the back.

She'd wanted to meet Sunday. He'd been booked, with another round of church repairs, then a family dinner with his widowed aunt a few miles down the Interstate. He'd invited Vanessa to come, saying they could work afterward. Her refusal had been more adamant than was totally polite, but he'd known he'd been pushing.

He had meetings until six, so then it became a matter of whether he could find a sitter, with Mrs. Mudge not available on Bingo night.

Fay jumped at the job, but not until seven-thirty. It pushed the edges of his comfort level for leaving Xena in charge at the house, but he'd agreed to meet Vanessa at seven, knowing Fay could be counted on to arrive when she said, if not earlier.

Now, nearly an hour into their meeting, Vanessa frowned at the screen she was consulting, checked her watch, and frowned more. "This is taking longer than planned, and I have additional items to go over."

"Yeah, I hear you've taken an interest in the classes to be offered here."

"Naturally, I'm interested in how the facility will be utilized."

"Uh-huh. Your suggestion about teaching high school seniors how to apply to colleges and search out financial aid wouldn't have anything to do with conversations with Fay O'Hearn, would it?"

She took off her glasses. "Oh, does she want to go to college?"

He laughed. Then he fought to keep from laughing harder at her flicker of dismay—she'd actually meant the question to make him believe she didn't know.

But Vanessa Irish didn't crumble.

She mustered a laugh herself, playing along as if she'd never intended to convince him of her ignorance.

"I'd like to think Fay told you her history herself. No, I can see from your expression she didn't." He caught another flicker, and guessed she was wondering what in her expression gave him that insight, and how she could prevent it from happening again. "So, I don't know how you—" He bumped the heel of his hand against his forehead. "What am I saying? Mrs. R., of course."

Her face went wooden in an apparent effort to keep her expression from confirming his conclusion. "Why would you like to think Fay told me about her situation?"

"She's too closed in, too reluctant to let anyone share her troubles. I have a feeling you understand her, and she needs that."

She hitched one shoulder in denial. "I don't understand people."

"She seems to feel you understand her, which is more important.

Besides, maybe you don't understand all people—who does?—but it seems to me you two have something in common."

She looked at him, not following—or, more likely, not prepared to acknowledge following.

"Feeling you're not in sync with the kids around you. And not liking that," he prompted. Then he tugged at her innate honesty. "Or am I wrong?"

"I hated it." For two breaths he expected that to be the extent of her revelations. "I hated being odd. Odd in the commune as the only one who cared about thinking ahead. Odd in the world for being part of the commune."

"But it ended—the commune, I mean—how did that happen?"

"My parents died in an accident. Without them, the last bit of the commune sputtered out."

She would have left it there. "What about you, Vanessa?"

"The nearby town had a high school, and I went there."

High school—Good God, she'd still been a kid when her parents died.

A kid and, from what she'd said earlier, with no one to turn to.

"How? I mean, without family—how did you do that alone?"

"The principal of the high school and his wife had me live with them for the year and a half before I graduated."

He pulled in a slow breath, and forced himself to keep it light, "And we know a principal's kids are always the oddest."

"Mr. And Mrs. Schmidt didn't have children."

"They had you."

She looked startled. Almost before he registered that, she dismissed his words. "They were kind. But I was not their child. However, you are right that living with them made me even more odd at school. As if coming from the commune, being somewhat out of sync academically, entirely out of sync in social interactions, and, uh, other things, weren't enough."

Those hairs on the back of his neck took notice of her abrupt turn away from Principal and Mrs. Schmidt, but he let that slide. "Other things? Like a Marilyn Monroe body?"

"No, that came later. At college."

He laughed, and saw an answering lightening in her. "You are honest. So high school didn't qualify as the best years of your life. What happened?"

"Nothing really. I already knew I was odd. The other students certainly did." She shrugged. "The benefit was that I had no distractions while making up ground where my self-teaching had been inadequate."

He kept his oral questions bland while the ones in his head screamed. *Self-teaching?* "Did you have to delay college?"

"No. I graduated at sixteen and began college during the summer session, thanks to financial aid."

He swore to himself again.

Graduated at sixteen. So about fourteen when her parents died—not all that much older than Xena, younger than many of his students, and she'd gone through all of that.

"And college? That's when the knockout body came in?"

"Knockout." She seemed to test the word. "When I … changed it did knock me. Mrs. Schmidt had bought me clothes to go to college. But she was much, uh, smaller. And the clothes she bought didn't hide anything the way my old clothes had. They … uh…"

"Highlighted your assets."

She glared.

He rather liked that. It was certainly an improvement over her iced-over expression. He grinned.

She blinked, and he liked that, too. Confusion was good for her.

"The, uh, attention was not pleasant," she said sternly. "I'd been left alone before. Only then did I realize what a benefit that was. You have no idea."

"I can make a fair guess, considering how much time I spend as lifeguard for an ocean of teenage hormones, not to mention distant memories of being a teenage boy myself. Guys in college are about a nanosecond more evolved than high school boys when it comes to matters like knockout bodies. So, guys came on to you. You decided the waters were too dangerous and got out of the ocean. Retreated—" His cell phone rang. "—right past the beach, over the dunes, through the parking lot and kept right on—"

A second ring. Checking the screen, he held up a hand, forestalling the words forming on her lips, which he'd bet were *I don't know what you mean.*

"I've got to get this, Vanessa. It's home. Hello?"

"Mr. Kincannon?" Fay's tone sent that immediate chill through him that every parent knows.

"What's wrong? The kids—?"

"They're fine. It's … I'm sorry, Mr. Kincannon, but I have to leave. It's an emergency."

"What kind of emergency? Can I help?"

"No. I'm so sorry … I just have to go. Right now."

He heard Xena's voice in the background, but couldn't make out the words. Then Fay came back on. "Xena says she'll keep an eye on Topher and Livvy until you finish your meeting."

"No. That won't be necessary. Fay, can you wait five minutes?" He barely waited for her agreement. "Okay, wait five minutes, then you go. I'll be there as fast as I can. I might even be there before you leave. If not, tell Xena to hold the fort until I get there. A few minutes, that's all."

As he disconnected, he said to Vanessa. "I know we have a lot to do."

"Yes, we do. Emergencies can't be avoided, however." Though she clearly didn't like the fact.

"True, but I have a solution. We move this to my house."

CHAPTER EIGHT

V ANESSA WAS UNEASY with the idea, but also… Was that curiosity about Josh Kincannon's home she felt?

She put papers into her briefcase. "Of course. Whatever it takes to get the work done."

"Thank you."

Outside, he gestured to a sturdy vehicle. "C'mon. I'll give you a ride. My car's right here and this will be faster than waiting for you to follow me."

Not until they had turned into a neighborhood of tree-lined streets did she break the silence. "Josh?"

"Hmm?"

"What present are you getting for Zeke and Darcie's wedding?"

He grunted with absent sympathy. "Tough, isn't it? Since he could buy whatever either of them wants."

"Yes," she agreed quickly. Too quickly.

"I've ordered lilac bushes. They're re-landscaping after the renovations. The bushes will have a great scent in the spring, and be a reminder that they found each other again when Zeke came back for the lilac festival."

The gift should come from the giver's thoughtful observation of the recipient's likes and needs.

"That's…"

"Sappy?"

"No. It's very … thoughtful." That sounded flat, but she meant it. Another thoughtful, personal gift.

While she had nothing. No observations. No thoughts. No ideas.

He pulled into the driveway of a frame house with a porch across the front.

For half a breath Vanessa feared he was going too fast to avoid crushing the jumble of bikes and toys between the front of the vehicle and the closed garage door. But he came to a stop just short with what struck her as practiced ease.

Josh came around the back of the car as Vanessa got out. She gathered a quick impression of big trees, moderately neat grass, and a row of bushes giving the porch privacy.

He grasped her elbow. "Watch your step—there's no knowing what might have been left out here."

The front door, situated on one side of the porch, opened to show Xena, holding Livvy on her hip.

Her gaze swung to Vanessa, then to her father's hand, and her brows dropped into a scowl.

"Are things okay, Xena?" Josh asked. "Fay…?"

"She left. Everything here's okay. But I've gotta talk to you. Alone."

"Vanessa and I have to work. We'll set up in the dining room then—"

"It can't wait. It's—" She shot a darker look at Vanessa. "It's about Fay."

"What about Fay? Xena?" he prompted when the girl said nothing. "You can talk in front of Vanessa."

"*Dad.*"

Inside, he took Livvy, who babbled her delight. "If it can't wait, you better tell us, Xena."

The girl huffed, turned a shoulder to Vanessa, and spoke to Josh.

"Fay went to the emergency room. She has a black eye, but not like anything I've seen before," she said, as if she possessed a long and wide-ranging experience of black eyes. "It wasn't really black yet, because it must have just happened. But she couldn't see out of it and it was swelling bad. I told her to go and I'd take care of things here."

"Xena, we've talked about that—you're not old enough."

She made a different sound this time, but Vanessa still heard disgust in it. "You've said it so many times that Fay would have sat here until her head exploded. She wouldn't budge. I finally told her she had to call you or I would."

The tuck was back between Josh's eyebrows, deeper than Vanessa had ever seen it. In the silence, she heard a muted jingle. It took an instant to track it to Livvy's foot jostling the keys in his pocket.

"Go check on her, Dad," Xena said.

"I'll call."

"You know they won't tell you anything on the phone. I'll take care of things here. Fay looked bad."

"Xena—" He broke off his protest and his gaze shifted. "Vanessa, I know it's a lot to ask—"

Xena looked over her shoulder, then spun back to her father. "*Her?* I can look after Livvy and Topher. We don't need her. We don't—"

"I'm not leaving you kids alone for more than a few minutes, especially at this time of night. That's not negotiable."

"You should go," Vanessa heard her voice saying. "As Xena said, Fay needs your help."

Xena shot a smoldering look over her shoulder, but said nothing.

What could she say?

Certainly not what she was thinking, which appeared to be along the lines of *Oh, never mind, Fay doesn't really need you. Stay here with us, and save us from this idiot woman.*

So, in less time than she could have imagined, Vanessa stood in the doorway of Josh Kincannon's home, holding his younger daughter—whom he'd plunked into her arms as he'd left—watching his car drive away. And wondering if she'd gotten into this predicament because she'd wanted to show a girl that she could not easily be run off.

Beside her stood Xena, who would have made a fine border crossing guard for a totalitarian state. All she lacked was the rifle.

"She needs a bath tonight," Xena said harshly, jerking her head toward Livvy, as she slammed the door, then stomped to the far end of the room.

On second thought, Xena did fine without the rifle.

"Then I will give her a bath." Vanessa was pleased she sounded normal. "And you shall do your homework."

They stared down the length of the living room, like gunslingers on a dusty Main Street at high noon in a movie she'd once seen. She sure hoped she, and not Xena, was Gary Cooper.

She gave herself a mental shake. She had to quit thinking of this girl as the black-hatted villain.

She was a child. That was bad enough.

Abruptly, Xena dropped her arms and spun away. "Fine. I'll do my homework. You give Livvy a bath."

Vanessa would have liked to believe she'd won, except she'd caught a nearly feral smile on Xena's face just before she turned away.

VANESSA'S LIMITED EXPERIENCE washing kids had involved buckets and a pull-rope. And those kids had been older.

For a child this age, she could draw on only vaguely remembered images from TV and movies. Plus the clue that a stack of folded bath towels sat on a counter near the kitchen sink.

She'd filled the sink with water of a carefully monitored temperature and found a fresh bar of bath soap in the pantry. The towels were at hand. All that remained was to put the naked child in the water and start washing.

She gripped the girl's shoulders, and re-discovered that hands wet from water-testing slid right off skin. She adjusted, gripping under the child's arms and half lifting, half sliding her into the water.

Water sloshed over the top of the sink.

Vanessa grimaced.

The child was the wrong size for this sink, barely fitting in. How had she failed to anticipate a simple volume problem and—?

The child gave a delighted sound and slapped her hands into the water, sending splashes high and waves wide.

Vanessa squawked a protest, trying to scoop overflowing water back into the sink with the sides of her hands.

Presumably taking that as encouragement, Livvy repeated the slapping maneuver, complete with sound effects, a half-dozen times in rapid succession.

Well, that took care of the volume problem.

The amount of water in the sink was now so low that no more slopped over the sides and the little girl's splashes sent barely a drizzle onto the water-skimmed countertop and floor.

The front of Vanessa's clothes were water-logged, while her back remained dry. Her shoes were wet all over.

She kicked them off, and dropped them around the corner into the dining room where they wouldn't get any more drenched. She hoped.

Back at the sink, a new problem became clear. There was so much child in so little sink and with so little water left—and she wasn't fool enough to refill it—that actually washing her presented a problem.

Then Vanessa spotted the solution sitting idly beside the faucet.

With renewed confidence, she soaped the child thoroughly, even congratulating herself a little because, no matter how slippery the girl became from the soap there wasn't room for her to go anywhere.

Livvy played with the froths of soap bubbles and chattered.

Reaching under the girl's leg, Vanessa found the plug and let the soapy water out. Next, she pulled the sprayer out, giving herself plenty of play in the cord so she could get all the angles, and turned it on.

It was like a firehose hitting a brick wall in miniature. Only the brick wall shrieked in glee and spread chubby hands under the nozzle, sending spray at impossible angles. Old Faithful had met an oscillating sprinkler.

"No! Livvy, wait, *No.*"

Vanessa tried to cup the spray into a stream that would rinse off the girl. But she had to fight off Livvy's efforts to commandeer the sprayer.

At last, seeing no lingering soap, Vanessa turned off the water, replaced the sprayer, and stepped back.

Livvy looked at her questioningly and said something in those odd words. The tone conveyed, *All done?* With a strong subtext of *spoilsport.*

"Yes, all done," Vanessa said firmly.

Just then a drop hit at her hairline and slid down her forehead. Wiping it away, she looked up and got hit with another drop on the eyebrow.

The kitchen was nearly as wet as she and Livvy were.

Well, she'd mop up later.

"They should make a machine to do this," she muttered.

"That's an interesting idea."

She spun around. Topher sat cross-legged on the floor, his back against a cupboard at the far side of the kitchen, well out of spray range.

"It makes sense," she said, too tired to care if he was secretly laughing.

She grabbed the top towel, then put it aside as too wet and took the second, wrapping the girl in it. A huge yawn shuddered Livvy's ribcage.

"They have machines to wash clothes, dishes, cars," she continued, drying the child's toes. "Why not babies?"

"Well, there are showers," he said.

"Xena said a bath."

He nodded. "I think she meant the bathtub."

"Babies can drown in bathtubs."

"True. And Livvy makes an awful mess in the tub. It was good she had less water to work with here. But she didn't fit real well."

"She's clean."

"Yes," he said, a trace of doubt in his tone. "But the kitch—"

"I've been waiting and waiting upstairs. Are you ever going to give Livvy her bath?" Xena started demanding even before she appeared in the kitchen. "It's way past her bedtime and—What did you *do?*"

Vanessa drew up to her full, dignified height.

"I gave Livvy her bath." She gathered up the sleepy child. "And now I'm putting her to bed." She paused in the doorway, looking back.

"Then I'll clean the kitchen."

"Leave her door open," Xena ordered from behind her, getting in the last word. "She'll scream the house down if she's alone in the dark."

VANESSA SLID THE last button through the last buttonhole of the pajama top, and this time they came out even.

"Done," she said.

She'd changed the child on the bed's mattress, so all she had to do now was draw the covers up.

She picked the damp towel up from the floor and went to the door.

"Good night, Livvy,' she said formally, flipping off the overhead light.

A soft glow remained, emanating from a nightlight and the hallway.

So, everything was done. Yet, she felt something more was called for.

Not sure what, she moved back into the room, to the child's bed-side.

Livvy's eyes tracked her as she neared. Vanessa leaned over, and brushed back one soft curl from her forehead, drawing in the smells of clean, warm child, and fresh sheets.

"Sleep well, Livvy," she said in a low voice.

Livvy pulled her thumb from her mouth and reached up to pat Vanessa's cheek with her palm.

Shocking tears burned Vanessa's eyes.

She blinked them clear, then got out of there, careful to leave the door ajar as Xena had instructed.

Speak of the devil…

As Vanessa emerged, Xena turned into her room, words floating out as the door closed behind her, "Way to flood the kitchen."

Downstairs, Vanessa found Topher standing on a chair, wiping an upper cupboard where water had sprayed.

"Thank you, Topher. But you better do your homework while I clean up." Then she added, "If you'd tell me first where to find a mop. I think that will be the most efficient way to get the ceiling."

He disappeared a moment, returning with a mop a foot taller than him.

"Here. And I can help. I've finished my homework." He looked at the towel in his hand. "Xena says you've used up all the just-washed towels and Dad will notice."

Concern showed through the lenses of his glasses—concern for her.

Shifting her hold on the mop so the head reached the ceiling, she set to wiping the area over the sink.

"Then, when we finish here, I'll do the laundry. Because there is a machine to wash towels, and I know how to run it."

He made a small sound she realized was laughter.

VANESSA PICKED UP the last of the newly washed and dried towels to fold it. It was oversized, and since she was sitting beside Topher on a bench behind the breakfast table, she had little room to maneuver.

"Livvy used to talk," Topher said abruptly. "I mean normal words."

She gave him her interest without speaking.

"Little stuff, but everybody'd say how smart she was to be talking so early." He looked at her, and she put down the towel. "Xena and I used to talk to her all the time. I think she wanted to keep up with us."

"That sounds reasonable."

"Yeah. A reasonable hypothesis." His solemn nod confirmed his words. Then he sighed. "Then her talking changed. You know, when our mom left."

"I'd heard that."

He eyed her a moment. She supposed a lot of people had told him they understood how difficult Melissa's departure had been for him, for all of them. From what she'd seen of this boy, he wouldn't easily accept that they did.

His skepticism was something she truly did understand.

"A lot changed after that," he said.

"Like what?"

"Xena got bossy. People asked how I was a lot. Dad's lines changed."

"Lines?"

"He has lines. Here." He placed his finger at the corner of her eye. "You have some, too. I don't, not unless I make a face in the mirror. After I'm done making the face, they go away. Dad's don't."

A scientific examination of the emergence of laugh lines in the Kincannon male. She bit the inside of her mouth to keep from smiling. "How did your dad's lines change?"

"They used to all go up." He drew curving lines on his own face with his finger. "Now a lot of them go down." When he drew these lines his mouth drooped in a corresponding curve.

"You're very good at changing expressions. I see exactly what you mean from your face."

"You mean like … acting?"

"I suppose so."

They sat in silence a moment before he said, "Mrs. Teramori asked me again to be in the play."

She was unsure if he considered this good or bad. "What did you say?"

"I said I'm still thinking. I don't like to just give answers like that when people first ask."

"Makes sense."

Another silence descended, settled, before he spoke again. "What you said before—about trying things we're scared to do—have you tried any?"

"Some."

"Did it end up okay?"

"It did when I joined Zeke's company."

"Any others?"

She considered. "Some of the instances were not at all comfortable at the time, however, they were necessary to get me to where I wanted to go, to where I am now. Others … I don't know yet how they might turn out."

He nodded his understanding. "But you had to be brave to try."

"I suppose I did." She hadn't seen it that way before.

He looked away. "If I tell Mrs. Teramori yes, will you come to the play?"

"Yes."

He peered at her. "Really?"

"Yes."

His sudden smile was as wide, as all-encompassing, as beautiful as his father's.

But before she could revel in it, it was gone, replaced by his solemn voice. "I've been thinking about what you said before—about a machine to wash babies. It would have to be adjustable."

She nodded. "But if the variables could be quantified…"

JOSH HAD HIS key in the lock but hadn't turned it when the door opened.

"You've been gone forever." Xena took his briefcase, placing it beside the bookcase where he always left his keys. "How's Fay?"

"She'll be okay. You did the right thing, but you should be in bed, Xena." He shrugged out of his raincoat and hung it up. "Why are you still up?"

She rolled her eyes. "Like I would go to bed."

Concern rose up. "Livvy?"

"She's in bed, asleep. *Finally.*"

His daughter's disapproval said Vanessa hadn't met Xena's schedule. But it wasn't unusual that a babysitter didn't reach Xena's lofty expectations. Josh's concern ebbed. "Topher?"

"Oh, he's having a *fine* time. Though he should have been in bed an hour ago."

Halfway down the length of the living room, he became aware of low voices from the breakfast area.

He stopped at the archway, taking in Vanessa and Topher, their heads close together. They were drawing on the same piece of paper, even though they had enough paper spread out to allow a score of pages each. The table also held a bath sheet that appeared to have been folded once, then dropped and forgotten. Paper drifted atop it.

"They've been at it forever," Xena said in disgust.

"At what?"

His daughter shrugged, disavowing any knowledge or interest.

"Vanessa?" Josh pitched his voice louder than usual. "How did it go?"

Topher jumped, looking not only startled but … wary?

Before he could double-check his son's expression—or his own reaction to it—Vanessa's acknowledgement of his presence caught his attention.

She raised her head as if in slow motion, blinking like she was waking up. When recognition came into her eyes, she smiled.

At him. Directly into his eyes.

Also like someone waking up.

Like a woman waking up after a long, satisfying night, and giving her lover that special, intimate morning-after smile.

"Hi, Josh." Her voice was morning-after husky, too. It brushed nerve-endings all through his body. "How's Fay?"

"She's doing okay. What are you two working on so intently?"

"A machine to wash babies."

It was his turn to blink. "What?"

"Not newborn," Vanessa amended. "They're too delicate."

"They got this stupid idea from giving Livvy her bath." Xena's contribution contradicted her earlier statement that she had no idea what they were doing.

"But once they're old enough to follow instructions," Vanessa continued as if Xena hadn't spoken.

"And you should see what she did to the kitchen," Xena added.

He looked around. "It looks fine."

"Now, maybe," Xena said scornfully, "but it was a disaster."

"In fact," Josh said, noticing gleaming surfaces. "It looks really good."

"Topher helped," Vanessa said.

"Did you?" Josh smiled, but the boy didn't raise his head.

"I better get to bed," he said in his usual mumble.

"That's a good idea," Josh said. "You, too, Xena."

His daughter glared, turned on her heel and pounded up the stairs.

What was that about?

He was about to call her to come down and say good-night and thank you to Vanessa, when Vanessa's words to Topher interrupted him.

"…so it could be an intriguing project for the Science Fair. Although, I do like your other ideas."

"Science Fair? You're planning to enter the Science Fair?" Topher wasn't old enough to qualify automatically. "You'd have to get a waiver."

"I haven't decided. It's not till spring."

"I know, but if you want to, you'll need a waiver."

"I dunno," Topher mumbled. He clutched the paper to his chest as he looked at Vanessa. "Good night, Ms. Irish. Thank you."

He said those words distinctly. Then, as he passed Josh on the way to the stairway, he reverted to his usual mumble for a "Night."

Josh sighed as he sank into Topher's deserted spot beside Vanessa, who was organizing the remaining papers.

"You've definitely made a conquest," he said.

Her eyes flashed to his, then away. "Topher?" Her would-be light tone carried a thread of strain. "If we get along well, that would barely bring me to the break-even point with your children."

"Oh?" Edginess rose up. He'd had this conversation with women before.

"Livvy and I wrestled to a tie. Xena hates me."

She said it with no heat, no emotion. But he knew his lines.

"I'm sure Xena doesn't hate you. I'm sure she holds you in high regard—"

"If you believe that, I have to adjust my assessment of either your intelligence or your honesty."

Taken aback, Josh met her eyes, and saw only facing-the-facts calm.

A spurt of sound escaped him. Part chuckle, part relieved sigh, part groan. He didn't need to mollify this woman's hurt feelings, or pretend his daughter adored her. He could be honest.

"Xena is—"

She stopped his words with a hand on his arm just below where he'd rolled back his shirtsleeve.

Not because the touch was a warning—it took several heartbeats to realize that's what it was—but because it was her fingertips on his skin.

Only after those heartbeats of warmth zipping gladly through his bloodstream from that spot to other spots far more sensitive and oh-so-happy to contemplate what Vanessa's touch on them might feel like, did he recognize the warning.

Following her gaze, he twisted around and saw a shadow on the stairs. Xena was listening.

"Xena thought I didn't know how to do things the way your—" Vanessa gave the briefest pause. "—family does them, and she's right. But she thought that's the only way, and she's wrong about that. Now, tell me, how is Fay?"

"You asked that before."

"Yes. How is Fay really?"

He tipped his head in acknowledgement of her point. "There shouldn't be permanent damage to the eye, though the swelling has to go down before the doctors will swear to it. A little to the right and it could have been a lot worse. They gave her something for pain and they're keeping her overnight."

"It's good that they're keeping her overnight?" she asked cautious-ly.

"Yeah, it's good. Gives everyone a cooling off period, plus gives Darcie time to find out what happened. Fay says she ran into a door."

"She won't stay with her aunt and uncle anymore?" She still spoke like someone testing a pond in winter, making sure the surface wouldn't shatter and dump her into freezing water.

"If I have anything to say about it she will." Then he caught on— God, he was tired. Of course, Vanessa didn't know. "This wasn't from Rose or Al. Fay went to her mother's. That much we know. After that, it gets fuzzy. But let's leave it until Darcie sorts things out. For tonight, I'm beat and there must be other things to talk about."

Like her. Like that look she gave him when he came in. Like the way he felt when she touched him.

Their look held. Her eyes changed, as if a haze were being wiped away.

Her breath hitched slightly and she looked around the room.

"It's too late." She cleared her throat, as if she hadn't liked how her voice sounded, though he had. "It's too late to dig into our work tonight. I better go."

"You don't have to go. You could stay, have a glass of wine. We could, uh, talk."

CHAPTER NINE

H E'D BLOWN IT.

Could have been the mention of wine. Or that Freudian hesitation before *talk*. Or possibly the mere fact of wanting her to stick around.

But if he ever wanted to know how to have CFO Irish wipe away Vanessa in an instant, he knew the trick now.

She stood abruptly. "No, thank you."

"Vanessa—"

"I have an early conference call."

She grabbed the bath sheet from the table, but he took it from her. "I'll do that."

"Very well. I'll see you at the meeting with Zeke and Quince at the end of the week. I'll see myself out. No need to—"

"You're not seeing yourself out," He guided her to the front of the house.

At the closet he took out her raincoat and held it for her. A flicker of exasperation showed, but she acquiesced. Even when she was in it, he retained his hold on one side, coming around in front of her. "And you're not going anywhere without me. I drove you here, remember?"

"Oh. But your children—?"

"Will be okay for ten minutes. Xena knows the drill." He pitched his voice louder. "Don't you?"

"Yeah," came the answer from the upstairs hall, where Xena had hastily retreated.

Vanessa withdrew behind her bland exterior during the quick trip to her car, but he didn't let that bother him.

It had developed thin spots lately, like an old curtain wearing out. Definite thin spots.

And he'd keep working on them.

They had not only the schedule to work out, but a whole lot of items on the schedule that would continue to demand that they work together. Plus, Zeke had apparently mandated that she come to home football games. And the next home game was this Saturday.

She got out of the car without waiting for him to come around and open the door, but he'd parked to give himself the advantage and beat her to the driver's door of her car.

She beeped the door open, he pulled it wide, but before she could slide past him, he stepped in and, taking care not to touch her—though whether for her sake or his own, he didn't know—drew the lapels of her coat together.

"It's getting cold out," he said.

"I'll be fine. I—"

"I know you'll be fine. I like looking out for you."

Her head snapped up, her eyes wide. Before she could produce a response that tried to discount the image of his looking out for her, he added, "I owe you big-time for tonight, Vanessa. Thank you."

"You're welcome. But there's no need—"

"Yeah, there is. And I'll make sure you collect this debt."

With a hand to her back he guided her into the car, closed the door firmly and walked to his car.

She didn't drive away for a long moment, as if she'd needed time to accept he wasn't going anywhere until he saw her safely off.

VANESSA HAD LONG ago learned the art of checking intra-office e-mail alerts without breaking her concentration on her primary task.

But this Tuesday morning, working on her laptop at Mrs. R's desk overlooking trees where green leaves had become a minority, this particular e-mail from Janine did break her concentration.

*Darcie Barrett asks that you call her at the police station. IMMEDI-
ATELY.*

When Vanessa called, Darcie didn't waste time.

"Fay O'Hearn is here at the station—"

Vanessa closed the lid of her laptop.

"—and she's asked if you'd be willing to sit in on the interview with her. Now."

"Me?"

Darcie didn't comment on her astonishment. "You wouldn't have official standing or bear any responsibility. It's simply to give her support."

"I…" Vanessa swallowed, then swallowed again. "I'll be right there."

Drago's police department occupied the basement of the town hall. Four doors, labeled "Interview," "Chief," "Evidence," and "Supplies," lined up along the wall opposite the stairs. In front of the doors were eight desks paired into four cubicles. Closer to the stairs, a round woman wearing a headset presided over an arc of computer screens and communications equipment.

The woman flicked a look at Vanessa, then spun her chair toward the console, and pushed buttons.

"May I help you?" offered a burly man in uniform who'd been filling a mug at the coffee station tucked under the stairs.

"Vanessa Irish is here," said the round woman. "Some policeman you are, Archibald. Don't even know the Zeke-Tech CFO when you see her. Darcie'll be right here."

It took Vanessa a second to unravel that the woman had directed the first sentence to the mouthpiece of her headset, the last one to Vanessa, and in between to the burly officer now swelling with indignation.

"Corine, I've told you a thousand times, call me Sarge like every-body else or address me by my last name and title, but you—"

Vanessa tuned out the rest as Darcie came out of the door marked

"Chief" and closed it behind her, but not before Vanessa had seen a dark-haired woman and a nearly bald man huddled on side-by-side chairs. Resolve structured their faces, even as worry dug lines into their skin.

"Fay's aunt and uncle," Darcie said, following the direction of Vanessa's gaze. Then she added briskly. "Thanks for coming. As I said on the phone, you won't have official standing or bear any responsibility."

"Does she need a lawyer?"

"No, no. She's in as a witness. You're here for support, strictly support. This way."

Vanessa had to consciously order her feet to follow.

Darcie opened the door labeled "Interview." It was a small room, windowless and outfitted with a rectangular table and four chairs. Fay sat at the table, her posture and expression echoing her aunt and uncle's.

"Fay? Here's Ms. Irish."

She turned, and Vanessa felt a burning in her chest.

The left side of the girl's face was purpling and swollen, her eye barely a slit.

"Oh." Fay sounded surprised, yet relieved.

Neither made sense.

Fay had asked for her, so how could she be surprised? As for relief, that made sense only if she expected help from Vanessa, but how could she help?

"Hello, Fay," she said cautiously.

Not cautiously enough, because a sheen covered the girl's uninjured eye, though her voice was steady. "Thank you for coming."

Before Vanessa's failure to come up with a response became obvious, Darcie gestured her to the chair beside Fay, and sat opposite them.

Fay shifted, bringing her arm in contact with Vanessa's. Quelling an instinct to regain space, Vanessa left her arm where it was.

Darcie leaned back, her posture, face, and voice relaxed as she talked about wanting to get a few things cleared up, Fay had to know she wasn't in trouble, that everyone wanted to make sure things were going okay for her.

It was a long, meandering, repetitious speech very unlike Darcie. Vanessa felt a pinch between her brows as she wondered when Darcie would get to the point of who had hit the girl.

She was distracted from impatience when she felt a lessening in the tension in Fay's arm.

Darcie's roundabout discourse touched on how every family had tensions and it was difficult when a girl wasn't old enough to be on her own, but was becoming a woman and—

"I swear I never came on to him, no matter what anybody says."

Darcie, apparently not surprised by Fay's fierce interruption, asked in the same easy tone, "Who says that?"

"He does." *He* twisted in Fay's mouth like it tasted bad. "And … and my mother. But I never have. Never. I dress like everybody else. It's not like my clothes show everything or I dress like a … a—well, you know."

"No, you don't," Darcie said, cutting through the tangle. "But even if you did, it wouldn't give anyone the right to touch you when you didn't want, Fay. Clothes can send a signal, so it makes good sense to dress, well, sensibly. But it's like stop signals—even if they go out, nobody is entitled to go speeding through the intersection. There are still rules. People who break the rules are the ones at fault. Anyone who's touched you inappropriately will be held to account."

Fay looked up. "Oh. No. Did you think—? He didn't—He talks about how I look and—well, you know. Talks and talks and talks when I'm around. It creeps me out, because he's gross, not to mention being about a hundred years old. But he hasn't touched me."

Darcie didn't show surprise by even a blink, but smoothly shifted. "Inappropriate touching doesn't have to be sexual. The blow to your face—"

"It's just a black eye."

"It's not just a black eye. It's a serious injury."

Something in Fay's expression caught at Vanessa's throat. She had a ... a *feeling* about where this was going.

"But it wasn't intentional. I mean, it wasn't an accident. Not exactly," the girl amended, clearly struggling to be honest. "But I don't think it was really on purpose, either. Not to hurt me like this. She was angry, because I'd asked for tax forms and stuff for financial aid, and I didn't back down. Then he came in and she was screaming and—But it wasn't like she meant to. It wasn't—"

Vanessa put her hand over Fay's wrist. "Saying what it wasn't can't make it stop being what it was, no matter how much you want that. Wanting people to not be what they are doesn't work. I know that."

A wash of tears covered the girl's visible eye and slid from the slit of the other.

Darcie spoke softly. "Who hit you, Fay?"

The girl snuffled. Finally, with a breath that shuddered her shoulders, Fay spoke.

"Mom." She sucked in another sob, then said, "My mother hit me."

RETURNING TO THE interview room after ushering out Fay and her aunt and uncle, Darcie flopped into the chair with a gusty sigh.

"I feel like a wet rag. You were great, Vanessa. You said exactly the right thing at the right time to get her to talk. I was afraid she'd never give up Ellie."

"You knew her mother hit her?"

Darcie grimaced. "Unless someone did fancy footwork, Fay was hit by a right-hander and the boyfriend's a lefty. Besides, he's more a burnout than an abuser. Then there's the jealousy thing. Fay's young and pretty and her mother's been drinking for years. Plus, Fay was showing up with way too many bruises a while back to be accidental. But Fay would never tell us. I needed her to say it this time, but she'd been giving me nonsense about running into a door. Told her aunt and uncle that, too."

"She was so adamant about not wanting you to do anything to her mother."

Darcie shook her head. "Talk about misplaced loyalty. But sometimes kids in that situation can't give up their hope."

"Perhaps."

Darcie quirked an eyebrow at her. "If you know something that would help…"

"I've only talked with the girl a handful of times."

"She seems to have connected to you. I don't want to pry, but if she's seeing a similarity in backgrounds, and there's something you can tell me…"

Vanessa shook her head, which didn't help the growing ache there. "She doesn't know anything about me—my background—not really. And I wasn't ever hit. We talked about the desire to go to college and that I didn't have parental support. I encouraged her to find out about scholarships and aid. You heard what she said about going there to try to get her mother to give her financial information. If I hadn't—"

"Don't you start taking on blame. Ellie O'Hearn is the one to blame—the only one." Darcie stood, and Vanessa did, too. "Don't worry about this, Vanessa. That's my job. We'll sort it out. You should feel good that you were a shoulder to lean on for a good kid when she needed it."

Darcie encircled Vanessa with her arms and squeezed.

Vanessa forced herself to release her held breath and to relax into the hug.

JOSH HADN'T BEEN sure Vanessa would be at Darcie and Zeke's house, not until he walked in Saturday evening.

They'd exchanged business e-mails, but hadn't talked since Monday night, when she'd looked after the kids. At this afternoon's game, there'd been no opportunity to do more than say hello. So he didn't know precisely how far she'd retreated after his *stay-and-uh-talk*.

She smiled. That was good.

But before he could approach her, Darcie handed him a plate and pushed him toward the buffet. General conversation kept him occupied while he ate, but then he tracked down Vanessa.

His luck was in, because the lone Zeke-Techer who'd been sharing her table left as he sat.

"How are you, Vanessa?"

"I'm fine thank you. You look tired." Blunt and accurate.

"I am." Their eyes met. "I heard you were great with Fay."

"I didn't do anything."

"That's not what Darcie said. Or Fay."

"She's talked to you? About what happened?"

"Not much. Just said you were very kind. You know, she reached out to you for a reason, Vanessa. Kids don't do things like that at random."

"I don't know why she would."

"Don't you?"

She looked up at the challenge he'd purposefully put in his voice. "She might think we have things in common. Disappointment in parents, seeing college—education—as a solution," she said. "But she doesn't know how different our situations are. Totally different."

"She will if you tell her."

Vanessa looked almost frightened. He wanted to take her in his arms to comfort her—hell, he just wanted to take her in his arms.

"I could, perhaps, see how her eye's healing and, uh, how she's doing."

"I think she'd appreciate that. If you want to talk about it, Vanessa…"

She squared her shoulders. "No. Thank you. No."

They sat in silence. He listened to Zeke and Darcie laughing at something as they stacked dirty plates, watched Trent bring a dish to Jennifer as she consolidated leftovers, then steal a kiss.

Sometimes this gig as high school principal, single father of three, and thus essentially celibate back into misty memory and forward into the foreseeable future was truly a pain in the ass.

Vanessa cleared her throat. "I want to ask to you about something."

"Okay."

"I have an idea for Zeke and Darcie's present, but it copies yours."

"I thought that was taken care of by your assistant."

"I, uh, it's a personal gift, not a business gift, so I'm selecting it." She rushed her words. "Only I had no good ideas until—only it came from what you're doing and if you think it's too close, or you don't want—"

"No points off for copying a wedding gift idea, Vanessa. But I'm curious now—what's the idea?"

"Holly bushes. Zeke has said they had some in his yard when he was growing up and he liked that they stayed green in winter. Many varieties won't grow here, but I researched through an arboretum near Chicago, and found a grower in Oregon who carries the kind the expert recommends. And it seemed right, because it takes a male and a female plant to, uh…"

"Make berries?" he prompted. "It's a great idea, Vanessa. It doesn't copy my idea, it complements it. The hollies will be green in the winter when the lilacs are dormant."

She let out a long breath and her shoulders eased. "Thank you, Josh."

"I didn't do anything, but my pleasure."

THAT FRIDAY, JOSH heard Vanessa's voice as soon as the whine of Todd's saw quit.

He followed it through the computer lab building like the scent of apple pie fresh from the oven—enjoying the aroma and anticipating the main event.

After Saturday evening at Darcie and Zeke's, she'd flown out the next day and had returned to Drago only yesterday afternoon, with work scheduled all day today, then Zeke and Darcie's wedding Saturday.

"…I would go even farther than that, Mr. Cottle," Vanessa was saying, "and contend that education is the one way a person can escape what he's been and become what he hadn't known he was capable of."

Despite the masculine pronoun, he'd bet she was talking about herself.

As he came around the corner, he amended that bet—herself and Fay O'Hearn. The girl was there, along with the rest of Malcolm's Citizen's Committee—Barry, Mrs. Richards, Mrs. Mudge, and Corine, chief dispatcher for the police department.

He'd heard that Vanessa had ice cream and a conversation with Fay within a couple hours of her return to town.

That news came to him by the usual Drago method. Barry had seen them, and mentioned it to Jennifer when he went to the auto dealership for his post-football-practice job. Jennifer had told Trent, who'd mentioned it to Josh last night at Zeke's bachelor party.

Remembering that decidedly low-key gathering, he smiled.

Zeke, Quince, Trent, Josh, Jorge O'Fallon from Stenner Autos, Police Chief Dutch Harnett, and Everett Hooper, a farmer Zeke liked, had played poker at Dutch's house, which he now shared with Darcie's mother, Martha. The refreshments had been lovingly provided by Martha Barrett and Mrs. Zeekowsky.

"I heartily endorse education, as you might imagine," Malcolm said. "But I fear you are asking education to carry a great weight. I have in my files a most fascinating study that shows that other elements—"

Josh, passing a stack of plywood, saw Vanessa shake her head.

"Education alone can allow people to change their lives completely. To break away. To go new places. Take this computer lab as an example. It can prepare some of Drago's students to enter the high-tech world that is doing so many exciting things, not only on the West Coast, but also in Virginia, and elsewhere. So this lab can give people a totally new life."

"Or allow them to improve the life they already have," Josh added.

Vanessa's head swung around to him. She straightened from a

comfortable slouch against a sawhorse and took up a stance like a fighter about to deliver a punch. Or back away.

"Ah, Josh," Malcolm said.

Josh never took his eyes off Vanessa. "You're talking about the lab as a ticket to send our kids to one coast or the other, but have you noticed *your* tech firm is moving here?"

From the corner of his eye he was aware of their audience. Fay and Barry looked thrilled and uncomfortable. Corine watched with keen attention. Mrs. R jogged Mrs. Mudge's elbows and hissed "Told you so!"

"A portion of it is moving here, true," Vanessa said. "A move based on its founder's ties to his hometown. Not a move Zeke ordered from any belief that Drago could become the next Silicon Valley."

"It doesn't need to become the next Silicon Valley to succeed. Not every decision should be based on dollars and cents. Emotional ties can be damned good reasons for decisions."

She arched her brows, popping the left one high.

"It occurs to me," Malcolm murmured in a soothing-the-quarrelling-children tone, "that this question cannot be resolved between the two of you. The result resides in the desires, hopes, and ambitions of other people. Vanessa maintains the people of Drago will use the computer lab as a tool to leave. Josh is adamant they will use it as a tool to remain. Time will tell which course of action more follow. In the meantime it is only sensible for Vanessa to become better acquainted with the people the lab will serve."

She muttered something.

Malcolm ignored it and went on, "You clearly possess an intellect that requires more immediate proof than someone else's experience. You must make your own observations. The perfect opportunity presents itself for you to observe the young people of Drago, gaining impressions on which to base your assessments and—"

"We already held a meeting with the citizens of Drago."

"But you don't accept what the people there told you," Josh said.

"It's not a matter of accepting what they say. It's a matter of having far greater experience in this field than anyone here has."

"The people of Drago have far greater experience at being them than you do."

Malcolm reclaimed the conversation. "As I said, what I have in mind would give you an opportunity, Vanessa, to gain information for making your own assessment at the same time you would be doing this community a service. All it requires is a few hours of your time next Saturday night."

"That's not—"

"And since you'll be in town for the football game and staying into the next week after having closed Zeke-Tech's books for the year—" Malcolm spoke over her. Vanessa's eyes widened, confirming her amateur status at dealing with Drago. As if everyone didn't already know her schedule in detail. "—that should work out wonderfully."

Vanessa's mouth closed with a snap.

"Excellent." Malcolm beamed as if she'd agreed with alacrity. "I know my dear wife, Bertie, looks forward to meeting you. And I shall claim a dance."

"Dance?"

"Oh, yes, my dear. We have been seeking an additional chaperone for the Homecoming dance, so it's providential that you've agreed to help us out."

"What a great idea," Fay said.

"Cool," Barry said.

"You want me to chaperone a high school dance?" Vanessa sounded as if Malcolm had suggested she run naked down Main Street.

Now, why the hell did he call up *that* image?

Before it could sink its teeth deeper into him, Josh said whatever came to mind. "Chaperone and dance the first dance with me."

And now the image was of dancing with her naked. Talk about into the fire...

"I don't dance." Vanessa's voice sounded strange.

"That's a shame, my dear, but not an absolute requirement. And now that we're all here, we must get to the work of the committee. Just let me add that it will be lovely to have you join us." Malcolm took her limp hand between both of his, a parody of a handshake to seal the deal. "So lovely."

CHAPTER TEN

"DO YOU ANTON Pavel Zeekowsky…"

Odd how familiar the words of the wedding service had become.

Only after Zeke-Tech grew and employees started inviting the bosses did she get wedding invitations.

Quince insisted she and Zeke go. He drove them to ensure they arrived on time and didn't leave too early. He guided them through the intricacies of social customs and refused to let them remain in a corner during the reception.

But on this bright, Indian Summer afternoon in Zeke and Darcie's backyard she was on her own.

Zeke stood with Darcie before the minister, saying his vows, and Quince stood beside him as best man.

She'd protested when an usher—a fellow officer of Darcie's, she thought—put her in the second row, just behind Zeke's mother. He'd quieted her with "Darcie's orders."

When Zeke and Quince came to stand before the gathering under a huge tree flaming orange, red, and yellow against sunwashed blue sky, Quince had winked at her and Zeke grinned.

Then the music started, and every fiber of Zeke's attention centered on Darcie. Looking only at his face, Vanessa knew the instant Darcie came into his sight.

That was the first time her throat constricted.

It happened again when Darcie came into view on the arm of Chief of Police Dutch Harnett. After the Chief delivered Darcie to Zeke, he'd taken a front-row chair from each side of the aisle and put them together in the middle, so Zeke's mother and Darcie's mother sat side by side, with him beside Martha Barrett.

"…to be your lawfully wedded wife?" the minister asked.

"I do!" Zeke said with enthusiasm.

Behind her, people chuckled. In front of her, the mothers joined hands and beamed.

Vanessa felt her mouth curve as the couple faced the gathering, displaying equally broad smiles. They kissed and hugged each mother. Zeke shook hands with the Chief and helped him return the mothers' chairs.

Zeke and Darcie started up the aisle, beaming, holding hands.

Married.

As best man and matron of honor, Quince and Jennifer followed, then the two mothers and the Chief.

Rising, Vanessa turned to follow the others up the aisle and encountered rows and rows of faces suffused with joy. It was like being dazzled by the sun. So many people so happy for Zeke and Darcie.

Darcie, looking fabulous in a simple and elegant dress, stopped her with a fierce hug or Vanessa, still dazzled, might have wandered past the informal receiving line.

"I'm so glad you're with us today, Vanessa," Darcie said.

Vanessa began to repeat the phrases Quince had shaped for her years ago. But with Darcie hugging her firmly, the words stopped.

"I'm so glad, too," she said, and hugged Darcie back. "You and Zeke are wonderful together."

To her astonishment, her eyes welled with tears. As she and Darcie released each other, she saw that the bride also had tears in her eyes.

Zeke grinned as he put one arm around each woman. "No crying, you two."

Vanessa stretched up to kiss him on the cheek.

A gesture followed immediately by a rush of awkwardness. But Zeke's hug tightened before he released her.

She moved on to Jennifer, murmuring a few shreds of Quince's phrases, but mostly smiling. In a suit of dusty green fabric with a slight shimmer, Jennifer was classically beautiful. And breathtaking, judging from Trent's expression as he arrived beside her.

Quince was next in the receiving line. He winked at Vanessa over the head of Mrs. Z as he leaned down to hear something the tiny woman said. Vanessa smiled and made way for other guests—those whose joy had so dazzled her.

Finding an empty spot in a corner of the yard, she looked back to the happy clot around the bride and groom.

Many times, she had felt she and Zeke and Quince were the odd trio amid a world of twos. Especially during stretches when nearly every weekend held a Zeke-Tech wedding.

Now Zeke had joined the twos, leaving only her and Quince.

She watched a heavyset woman with red hair smile at Quince with the expression Vanessa recognized from observing many females dealing with him.

Women at Zeke-Tech considered him a hunk. To her, he was simply Quince.

More evidence that she was out of sync with her gender. For that matter, with humanity.

She turned toward the lowering sun glowing through the trees.

She felt a hand at her back. A touch. The warmth of human contact through the fabric of her dress sinking into her. Into her skin, yes, but deeper. Into her.

Turning, she already knew.

No, that was ridiculous.

Her brain had instantaneously sorted probabilities and landed on the most likely person. That was all.

"Come spring, this will be a great spot when those bloom lilacs." Josh pointed. "The bushes that led to Drago's annual Lilac Festival, which led to Zeke's return, which led to the computer lab and Zeke-Tech's division moving here, and to this terrific wedding. Not bad for humble bushes, huh?"

"It was a wonderful wedding."

"Was? The celebration's just starting. Here tonight, and later on in

Virginia, right?"

"Yes, there's a reception planned at Zeke-Tech. Darcie didn't want people to feel obligated to travel here. So they'll stop in Virginia on their way back from their honeymoon in Paris. Zeke's assistant, Roberta, is handling the details."

"Ah, I've met her. So, the reception will go off without a hitch?"

Vanessa nodded. "Without a hitch. It will be low-key because that's what Darcie wants, and Roberta respects her. And it will be lovely because Roberta adores Zeke."

"She doesn't strike me as the adoring kind."

"Adores him in a totally clear-eyed way."

"That's more like it. Speaking of adore, my youngest's smitten."

"With whom?"

He pulled his head back in a quick gesture she interpreted as meaning: *Are you kidding?* "With you, of course. Topher was talking about you, and Livvy joined in, and it was clear she was singing your praises." Josh sobered. "I really appreciate your talking to him."

"I didn't do it as a favor to you." Oh, God, that came out wrong. This was why she avoided talking. "I'm sorry. I did enjoy—I didn't mean—"

"It's okay, your bluntness is an old friend by now. Besides, what kind of father would I be if I *wanted* you talking to my son as a favor to me? I'm glad you enjoy talking to him. And I'm especially glad he enjoys talking to you, because he sure doesn't talk to me."

She should say something. Something about how she was sure Topher would talk to him. But that wasn't true. She'd seen Topher's discomfort, and how it hurt Josh—

"Hey, you shivered," Josh said. "With the sun going, it's getting chilly out here. Let's go in. Everyone's headed that way."

The moment to respond was gone.

She couldn't deny her relief, yet she felt she'd let Topher down. And Josh.

They followed other guests in through new French doors to a bookcase-lined room with a bar set up across one corner. A wide archway opened to the large room destined to become the living room. A string trio played softly. Servers distributed champagne.

Josh took two glasses from a tray, his arm brushing hers as he handed her one. How could that set off friction that translated to a charge that passed through her?

"I hadn't seen this area before," he said. "Looks like they've taken down several walls."

So *his* mind wasn't on friction and charges.

House renovations had taken a break to let Martha Barrett and Mrs. Z work magic by draping silky white fabric to soften corners and mask unfinished surfaces. Round tables with white tablecloths over russet skirts and chairs covered in similar fabric were grouped around the rooms, and everywhere candles in hurricanes glowed.

As the sun set outside, it was like lights coming up on a stage inside.

"Hey, Vanessa." Quince's voice didn't surprise her, but his hand on her shoulder as he reached across to shake hands with Josh did. "Nice to see you again, Josh."

She studied Quince's profile as he leaned past her.

She and Zeke and Quince weren't touchy-feely people. Her kissing Zeke's cheek and his hug could be put down to this being his wedding day, but Quince's gesture couldn't.

"Good to see you, too, Quince."

"I hear great things about the progress on the computer lab."

"We're two and a half days behind," Vanessa said.

Quince's hand squeezed her shoulder. "That's our Vanessa. Keeping everyone on the straight and narrow." He smiled, then took stock. "You look great. I like that dress, Vanessa."

She looked down at the dark green silk. "I've worn it to a lot of weddings, since you and Janine said I couldn't wear the brown one."

"Well, you look particularly good in it today. I—"

"Quince, time for the toast." Martha Barrett glided up, smiling at Vanessa and Josh. "You don't mind if I steal him, do you?"

They said the appropriate "not-at-alls" and Martha and Quince headed toward the staircase.

"I don't mean to monopolize you," Josh said.

She checked his expression to see if it helped her make sense of that odd tone. No. She waited for him to say more.

"Quince seemed to be making a point," he said.

"I know. But I have no idea what." She adjusted her hold on the champagne flute.

"As long as we're being blunt, the way he acted, sort of possessive, I wondered if I'd missed something."

"What?"

"Like maybe you and Quince are involved."

"No."

"You don't sound totally happy about that." He was watching her.

"You mean like I'm … pining for him? No. Nothing like that. He's a colleague." She hesitated, then added. "A friend. If I absolutely had to be with someone, it would be convenient with Quince."

He laughed. Full out, and loud enough to draw attention from every corner. He did have a nice laugh.

"Oh, Vanessa, I do love—I do love that about you." When he continued, he spoke fast. "Most people don't look for convenience first in a relationship, you know. So, you're saying Quince was being protective of a friend."

"I don't know why he would be."

"Don't you?" He took another sip of champagne. She couldn't see his expression, though she doubted that would have helped her much in untangling the subtext in his words. "He was certainly right though, you look very nice."

"Thank you."

He angled his head. "Now why don't you like hearing you look good?"

She said nothing.

"For the same reason you usually wear those suits of yours?"

Would she have answered him? Didn't matter. The sound of champagne glasses being tapped halted all conversation.

"I hope you'll all raise your glasses to join me in saluting Darcie and Zeke." Quince stood on the bottom step, with the newly married couple two steps above him. "We should all be so lucky to be as happy as I know they will be. We should all be so good as to deserve that luck even half as much."

He raised his glass, smiling up at them.

"To Darcie and Zeke."

Vanessa's throat constricted again as she raised her glass and her voice joined everyone else's, including the deep voice beside her in saying, "To Darcie and Zeke."

EVEN AS HE'D laughed, Josh had felt a prod of pain.

...if I absolutely had to be with someone...

Why did she view it that way? She deserved more. She deserved everything that joyous robe indicated lived inside her.

He wanted to know why she kept it hidden.

More, he wanted—oh, yeah, no denying this—he wanted to be there when she stopped hiding it.

And making the whole matter a hell of a lot more complicated as well as dangerous to one Josh Kincannon—high school principal, single father of three, and thus essentially celibate both back into misty memory and forward into the foreseeable future—he wanted her to *want* to do that with him there.

His mouth twisted.

There he went indulging in grandiose goals again.

If you had any ambition at all, you'd...

How many of Melissa's complaints had included that phrase?

And he was unquestionably guilty as charged when it came to the kind of ambition she'd meant. He'd wanted a good life, with a woman who loved him and their kids. A woman who'd be his partner in their community, in their family, in their bed.

No, he didn't want much. Just more than the woman he'd married could deliver.

When she'd left he'd vowed his kids would never again suffer for his Wrong About Women track record.

Not to mention that Vanessa had not shown the least interest in a relationship with him.

In fact, CFO Irish backpedaled so fast when any connection sparked between them that if he truly fell for her, he'd surely fall flat on his face.

So he wouldn't fall.

For his kids' sake.

And for his own.

Oh, Vanessa, I do love—I do love that about you.

A slip of the tongue. Nothing more.

Although not another woman in a million would have let it slide the way she had.

Josh bobbed along with the familiar flow of the reception, enjoying the celebration, spending time with nearly everyone, having plenty of champagne, and never losing awareness of one particular guest.

That's when it occurred to him.

Vanessa, that woman in a million to let his slip of the tongue slide, could be just what he needed.

It could work.

It could.

With both of them determined not to fall, they could explore this attraction.

And in the process, just maybe that doe-in-the-headlights look that lurked under the assurance and intelligence in her eyes could be erased.

He'd like to be the one to do that.

He'd really like that.

"Leaving already?"

Josh had timed it perfectly to reach Vanessa as she stepped beyond the light spilling through the French doors.

"Yes."

"You can't go without seeing the garden." He cupped her elbow, guiding her off the paved path, and into deeper shadows.

She looked toward his hand, then into his face.

"I saw the garden during the wedding. And it's too dark to see anything now." He brought them face to face. "Josh, what are you doing?"

"Getting ready to kiss you." He moved his hand from her elbow to the back of her neck, his index finger sliding into the soft hair at her nape. "It's a wedding custom—like kissing under mistletoe at Christmas time."

She frowned. Not the reaction he'd been going for. "I've been to weddings. It's not a custom."

"Maybe not where you're from, but it is in Drago. Kissing under the lilacs. No reason to be afraid."

"We're not under—"

"Close enough."

He brushed his lips against hers, then a second time. Giving her a chance to bolt.

She didn't.

So he brought their mouths together. Not hit-and-run this time, but firmly G-rated.

He felt the smallest shift from her, a slight adjustment that changed the angle, brought her lips to meet his more fully.

He eased back to look at her.

She held perfectly still, her eyes wide open. Stunned, but with a flicker of flame in their depths.

As he watched, the flicker grew stronger. He shifted his focus to her mouth, letting her know what was coming.

A real kiss this time. A kiss between two adults.

He leaned in.

"Ah, Josh, Vanessa." The familiar voice registered simultaneously with the rustle of bushes. "How nice to see you both. Don't let me intrude. I'll slide right past you and be on my way to retrieve the car and pull it around for my dear Bertie. Tight shoes you know. Doesn't want to walk far."

"Malcolm—"

The older man talked over him. "And we are not alone. Quite a contingent preparing to depart in my wake."

Vanessa stepped around Josh to return to the walkway, dropping her head, but not before Josh had seen that her cheeks were darkened with color.

"Ah, yes." Malcolm made way for her. "See you bright and early Monday morning, Josh. And I will see you one week from now at the dance, if not before, my dear Vanessa. Well, good night! Good night!"

SHE WOULDN'T GO to the dance.

Vanessa stood at her office window, fiddling with the blinds' wand.

Why should she? She'd made no promises.

Malcolm had made all the promises on her behalf, while Josh had watched her. The way he so often did.

Though the way he'd watched her at the wedding—

No, that wasn't the issue.

She'd returned to the office Monday to discover *Drago High School Homecoming Dance* on her official schedule. If she waited much longer to tell Janine to remove it, she would appear indecisive.

So, on a day she needed to check progress in consolidating the year-end accounts, she was thinking about this dance—only the dance—and how she'd been tricked into it.

While Malcolm had set his trap of words, Josh had watched her, his expression going from irked to speculative to pleased.

She'd liked that last look the least. He'd known she was being manipulated into going, and it had pleased him because he reveled in "community."

But she was happier alone, was better off alone.

So, she wouldn't go.

No reason to be afraid.

Josh hadn't said that about the dance. He'd said it about... Oh.

Her fingers touched her mouth.

No reason to be afraid.

A kiss.

Barely even a kiss.

Did he think she'd never been kissed before?

Well, she had, and it didn't scare her. Not at all. Especially not a kiss certainly borne of too much champagne and the emotion of the wedding.

If she didn't go to the dance this weekend, however, he would think that was her reason.

He'd think she was afraid.

She wasn't.

So, she'd have to show him.

CHAPTER ELEVEN

"Would you dance with me, Ms. Irish?" Barry asked.

"Barry," Josh started, sounding faintly amused. "Ms. Irish doesn't dance—"

"Yes, thank you, Barry. I would like to dance with you."

She flicked a glance at Josh, and saw a man accustomed to hiding his reactions in public letting *thunderstruck* show around the edges.

She'd had no intention of dancing.

She'd repeated that fact when Josh asked her earlier, adding that he, however, should feel free to dance all he liked. That would have provided a welcome respite from him standing beside her, making idle conversation.

But he'd replied that he didn't dance at these functions because the only possible partners were usually students or faculty.

So they'd stood there, not talking about exactly what she didn't want to talk about—really, truly didn't want to talk about—as if it had never happened at all.

Until Barry offered her this escape.

Beaming, Barry backed up a few feet and curved his arms into the formal dancing pose.

Panic wiped out Vanessa's relief.

What if Barry was the one kid in this gymnasium who knew how to dance?

All the others were shuffling around the floor. That, she could manage.

As long as the boy didn't expect them to drape over each other the way a few couples did back in the dimmest corner.

Though even that she could deal with better than if he expected her to truly dance.

She placed one hand on Barry's shoulder and the other in his faintly damp palm, and they headed off in a mid-speed shamble, to her infinite relief.

After a half dozen shuffling steps they both relaxed. Barry looked up from his feet and smiled.

She smiled back. "Do you come to all the dances, Barry?"

"Unh-unh." Apparently, talking while dancing was asking too much.

That left her attention to wander.

It wandered right to Josh, standing where they'd left him, watching her. Over Barry's shoulder, her gaze met his.

His face was drawn tighter than usual. His mouth almost grim. He stood with his feet slightly apart, poised for movement. An athlete's pose.

He's probably a marvelous dancer.

And then, in a slice of wanting too fast to turn aside, she wished she were dancing with Josh.

His hand on her back would be warm and sure, spread wide as he guided her through steps that would tilt and whirl. Their bodies would be close, but with the difference in their heights, Josh's breath might stir her hair, and the line of his mouth and jaw would be at perfect eye level.

The music drifted to a slower, contemplative patch.

Vanessa must not have been paying attention, because somehow she and Barry had come to be only inches apart. His hand, once at her shoulder blade, had dropped below her waist.

She reached back to reposition his hand, but just as she touched his wrist, his hand flew off as if she'd become too hot to touch.

"Cutting in, Barry," Josh's voice was unmistakably commanding.

"Mr. Kincannon—?"

Josh had already displaced Barry, one arm around her back, his other picking up her fallen hand. It took her a couple steps to get her left hand to his shoulder where it belonged.

"You never dance," she said stupidly.

"You're not a student. Or staff."

He sounded strained.

No doubt irked that he'd felt obliged to rescue her from Barry's sliding hand by breaking his rule.

She'd have taken care of it, if he'd waited instead of looking after everything and everyone, including her.

She turned her head to deliver that indictment.

She'd been wrong.

Her eye level was even with the top of his sharp cheekbone and the bridge of his nose. She hadn't calculated the heels of her shoes, when she'd imagined looking at his mouth and jaw.

With her eyes lowered, however, she could see that area quite well.

Especially his mouth.

His lips were parted, and his face turned a bit toward her. She'd been right about his breath stirring her hair, though. It teased the hair at her ear, making her shiver.

She pulled in a breath, her gaze jumping to his eyes, to see if he'd noticed.

Only a slit of brown showed between his lashes. His hands tightened. The one around her hand, and the one at her back—with two fingers dipping even lower than Barry's had.

And she did tilt and whirl, but not from the motion of the dance.

The music stopped. For one instant she willed it to go on, to hold onto it with only the force of her thoughts.

The futility of that rushed up, along with heat into her face. She stepped back, in recalcitrant jerks.

"Thank you." Her voice was equally jerky.

"I enjoyed it."

"For rescuing me from Barry," she clarified. "I'm going now."

"The dance doesn't end for another half hour."

"You can do without one chaperone for the last half hour. I have a lot of work tomorrow."

"Sunday?"

"You work on Sundays."

"Yeah, but…"

"So do I."

"I'll walk you out."

"No need."

He ignored that, following her to the coat racks in the hallway. When she said good night there, he cupped his hand under her elbow again and said he'd walk her to the door.

WALK HER TO the door, that's all Josh intended.

But the last hallway before the exterior door stretched out dim and unoccupied to their left and he steered her there before he could think about it.

Then, as in the garden at the reception, he turned her toward him.

"Josh, this isn't—"

"Vanessa, I want to be absolutely clear about this, so I'll be as blunt as you usually are. You said Quince is a friend, but do you have feelings—or have you had feelings for Zeke? Is that why Quince was protective of you at the wedding?"

"*Zeke?* Zeke's in love with Darcie." Every syllable echoed with *Are you out of your mind?*

"I know. But you can't help who you fall for. Attraction can't be controlled. You can be powerfully attracted to someone, even when you know they'll never fall for you."

She would have run—he was certain of it—except he was between her and the exit.

"What's wrong?" he demanded.

"Nothing. It's—I was thinking of material I read that would interest Malcolm. About human attraction. I'll have my assistant send him the study." She could have won a prize for speed-talking. "Scientists have found a specific relative proportion of facial features is most pleasing to the human eye. It can be expressed as a mathematical formula. The quotient…"

He stopped listening, narrowing his eyes as he watched her.

Then he had it.

He could have sung a couple rounds of the Drago High School fight song, or the Halleluiah Chorus. Instead, he kept it simple, cutting across her stream of words with a fervent: "Thank God."

She blinked. "What?"

"You're attracted to me."

"What? Why would you—? What on earth gave you that idea?"

"You revert to robot talk when you're pushed beyond your comfort zone. And what is there to push you beyond your comfort zone here except me? Therefore, I deduce that you are attracted to me. And—"

"That's not at all—"

"And that," he overrode her protest, "is why I said *Thank God.* Because I was damned tired of feeling like this alone."

She opened her mouth, closed it, opened it again. Nothing came out.

He leaned closer. "I thought you were. I hoped you were. But I wasn't entirely sure. I thought possibly Quince or Zeke… But now I know. We're both—"

She sidestepped and walked past him. Fast, but not running, turning the corner into the main hallway.

He stayed where he was, facing the dark, until he heard the outside doors close.

JOSH LOCKED THE door of Drago High School behind him.

Only when he turned into the chilled air and dropped the keys into his pocket did he realize his car did not sit in splendid isolation, as it so often did at the end of the day.

The other car was Vanessa's rental.

Heat flared so fast and intense he thought smoke might pour out of his mouth along with the trail of vapor.

She'd felt what he'd felt during that dance.

When their eyes met in that long moment while she danced with Barry, he'd hoped. In the hallway he'd been sure.

So sure, he'd blown it.

The woman who hid that robe wasn't ready for that kind of blunt.

And yet… She was still here.

Could she have reconsidered?

Then realism took hold, nudged along by recognizing that she was huddled in the seat against the cold.

Not the pose of someone waiting to continue what hadn't really started.

He knocked on the driver's window.

She jumped a good foot.

"Vanessa? It's Josh." He backed up as she scrambled out of the car. "Stay in the car, where it's warmer. Just put down the window."

"I can't," she said bitterly. "Nothing's working on the wretched thing, including the engine."

"I can take a look—"

"No need. I called the rental car company. Three times. The last time, I talked to someone high enough up to be assured they are, in fact, sending someone." She checked her watch. "They should be here any minute."

"You've been out here all this time?" He took her arm, hoping his gloves and her coat to insulate him from the sensations of temptation. No such luck. "C'mon."

"No. I can't leave."

"We'll talk about that in my car, with the heat on."

He suspected her thin coat and stiff lips did more to win the argument than his words.

"They should be here any minute," she repeated, even as his car's heater kicked in with a stalwart spew of warmth. "You should go."

"No way I'm leaving you here on your own. So relax."

"I am relaxed."

Yeah, right.

He searched for a neutral topic. Something that didn't involve kissing and desire.

"Topher's got a role in a play at school. Did you know that?"

"Oh. No. I didn't."

There was something not quite right about her answer, but among the universe of mysteries that was Vanessa Irish, it was a minor star, and would have to wait its turn for exploration.

"I didn't either, not until well after rehearsals had started."

She faced him, frowning. "Are you displeased?"

"Not at all."

"But there's … something?"

He might have blown off anyone else, but her hesitancy drew his words. "I'm worried."

She considered that. "Because you fear he will do badly. That's not impossible, but he'll work very hard and that decreases the chances of failure. Also doing this could build his confidence."

"If he doesn't back out at the last second, leaving everyone in the lurch and dropping himself into a deeper pit than ever."

His own words surprised him—he hadn't defined the gnawing concern that had shadowed the support and enthusiasm he'd addressed to Topher and everyone else—but they didn't appear to surprise Vanessa.

"He won't."

"He avoids any attention, and then to be in a play—if he hasn't considered what it'll be like on stage with everyone looking at him, and it hits him at the last moment… Oh, hell, maybe I'm all wrong. He sure doesn't let me see inside him. I ask a question, and it's like I'm pushing him off a cliff."

"You rush him. Give him time."

"Time? How much time? How much *more* time?"

"More is counting by your system. Give him his own time. He has his way of processing—information and emotions. Being inside himself doesn't mean he wants to get away from you, just that he needs time with himself."

His frustration ebbed, released by the sudden certainty that she was not only telling him about Topher, but also about herself.

That's how she understood Topher so well, that's why they connected.

"And you do know him," she said. "You know Topher doesn't jump into things without thinking them through. He will have considered the commitment he's making to himself and others before he agreed. Since he is very like you in that aspect, once he has made the commitment, he will not let anyone down."

"Like me?"

"Are you trying to make me compliment your reliability?"

"Heaven forbid I coerce a compliment out of you." His grin faded. "But Topher in a play... You could have knocked me over when I found out."

"Did he tell you?"

"No, Xena did."

"Oh."

He hitched his right knee up on the seat between them to face her as he probed that syllable. "Xena keeps me up to speed on a lot that's going on."

"I've witnessed that."

"You don't approve?"

"It's none of my business."

"Sorry. Shouldn't have snapped. Some women I've dated have said things. All the kids have had issues, but Xena... Well, Malcolm's forever quoting studies saying it's natural for kids to try to preserve the status quo in hopes their parents will get back together. And I'll admit Xena hasn't been warm and welcoming to other women."

"It's not my business."

If she hadn't been so in control, he'd have said he heard a hint of panic in her voice.

He'd steered away from what had happened in the hallway ... until now. "Other women I've been interested in. Attracted to."

She made a show of peering toward the street.

"And who are attracted to me," he added to the back of her head.

She clicked her tongue. "I put too much trust in the supervisor I spoke with. I'll have to call again."

She reached for the door handle.

He leaned across her, grasping the handle her questing hand hadn't found. Instead of opening it, he held on.

Their faces were close, their eyes connected. She breathed two rapid cycles of in and out. Her tongue darted between her lips, then disappeared.

"The number's in my car," she said.

His impulsive gesture deflated, not from that prosaic prick of practicality, but from something darker he saw swirling in her eyes amid other, more welcome reactions.

He drew back to his side of the car and said, "Of course."

"Josh. There's no reason for you to get out," she protested as he followed her across empty parking spaces. "In fact, there's no reason for you—"

"I'm staying. Unless you'd rather have a ride to Mrs. R's and deal with it tomorrow."

"I'll deal with it tonight."

She opened the driver's door of her rental and reached to the other side.

Her motion swung her raincoat to one side, highlighting her rounded bottom under the fabric of her dress.

The sight ended far too soon, as she secured a paper and backed out of the car.

She locked the door, turned, then stopped. "Josh? Is something wrong?"

"Yes."

He leaned in and kissed her, fast, mouths alone touching.

Her lips tasted of coolness over a heat so profound he thought he'd melt right there.

He was aware at some level that her hands rose, hesitant, fingers stretching, then curling in, as if caught between reaching for and pushing away.

But there was no uncertainty in her kiss.

Her lips met his with fervor. Not only accepting when he caught her bottom lip, but reciprocating with quick, feathery kisses to the corner of his mouth, then around the line of his top lip.

He bent his head more to accommodate her, and that angled them perfectly for him to kiss her once more, fully on her parted lips.

His tongue slid inside, experiencing the sharp, smooth line of her teeth as the soft, heated sigh of her moan came into his own mouth.

He was hard and aching and nearly shuddering with desire.

From a kiss. From her kiss.

She broke away, sidestepping.

He didn't try to recapture her, but echoed her motion, so they still stood face to face.

She was as shaken as he was.

No, she was *more* shaken.

Her eyes were wide and … God, frightened? She was frightened of him?

"Nothing's going to happen between us that you don't want to happen, Vanessa. Not now, not ever."

"I know." The fear in her eyes flared. "I have to…" She shook her head. "It's the tow truck. I have to go."

That wasn't what she'd started to say.

Yet it was true. The tow truck was chugging up the slight incline.

He would have happily sent it to oblivion.

CHAPTER TWELVE

"WELL, WELL, WELL."

Josh mentally winced at Malcolm's greeting Monday, but responded with a measured, "Morning, Malcolm."

He would have left it at that, but Malcolm blocked his exit from the narrow U of staff mailboxes simply by occupying the opening.

"I sincerely hope it is a good morning for you, Josh. I could wish it had been a good weekend for you as well, but as dear Bertie pointed out, that was most improbable since your whereabouts were quite public all day Sunday and the lady in question was never in the vicinity at the same time."

"I have no idea what you're talking about."

"Ms. Irish, of course. After your dance Saturday, why even the students, who are otherwise so engrossed in their own dramas as to be blind to, ahem, fireworks going off in front of them, are talking about a romance."

"Oh, God," Josh groaned. "The rumor mill is exactly why I usually don't dance with anyone at those things."

"Usually? *Never before* have you danced at a school function. I assure you, the significance was not lost on a soul who witnessed or heard about Saturday."

"No significance. Except that Barry got too into the dance and Vanessa isn't accustomed to corralling a hormonal teenager."

"That might serve for many, Josh, but you should recall that I witnessed—purely by accident of course—your embrace at Darcie and Zeke's wedding."

Accident his ass. The old coot had tracked them three yards off the path.

"In addition to witnessing other occasions when the *frisson* of attraction crackled around you and the lady in question like an electrical storm. I remarked on it from the first to dear Bertie. Initially, she was doubtful, citing your history as well as Vanessa's demeanor. I held to my position, and after seeing you together at the wedding, Bertie now concurs."

"I hate to disappoint Bertie," he said dryly. "But nothing's going on."

Nothing's going to happen between us that you don't want to happen, Vanessa. Not now, not ever.

I know.

That's when she'd panicked. *After* she'd said she knew.

He'd been mulling that non-stop.

"Don't despair." Malcolm rested an avuncular hand on Josh's shoulder. "Many a good knight has been tested by hard battle to win his fair lady. Why, I courted dear Bertie for four years before she agreed to be mine. Someone raised as Vanessa was is bound to have issues with boundaries. Ha! I jested without intention: Bound to have issues with boundaries."

Josh straightened and stepped nearer, dropping his voice. "What do you mean, someone raised the way she was?"

"I refer to the commune, of course."

"What do you know about that? How do you know?"

Malcolm raised his eyebrows, as if wondering what Josh was getting so wound up about.

"I know what I have said, that she was raised in a commune. A commune that it would be safe to say was well off the grid before that concept was fashionable. In addition, I have been informed that after her parents' death she entered the school system for the first time and was viewed as an academic marvel who garnered no end of awards and scholarships." Malcolm's expression edged toward coy. "I also know that she lived for a time with the local high school principal's family."

Josh got the implication.

Vanessa had baggage when it came to high school principals.

Maybe she associated them with rescues or maybe with misery. Either extreme or anywhere in between, she also might associate with him. But if he cracked open the door of his reactions, Malcolm would walk right in and root around. Oh, he meant well, but it wasn't Josh's idea of fun.

"How'd you hear this gossip?"

"As to how I acquired this *information*, you should know your town better than to need to ask, Josh. As it happens, it was an interesting combination of modern technology and old-fashioned grapevine. Warren was demonstrating his expertise with search engines to Mildred Magnus. Mildred suggested he look up Vanessa Irish."

Josh stifled a curse. Mildred was the nosiest resident of Drago, and that was going some.

"He Googled her and retrieved many references to her work with Zeke-Tech," Malcolm continued. "To display narrowing a search, he did another that disallowed Zeke-Tech. That attempt produced items about her academic awards, as well as articles in a small newspaper in Pennsylvania. The articles included matters of her background. Using the location and the reference to the commune Warren tracked down further information on it, as well as tracing the land's title. Quite impressive, actually. Mildred, no doubt, repeated the information to several others, and it came to me via dear Bertie."

Malcolm's wife was frequently a source for his information.

"It's such an interesting background," the older man added. "I would enjoy hearing about her experiences. With her keen intellect, I'm certain she would have many insights. But her reserve does not invite such questions."

"No, it doesn't."

Malcolm's eyebrows arched. "Does that tone mean that her reserve has prevented you from asking questions that you would like the answer to, or is it a warning to me not to intrude on her privacy?"

"Both."

The arch went up a couple more stories. "I see. Yes, I do believe I see."

"I hope you do. And I hope you'll make sure everybody else in town does, too. And for God's sake, keep a leash on Warren. Vanessa's life is off-limits."

VANESSA SWEPT A second look around her rented room, even though she'd already checked that she had everything she would need for back-to-back computer lab meetings.

No more excuses to delay.

Time to go.

She had reached the top of the stairs when Mrs. Richards appeared at the bottom.

"There you are, dear. There's someone waiting for you."

Vanessa tightened her hold on her laptop case.

She wasn't ready.

She would see him at the second meeting today for the first time since…

Anyway, she'd see him at the second meeting. By then, surely, she'd be ready.

But not now.

Not yet.

"Ms. Irish?" Fay O'Hearn joined Mrs. Richards at the base of the stairs, looking up. "Uh, I wondered if I could talk to you—ask you some questions?"

Fay. Not Josh.

Not. Josh.

"Vanessa, dear? Are you all right?"

"I'm fine." She started down. "What kind of questions?"

Fay cut her eyes toward Mrs. Richards, then back. "Uh, I hoped we could talk on the way to the meeting. If you're walking—"

"You are not walking in this rain—not either one of you," proclaimed Mrs. Richards. "Why, Fay, you're nearly soaked through as it is. If Vanessa doesn't want to drive, I'll call Josh—"

"I'm driving." She might have said that louder than necessary. She buttoned her coat and got out her umbrella. "Let's go."

In the car, she stopped Fay's thanks for the ride, her time, and her general saintliness by saying, "What are the questions?"

"I heard you did that legal thing where your parents don't have control over you anymore."

Vanessa slowed for a stop sign, feeling the tires skid slightly on rain-slicked leaves. Mrs. Richards had told her there were rumors going around about her background. Here was confirmation. "Emancipation?"

The girl nodded. "That's it. Can you tell me about it?"

Vanessa shook her head. "That wasn't my situation. And even if it had been, it was another state and years ago. I doubt it would apply."

"Oh." Fay did that deflating balloon thing Josh did now and then. "You went to college at seventeen, right?"

"Sixteen."

"Wow. You must be brilliant."

Vanessa never knew what to say to comments like that.

This time her failure went unnoticed. "It must have been hard, though, to go to college so young," Fay said. "I know I wouldn't have been ready at sixteen."

"I'd tested well, so I felt ready."

"I meant socially. Boys."

"I doubt I'll ever be ready for that."

Fay giggled, and Vanessa debated telling her it was the absolute truth. Her decision was made for her when the girl instantly sobered.

"But you said your parents didn't support you—and for financial aid you have to have your parents' financial information. How did you afford college?"

"My parents were dead, so I had a legal guardian."

The sound of rain filled in the silence in the car. "Oh."

"Your mother still won't give you the necessary papers?"

"No. Even after Officer Barrett talked to her."

"Your aunt and uncle—"

"They're not my legal guardians. I don't want them to be, because then they'd be responsible for all my expenses. I mean they take care of me, even though she promised… But college is *so* expensive. They can't afford that, even with Uncle Al back at work. Plus, if they were my legal guardians, his job would count against me getting aid. And to make them my guardians we'd have to go through the legal system and pay a lawyer and it would take so long. And after all that it still might not make any difference because what if the schools I applied to don't admit me because I don't have community service, because I've worked instead, because I knew—I *knew* she'd refuse the one thing I want most. And she said—I wasn't asking for money, just papers to get aid. So it doesn't matter if any schools accept me because I can't afford to go anyway."

Vanessa unwound the tangle of words while Fay slumped in the passenger seat, blinking rapidly, and pulling in air through her mouth.

"That day you went to your mother's house, what did she say when you asked for the papers you need for financial aid?"

"She said tramps don't need a college education, and that's what I am. Then she started in about *him*, and how I dress."

Vanessa stood in an emotional minefield, a minefield that—off the top of her head—she could think of twenty- or thirty-thousand people better equipped to negotiate than she was.

Unfortunately, not one of them was here in this car, now parked around the corner from the computer lab, isolated by rain.

"Fay, I don't know about the situation you described or—"

"I shouldn't have said anything. I'm always having to beg for help, and it's so—" She reached for the door handle. "I'm sorry. I'll—"

"Wait. Let me finish. I don't know anything now, but let me research it."

Fay turned. "You'd do that?"

"I can't guarantee a solution, but let me investigate."

"Thank you. Thank you so—"

"Don't thank me. There's something I need from you."

"Of course. Anything."

"I need to tell my assistant at Zeke-Tech an outline of the situation."

"Oh. Yes. That's okay."

"And I want you to talk with Officer Barrett and Mr. Kincannon."

"*Ohhh.*"

It was more a wail than a word. Vanessa persisted. "And probably your aunt and uncle eventually."

"No! I don't want them to—"

"I know. But sometimes you have to accept help. Sometimes to get where you—to where you can be the person you know you need to be—you have to accept help. And keep accepting it. Until you can pay it back."

ONE MEETING DOWN, one to go.

Vanessa felt as if she'd pulled all-nighters for a week the way she and Zeke and Quince used to.

But it wasn't long hours and brain work that had depleted her.

It was unfamiliar emotions.

Fay's emotions, and the emotions of her own past they'd stirred.

Plus, another set of emotions.

Emotions that jangled nerves just under her skin and did strange things to her breathing and heart rate just now when Josh walked in as the meeting of the community committee wrapped up.

He tried to catch her eye.

She made sure he didn't.

Voices from the doorway reached her. Xena, Topher, and Livvy were there, with Mrs. Mudge putting on her coat as she greeted them.

While Vanessa carefully didn't look at Josh, she did listen, while he—as he called it—made the kid handoff to the babysitter who would take them home.

Vanessa raised her hand in greeting to the kids. Topher raised his hand in a similar gesture, Livvy waved madly, Xena looked away.

Topher and Xena then had a fast, intense exchange in low voices.

It concluded with Xena snapping, "Well, then ask her." She grabbed Livvy's hand and headed off over the toddler's objections, leaving Topher alone in the no-man's land between the front door and the back room.

"Topher? Something wrong?" Josh said.

"I, uh, I want to ask Ms. Irish something."

She walked toward him, trailed by Josh. "Yes, Topher?"

"Will you come to the play I'm in? It's next month. Thursday night for grown-ups, then the next day we'll do it two times for all the students. Will you come? To the grown-up one, I mean."

"Topher, Ms. Irish is very bus—"

"Yes, I'll come."

Without looking, she felt Josh's surprise.

She was looking at Topher.

She'd already promised to come if he was in the play, yet he'd felt the need to ask again.

What was it Josh had said about his wife?

All the promises to be there for the kids, and the phone calls saying something had come up, she'd be late, she couldn't make it, another time—all the damned *phone calls.*

"I'll need the exact date, time, and place." If she had to reschedule the auditors, earnings release, board meeting, or all three, she would be there.

"Dad has all that." He looked at Josh. "Will you tell her?"

"Sure. But, Vanessa, I know you're busy. You shouldn't feel obligated."

"I want to see Topher in his play," she said firmly.

"Great. The other thing—" The head of steam of achieving his first goal seemed to propel Topher. "—is supplies for my Halloween costume, Dad."

"You sure you don't want to go as Harry Potter?" Josh turned to Vanessa. "You know who that is, don't you."

She nodded. She wasn't a maven of popular culture, but she considered it part of her duties to be aware of major movements.

"Everybody says I look like him." Topher didn't sound pleased. "Skinny, with big ears and glasses."

"Oh, c'mon, Topher. That's not what I—"

Vanessa interrupted without hesitation. "I can see the resemblance." She tipped her head, studying the boy, and had the satisfaction of seeing the veneer of oh-brother-cynicism that froze his features at his father's words, slide away in surprise. "Yes, I can definitely see a resemblance to the actor Daniel Radcliffe as a boy. Now that he's grown up, he's quite good looking. A hunk." She felt silly using the term, but it caught Topher's attention. "However, even when you resemble a celebrity who's a hunk, I can see that you might not want to look like your everyday self for Halloween."

"Good point," Josh picked up. No one ever said the man was stupid. "You're right, and I apologize, Topher. The whole idea is to dress up so you look like somebody other than yourself. So what supplies do you need?"

"I have to make my hair white and get it to stick out. A white mustache. Lines on my face to make me look old. And a jacket." He considered. "Maybe a lab coat?"

"A white shirt with a high collar and a black floppy tie," Vanessa added.

"You know who he's going as?" Josh asked.

"Yes." Then she wondered. She looked at Topher, "Albert Einstein?"

A huge grin split his face. Oh, yes, he would look so much like his father when he grew up. Definitely a hunk.

"Yes!"

Josh stared.

Only when the boy's grin faded and he became self-conscious did Josh rally. "Okay. Albert it is. Let's see, for your hair—they have temporary colored spray. Unless you want powder. What about flour?"

"What if it rains? The spray's better."

"And hairspray," Vanessa contributed. "To make it stiff."

"Right. And a mustache and—" Josh frowned. "Some sort of

makeup pencil to make lines."

Both males looked at her. "Uh, eyeliner pencil?"

"Okay," Topher said. "The drug store should have most of that. But what about the lab coat and high-collared shirt and tie?"

"Tell you what," Josh said. "How about one day next week after school we check the thrift store over in Pepton. Just you and me."

The boy looked a little cautious. "Maybe Ms. Irish—"

"I won't be here next week," Vanessa said. "I'll be in Virginia for work."

"Oh. Sure. I understand." She felt a prickle in her throat at his off-hand tone. "But you'll be back by Halloween, right? So you could come over and help me get ready. We get in our costumes at lunch, then we go back to school and there's a parade."

"Topher—"

The boy's enthusiasm evaporated under his father's one cautious word. "Sure, sure, I know you're busy. And coming to my play, that's really nice, so—"

"I would be happy to assist you with your costume, Topher." That would mean condensing her schedule even more. She'd just have to do it. "But I'm not adept with makeup."

He beamed at her, and she forgot her schedule. "That's okay. You know what Albert Einstein should look like, and that's the important part."

She went to the back room to note the appointment, with Topher urging her to add the play immediately, too. *To be sure.*

Just then, Xena reappeared in the front doorway, hands on hips.

"Are you ever coming?"

"You go ahead, Topher," Josh said. "I'll give Vanessa the details."

"Okay. Thanks!" He divided a grin between them and ran out.

Josh watched him an extra beat before following her to the meeting table, He pulled a battered pocket diary out and read the time, date, and place.

"You're generous with your time and I appreciate it, Vanessa. In case you couldn't tell, so does Topher. I haven't seen him like that in a long time."

She mumbled something—even she didn't know what. As she closed her tablet, Josh leaned closer and covered her hand with his, stilling it.

"Thank you."

She slid her hand free and tucked the tablet away. "I like him."

"I know you do. And he likes you."

There was something in his tone she couldn't be sure she'd read right. She took out the meeting agenda and tamped the pages on the plywood top.

"Vanessa," Josh said in a low tone. "Relax. I know the others will be here any minute. I won't jump you in public. I promise. Now, if we ever get some privacy…"

"Don't be absurd. I had no such notion."

"Good, then you won't mind moving our working session Friday evening from here to my house."

Her head snapped up. "Your house? That's not public."

He laughed, as she felt heat flood her face. "Maybe not public, but we'd stand a better chance of getting privacy in the middle of downtown Chicago."

"I meant, there's no reason to move our meeting to your house."

"There's an excellent reason. Xena's having a birthday sleepover and there's no way I can ask Mrs. Mudge to ride herd on it. They'll be in the family room with the door firmly closed against hideous intrusion from adults. So don't worry, you won't have to interact with them."

"I'm not worried. But—"

"Good. You're not worried about the kids and you've said you're not scared of me, so it's all set."

She glared at him. "You tricked me. You … you *played* me."

To her surprise she felt the edges of her glare giving way, and he clearly saw it, too, because he was grinning at her.

Before she could be caught in that grin, she snatched up the agendas to place them around the table.

But there was no denying that somehow they'd gotten past the awkwardness she'd been certain would last forever.

"Vanessa, I have something to tell you."

She stopped, instantly wary. "What?"

"Word's gotten around about the commune. I'm not the source."

"I didn't think you were."

"Good, because—Wait a minute, what do you mean, you didn't think I was?"

"Mrs. Richards told me two days ago about it."

"You didn't tell me."

"You already knew my background."

Lines fanned across his cheeks but different lines dug into his forehead. "Sometimes you are so damned logical—I meant, why didn't you tell me about word being out?"

"Why? There's nothing to be done about it. And you have said this is part of a community."

"Not my favorite part. But you're taking it so well, I'll start believing you think the nosiness is outweighed by everything that's good about community."

She only had time to say, "You're wrong" before the others arrived in a swirl of laughter, conversation and rain-chilled air.

CHAPTER THIRTEEN

Friday evening, Josh smiled as he opened his front door and stepped back to let her in.

Vanessa's neutral expression froze as a rush of noise slammed into her.

The sound was unlike any she had encountered.

Perhaps a flock of excited parrots would make as much racket. But to be this high-pitched, the entire flock would have to have been sucking on helium balloons.

"I told you it was a sleepover." Josh raised his voice.

"Yes, but I thought a friend or two…"

"That goes against the very core of sleepovers. Their whole purpose is excess. A horde of girls. Enough food to make an eating contest champion blanch. Way, way too much talking. Incessant giggling." He raised a finger with each point, and now added the thumb. "And no sleep. For the girls or parents. They're limited to the family room so that leaves us the relative peace of the kitchen."

Belatedly, she recognized that the noise was muffled by the closed doors to the family room. Good heavens.

The noise had shaken her out of the distant, professional mode she'd determined was the only way to handle herself tonight.

Now, he placed a large, warm hand at the small of her back. Apparently to guide her toward the kitchen. Though surely he knew that she knew the way.

She could point that out, let him know the gesture was unnecessary. And she would, if he didn't remove his hand … soon.

"Of course we have to share the kitchen with Livvy and Topher, but—"

His cell phone rang and he excused himself to step into the living room to answer it. She couldn't miss the change in his voice from his first, cheery "hello" to a clipped "Give me a minute."

He pressed a button, then faced her, expression strained. "I hate to ask, but could you look after Livvy? And Topher. They're in the kitchen. Xena and the girls will be fine in the family room. I'll be off before they need anything."

She wanted to say no. After studiously not thinking about it, she recognized now that the bathing-Livvy evening had unsettled her in undefined ways.

But looking at the newly rigid lines of his face she nodded and said, "I'll go say hello to them."

"Thank you."

Topher and Livvy greeted her with pleasure, one quiet and one exuberant.

She smiled at both, explained their father's absence, and sat at the table where Topher had homework neatly stacked in front of him and Livvy had a coloring book askew on the tray of her high chair as she skidded crayons across the page—one in each fist.

Vanessa had barely set up her laptop when the double pocket doors to the family room opened, letting loose a torrent of high-pitched noise like steam from a broken radiator.

Xena snapped the doors closed behind her, and was nearly to the kitchen table before she stopped.

"Where's Dad?" she demanded, as if Vanessa might have done something nefarious with him.

"He had to take a phone call."

"Oh." She started to return to the family room, then stopped.

When Xena turned back toward the kitchen, Vanessa was reminded abruptly of a certain financial analyst.

His predictions of doom had been pulverized by Zeke-Tech's results and his reputation had suffered. Since then, even Vanessa picked up on his bristling animosity.

Loaded for bear. That's how Quince had described the man.

And that's what Vanessa saw in the young eyes of Xena Kincannon.

"It's time for the popcorn," the girl announced. "Dad says an adult has to make it. He's not here, so that's you."

It was a challenge, all right.

Just as the financial analyst's demand to visit Zeke-Tech headquarters had been. She and Zeke and Quince had been unanimous that facing the challenge was the only way to deal with it.

"I see." She took off her glasses and stood. "Where are the bags kept?"

"Bags?"

"To put in the microwave."

"That's not how we do it," Xena said with disdain. "We could do *that* ourselves. We do it on the stove, that's why Dad won't let us do it ourselves."

"Okay." Really how difficult could this be?

Oh, yes she understood that the girl expected her to fail. Vanessa couldn't deny Xena had some basis for that expectation, considering what had happened with Livvy's bath.

On the other hand, Xena had also clearly expected Vanessa to botch washing the towels afterward, standing across the kitchen with her arms folded, and a hint of a smirk.

"There's one pot Dad always uses," Topher offered from the table. "It's the one with the black lid, over there."

Vanessa followed his pointing finger to a cabinet, and found the pot. He directed her to the oil in another cabinet and the popcorn in a drawer in the refrigerator. Vanessa found the right knob on her own, and turned the smooth-top burner on high. Xena watched it all with sharp eyes.

Vanessa carefully poured in oil to coat the bottom of the pan.

The girl immediately scoffed, "That's not enough. That wouldn't make enough for even half the girls. You have to put in lots more."

Vanessa tipped in more oil.

"Put in three kernels and when they pop you know it's hot enough for the rest," Topher instructed.

The atmosphere shimmered with an anxiety Vanessa remembered surrounding final exams. Even Livvy sat still and wide-eyed in her high chair.

Crack!

Vanessa jumped and Xena's snort carried a boatload of derision.

Two more cracks followed as Vanessa got the bag of popping corn and adjusted her hold so she could pour kernels in quickly and with control. She lifted the lid on the sizzling oil, and added the corn.

"More."

"Xena—"

That was all Topher got out before his sister rounded on him.

"Shut up, Topher. This is none of your business. This is *my* sleepover."

The bag shifted in Vanessa's hand and more popcorn slid into the pot. But she barely noticed, because the sounds behind her indicated Xena had reached her brother and some sort of scuffle was going on. She clapped the lid on the pot and spun around.

Xena was trying to put her hand over Topher's mouth, while he fended her off with an elbow.

"You're trying to—"

"Mind your own business."

"Stop it," she ordered. "Both of you."

Neither paid any attention. Topher's chair want over backward. To get away from his older sister he scooted around the table toward Livvy.

As Vanessa headed for them, a tattoo of popping sounded behind her, signifying the newly added kernels were hitting the critical temperature.

"Vanessa, she's trying to—"

"Shut up. You don't know anything—"

Xena grabbed for Topher. He bowed his back to avoid her. Off balance, Xena lunged, knocking her shoulder into his hip. They both rammed into Livvy's high chair.

The tempo of popping behind Vanessa had picked up to an alarming rate, but Livvy's chair was teetering. That captured all of Vanessa's attention.

And when Livvy emitted a high-pitched *Eeeee*—excitement, fear, she couldn't tell—Vanessa heard only that amid the racket.

With the flailing bodies of the older kids between her and the high chair, Vanessa reversed direction and ran around the table. The chair, with the little girl strapped in, was falling. Vanessa could see it as if in slow motion.

Desperately, she lunged her left leg forward.

The edge of the seat crashed against her shin with enough force to bring immediate tears to her eyes and she uttered her own *Eeeee*.

But her leg slowed the chair's descent and held it short of crashing to the floor.

Fighting to maintain her balance, she got her left hand under the side support of the tray and lifted enough to let her pull her leg back.

Livvy, with tears sliding down her smooth red cheeks, lifted her arms pitifully toward Vanessa. The girl didn't need words. She wanted out of that high chair. Now.

"Just a minute, Livvy. Just a minute and I'll get you, baby," she muttered, regaining her own balance. She pushed the chair upright. "There. Now, we can get you out."

Standing beside the chair as she pulled at the plastic lock on the end of the now-twisted webbed belt, she saw Topher and Xena beyond it.

They had frozen in mid-tussle.

Xena grasped her brother's shoulder with one hand while the other had slid off his mouth to one side of his jaw. Topher had his arm—elbow raised almost to his ear—between them. His other arm was locked straight as he pushed against her ribcage. Both were gasping for air, but almost absently, because their eyes-bugging, cheeks-whitening attention was focused on their little sister.

"Do you see what almost happened?" Vanessa demanded. It was

the sort of inane question she hated—they clearly did see. But that didn't stop her. Something bigger than herself spit out demands. "Do you realize Livvy could have fallen? Do you have any idea how badly she could have been hurt?"

The latch came free, and Vanessa scooped up the little girl, who clasped her around the neck and snuggled into her shoulder.

"What were you thinking? How could you—?" She drew in a deep breath, fighting the adrenaline of fear.

And nearly choked.

The smell was unmistakable.

"Oh. Kwyly!" Livvy squealed, hands outstretched over Vanessa's shoulders toward the stove.

She hitched the little girl around to let her move faster. Excitement lighted Livvy's eyes even as a final tear leaked out.

Vanessa wished to heavens *she* recovered that fast.

Popcorn waterfalled from the overflowing pot.

For each escaping kernel three took its place, lifting the lid higher and higher on a volcanic eruption of fluffy white.

Overflow hit the gap between the pot and the outer ring of the burner, bursting into puffs of flame. Most of the mini-fires were self-contained and self-consuming, but some ignited popped pieces burned beyond the burner, threatening a conflagration by spreading to drifts built up on the stovetop and dropping to the floor.

"Stay back!" Vanessa shouted in general command.

She shifted Livvy again, holding the child with her left arm, and continuing the motion to swing the toddler almost entirely behind her. It was awkward, straining her arm, but it kept her body between Livvy and anything that could burn her. It also freed Vanessa's right arm.

She pulled the pot off the burner, but it kept pumping out plump popped, flammable morsels.

They spilled onto the burner as the pot exposed more of it and more mini-poofs of flame spouted up.

"Turn it off!"

"Get the fire extinguisher!"

"Use the hot pad!"

The high-pitched suggestions came from girls piling up in the kitchen doorway, drawn either by the smell or the shouts.

"Topher, get them out of here," Vanessa ordered.

She heard complaints as he herded the girls back into the family room, then closed the pocket doors.

She put the pot on another burner, snatched off the lid and used its edge to flick unignited pieces away without touching the cooking surface, then grouped the flamers.

"Don't put them back on the burner!" Xena yelled from beside her. "That's stupid. You don't do anything right. Our mother wouldn't have—"

"Be quiet, Xena. Right now."

Vanessa spoke in her CFO-in-charge voice.

It had stopped Zeke and Quince dead in their tracks from the start, and she'd heard Zeke-Tech employees lived in fear of it. Good to know it worked on ten-year-olds, too.

Vanessa dropped the lid over the gathered burning pieces, smothering them all at once. Then she turned off the burner.

She lowered Livvy to the floor, holding onto the girl's shoulder, while she faced the elder Miss Kincannon.

"I'm going to say this once, Xena. I am not your mother. I'm not trying to be your mother. I'm sure I can't do half of the things your mother did. More power to her, but I don't particularly care about her skills. I would have preferred not to burn this popcorn, but in the scheme of things, this doesn't make or break my self-esteem. Livvy is okay and that's the important thing."

Xena gaped at her. Vanessa considered that a good sign.

"As for you and me. I am not trying to take anything away from you. I—"

"You and Dad—"

"Are working together. You're smart, Xena. You know about when people work together."

"You swear nothing's gonna happen with you and Dad?" she demanded.

"No," Vanessa shot back, shocking herself more than the girl, who gaped at her. "I don't predict the future. And I have no reason to make that kind of promise to you. Nor do you have any right to demand it. You'll have to be satisfied with my promise that I'm not trying to take over your spot or your mother's. I couldn't even if I wanted to. I'm not either one of you. I'm me."

The girl's mouth snapped closed. She stared at her, her posture never relenting, but was that a softening in Xena's eyes?

The girl broke the look and stomped over to a deep cabinet drawer. She pulled out a bag of potato chips and dumped them into a wooden bowl. "Guess this'll have to do since you ruined the popcorn."

"Way to adapt," Vanessa said to her back, echoing Xena's *way to flood the kitchen* crack.

Xena shot a look over her shoulder that some might have deluded themselves into believing held a shred of amusement.

But Vanessa was a realist.

When the family room doors closed behind Xena, Vanessa contemplated the mess on the stovetop.

Livvy whimpered at her side. Vanessa turned, intending to pick her up, when she saw Livvy was heading toward the figure of her father, emerging from the shadows at the base of the stairs.

"Looks like you had some excitement." The lines around his mouth and eyes that showed up when he grinned flickered. It made the grimness in his eyes more stark.

"I burned the popcorn."

"No kidding."

So his grimness wasn't over the mess on the stove. Or, she surmised, whatever he might have heard of her confrontation with Xena.

"I fear I rank with Mrs. O'Leary's cow," she said. "If this has caused permanent damage—"

"It won't. But even if it did, it's not like this house—and this family—haven't sustained permanent damage before. All kinds of damage." He scooped up his daughter and looked into her face like it held the answers to the universe.

There was a secret in his tone other women no doubt could unlock.

Not her, not at her best moment. And this was far from her best moment.

"Damaged, but still standing," he added in a mutter, then seemed to shake himself. "Now let's take a look at this."

Together, they cleaned up the charred popcorn. They salvaged enough for a bowl for the revelers and a smaller one for the kitchen group.

Amid half-formed questions and doubts and thoughts swirling through Vanessa's brain, one formed clearly.

That must have been quite a phone call.

JOSH LEANED BACK, stretched his arms straight, rolling his shoulders.

Vanessa glanced at him, then immediately returned her attention to reordering the papers he'd spread out so he could see them all together.

Too late, Vanessa, he said, but only inside his own head.

He'd caught a whisper of heat in her gaze. And he liked it. Liked it a lot.

"You did well with the girls. Guess it was that commune upbringing."

"It wasn't—oh, you're kidding."

"Yes, but I probably shouldn't have."

"People assume living in a commune was like summer camp all year long. Or a huge—" She waved a hand toward the family room. "—sleepover."

"What do you usually tell people?"

"Nothing. I've never been to camp or a—"

"Sleepover? You can't say that anymore. So, was growing up in a commune like a fifth-grade sleepover?"

The corners of her mouth tipped slightly. "For my parents and a few of the others, it was remarkably like a fifth-grade sleepover."

"But not for you?" He tapped the pen he held on the table.

"No. The active, energetic members had left long before. When Starlight and Sol died in the accident—in the truck—that was the final straw."

"I'm sorry."

"Don't be."

"I meant about your parents. I know how hard it is to lose someone you—" He veered away, uncertain if he avoided the word because of what he read in her eyes or what he felt in himself. "Who'd been a big part of your life."

"Like your wife."

Vanessa, on the other hand, didn't veer.

Not when it came to *his* life, anyway.

"Yes, like my ex-wife," he said. "I suppose you've heard all about that."

"I doubt all, but I have heard a great deal."

Blunt and honest, that was Vanessa Irish.

"As you've learned, that's one of the things about living in a town like Drago. Not only does everyone know your business, most of them are willing to tell anyone who comes along. With Zeke and Darcie it was—"

An echo of her voice stopped him mid-sentence. *You turn talk about yourself to talk about the community.*

Damn.

She was right.

He pulled in a breath, and started again. "It was a shock when Melissa left. I don't know, maybe I wasn't paying enough attention. Or the right kind of attention. I mean, I knew she had ambitions. But she didn't seem unhappy."

Was that true? Or had he been so busy being happy with exactly the life he'd wanted that he'd stopped noticing that Melissa wasn't happy.

In earlier years, she'd expressed her views of Drago's deficiencies.

Endlessly.

That had stopped. He'd thought that as the kids came along she'd found satisfaction, if not the pleasure he and the kids had, in their life here.

But maybe she'd stopped complaining because she'd realized it wouldn't make him pick up his kids and his life and move to the big city because she wanted better shopping and restaurants.

And maybe that wasn't entirely fair.

But, dammit, the woman had left her kids. He could be as fair as a saint, and nothing changed that fact.

He looked up to find Vanessa watching him.

They connected, like a plug into a socket.

She felt it, too. He knew she did.

Then her chin dropped, breaking the look.

"That was Melissa—my ex—on the phone."

Her head came back up. But this look held less of the connection and more of the inquisitor.

"Yeah," he said. "I was surprised, too."

CHAPTER FOURTEEN

*S*URPRISED?

Maybe, she thought, but it went beyond that. More like a man having a delayed reaction to shock.

Despite the grimness in his eyes, he'd been calm when he'd entered the kitchen. Not even blinking at the popcorn fiasco.

After they'd cleaned up, she'd thrown herself into work. For once, he'd shown no inclination to stray from business.

Until now.

"When she left…" He stared at the pen he held. "The last thing she said was she didn't feel about me and the kids the way a wife and mother should. Other than through lawyers, not a word from her."

She should say something.

What?

She didn't know about family.

Certainly not about his family now, much less how it was before the wife and mother walked away. A woman who *didn't feel about me and the kids the way a wife and mother should.* She had no idea what a woman would feel about being a wife and mother.

Except … if you felt enough that way to *become* a wife and mother, how did you lose the feeling?

"It caught me by surprise," Josh was saying. "I didn't want it to hit Xena that way. I told Melissa she couldn't talk to her. It's not that I'm trying to punish her, but to pull Xena from her friends, from her party, with no warning, that's not fair. She could have called Xena any time today to say happy birthday. Hell, she could have made time in the past two *years* to call her kids. Just because it came into her head to call doesn't mean we drop everything."

"Xena will be happy to hear from her mother," she offered tentatively.

His eyelids lowered in what seemed a deliberate masking of his gaze. "I told her not to call unless she's prepared to follow through. God knows she disappointed the kids enough with her I'll-be-a-little-late calls before she left."

There was something else.

Wasn't sure how she knew, but she did.

It was a strange sensation. Oh, she could read Wall Street types, tell if they were pleased with Zeke-Tech's bottom line, but that was numbers. This was another case entirely.

Yet she knew for sure that Josh was holding something back.

"Follow through?"

He slapped the pen on the table under his wide-spread palm. "She says she wants to see the kids. Wants us to come to New York."

"Oh." He didn't sound happy to have told her that. So why had he? She wouldn't have—couldn't have—made him tell her. And she wasn't entirely sure she'd wanted to know, especially now that she did.

"After all this time, she thinks she'll drop back into their lives."

"You don't want them to see her?"

He looked at the window beside him. "It's not a matter of what I want. It's what's best for the kids. Why stir that up, get them excited about seeing her, then go into a funk when she forgets because her life's so busy. Forgets birthdays and Christmas. Forgets everything. Forgets them."

Vanessa said nothing.

His gaze came to her. "What?"

"Nothing." Damn. That sounded as flustered and guilty as she felt. Feelings that multiplied at his skeptical snort. "It's none of my business."

"You won't ever get the hang of Drago if you don't comment on things that aren't your business." His mouth twisted toward a grin but didn't reach it.

"I don't want to be like that."

"You don't want to care about other people?"

No, I don't zipped into her mouth, but it stayed there, behind lips she firmly closed, for reasons that didn't matter enough to sort them out.

"What, Vanessa?" Josh insisted.

"You worry about Topher. Livvy isn't talking, not in English. Xena…"

"I know Xena's given you a hard time. She's pretty tough on people in general. But she's fine. She's more than fine. She's my rock."

"Your rock could shatter."

Damn, damn, damn.

What was it about this man that made words bubble out of her like the popcorn bursting out of the pot tonight?

"You sound like you speak from experience."

She shrugged. But her shoulders felt weighted. "As I said, my parents weren't practical. Someone had to keep things going."

"I'm not relying on Xena to keep this family going."

"Not like my parents did, no. But who makes sure Topher and Livvy follow a schedule no matter who's babysitting? Who watches your schedule?"

"Yeah, but—"

"She wants to do anything—everything—to make you happy. And she misses her mother."

That did it. Expression closed down, he pushed back from the table.

Definitely time for her to go.

Her foray into minding someone else's business had been about as successful as her stove-top popcorn-making.

SEVEN-THIRTY A.M. AND hours to go before the sugar infusion began, yet already all three of his kids were in Halloween overdrive.

"Listen up." Josh said, trying to damp down the excitement

enough that they'd finish their breakfasts, "I won't be back until just before the parade. I can't get away for lunch this year. Mrs. Mudge will help you two—" He nodded toward Xena and Topher. "—get in your costumes at lunchtime and I'll—"

"And Vanessa."

He stared blankly at his son.

Josh hadn't talked to Vanessa this whole week she'd been back in Virginia. A few professional emails had been it.

He'd been reeling that night from Melissa's call.

Probably hadn't been the most receptive to what he saw—in hindsight—were Vanessa's tentative efforts to connect.

Would they regain any ground they'd lost?

Would she give them that chance?

"Vanessa's coming," Topher said. His expression tightened and so did his voice as he added, "She said she would. At the computer lab. She said it."

How many times had Melissa said it, then failed to show?

"Right." Xena laughed like a jaded thirty-year-old.

Or maybe she sounded like a high school principal and single father of three?

Had he let his distrust of Melissa—well-founded as it was—infect his kids?

"Well, that would be great wouldn't it?" he said neutrally. "But no matter what, Mrs. M will be here and—"

He ran through the day's schedule again in detail.

Finally, all three kids settled enough to ingest a passable amount of the homemade oatmeal Mrs. Mudge bought from a nearby farmer.

As he cleared the table, Xena patted his shoulder. "Don't worry, Dad. I'll make sure everything goes right at lunch."

Your rock could shatter.

"VANESSA!"

Josh wasn't the first to greet her as she waited at the blocked off intersection for the elementary school Halloween parade.

She'd had conversations with members of the computer lab committees, as well as Martha Barrett and Zeke's mother.

Josh's was the only voice that accelerated her heartbeat, however.

She avoided looking at him by bending to the stroller to admire Livvy's bunny costume. The child babbled at her happily.

People around her cheerfully made room for Josh to edge in with the stroller in front. But not so much room that her shoulder didn't brush against his chest.

She had to stop thinking about things like that.

She'd spent far too much time on those thoughts. And dreams.

"When I picked up Livvy, Mrs. Mudge said the costume-donning went great. What did you think, Vanessa?"

"Mrs. Mudge had things well in hand when I arrived." Catching the flight that got her here just in time to help Mrs. Mudge, had meant a pre-dawn session at her Virginia office.

The older woman had helped Xena change into her costume as Amelia Earhart, while Vanessa facilitated Topher's transformation into Albert Einstein. She also listened to the boy's cautious comments about rehearsals, and promised once more that she would attend the play.

"Are you interested in flying?" Vanessa had asked Xena after complimenting her costume.

"I like her, that's all," she'd said before clomping down the stairs.

It was Topher who said, "Mom gave her a book on women explorers for her birthday right before she left. She reads it over and over."

Josh's voice brought her back to the present. "Mrs. M said you were great. And as long as you're doing so much for the Kincannons today, I'm asking another favor."

"What?" She knew he'd caught her wariness when he grinned.

"Give out treats at the house while I take Livvy around. It won't be long—a few neighbors and friends. And there's something in it for you—spaghetti when the older two get back from trick-or-treating.

That's when the kids—"

"I know what trick-or-treating is."

"Wasn't sure. The commune celebrated Halloween?"

"No. But I was curious about things on the outside. And I witnessed it while I was living with—in high school. And later."

"So you greet ghosts and goblins at your front door in Virginia?"

"No. I'm at work."

"It's about time you had the experience then. It's easy. Mrs. M will have candy in a basket. Kids'll ring the doorbell. They holler *Trick or Treat!* You give them a candy bar—one. Don't let the greedy ones dig a fist in or—"

"Vanessa! Josh!"

Darcie, in uniform, was coming down the street, asking people who had crept too far forward to keep the parade route clear.

"Working already? I heard you just got back last night," Vanessa said.

The other woman straightened from saying hello to Livvy. "I'm filling in to let one of the guys play in the Drago Band. You can hear their drums."

"How was Paris?"

"Wait a minute," Josh said. "Before we get onto Paris, say yes, Vanessa."

"Yes to what?" Darcie demanded.

Josh explained.

"Oh, you definitely should, Vanessa," Darcie said. "Lots of kids having a good time. You'll get a kick out of it."

Josh turned to Vanessa. "Well?"

"Okay, but—"

"That reminds me," Darcie interrupted. "We're having Thanksgiving dinner at our place and we'd love for you guys to come—and the kids of course. It'll be pretty simple. The house isn't done, but we have the important things—functioning bathrooms, the kitchen, a table, and a big-screen TV for football."

Before Vanessa could reply, Josh said, those telltale lines flickering,

"Uh, Darcie, are you cooking?"

"Good heavens, no. Maybe appetizers—that I can do. But Mom'll do the turkey. She's itching to use the doo-dads in the kitchen. Mrs. Z is making pies and rolls. Jennifer will bring mashed potatoes and green beans."

"In that case, we'd all be delighted," he said. "What can we bring? Wine?"

Josh and Darcie went on talking, as if it were perfectly normal for Darcie to make her part of *you guys*, for Josh to include her in *We'd all be delighted*.

Darcie shook her head. "Quince signed up for wine. I think we've got everything covered. Maybe carrot sticks, celery, olives, things like that."

"Sure. But that's not much. There's got to be something else."

"I can't think of a thing. We're not going whole hog with five kinds of potatoes and six kinds of vegetables. We're keeping it basic, so—"

"Cranberry sauce," Vanessa said. She could have sworn she was barely listening, stuck on *We'd all be delighted*. But even someone as high and dry on the banks of mainstream culture as she was knew cranberry sauce was a staple of Thanksgiving dinner.

"Oh, no—how did I forget cranberry sauce? Maybe I can make it. Or—"

"We'll bring it," came out of Vanessa's mouth.

We was contagious.

"You will? Fabulous." Her eyes glinted. "I asked Mrs. R, but she's visiting a nephew in Indiana that weekend, so you'll have the house to yourself. Whoops—better get back to parade duty."

Only after Darcie was out of earshot did Josh lean in and ask, "Do you know how to make cranberry sauce?"

"Not a clue. It can't be any worse than popcorn. Can it?"

He chuckled, and he was so close that the reverberations traveled from his body to hers. She made the mistake of looking up.

Their eyes met. Held.

He murmured, "Public be damned" and leaned close.

"Here they come!" someone shouted.

He held her look for the time it took her heart to perform two hard, erratic beats.

He said, very low, "Saved by pint-sized ghosts and goblins."

CHAPTER FIFTEEN

T HEY DROVE PAST the last flickers of jack-o'-lanterns, remembered shrieks of excitement echoing in now quiet and darkened streets.

"You do know you made the Kincannons' Halloween, don't you?"

He caught her smile reflected in the passenger window. "I had fun. This isn't the way to Mrs. Richards' house."

"No. I'm taking you to a Drago landmark."

He'd plotted for time alone by picking her up at Mrs. R's before the start of trick-or-treating.

With Mrs. Mudge dozing on the sofa and the kids counting their booty he wasn't about to waste the opportunity.

He pulled onto a rough road through woods to the Drago River, and stopped. After checking that no other cars were around, he turned off the engine.

She peered out. "It might be scenic during the daytime, but—"

"It's not all that scenic then, either. But it provides something we seldom have—privacy. I told you I wouldn't jump you in public, but in private…"

She slowly turned to him. He shifted, sliding one arm around her shoulders and drawing her to him.

He gave her time—a little—to protest or dodge.

She did neither.

She met his kiss and matched it.

The element of uncertainty was gone. And for his money, that beat the hell out of any aphrodisiac he'd ever heard of.

She rested a palm on his jaw and he had no consciousness left for anything but her.

The taste of her. That crisp, tartness with softness down deep.

The feel of her. That strong, upright posture with the rich curves.

The smell of her. That no-nonsense soap clean, with the heat of woman beneath it.

He pulled pins from her hair until he could sink his fingers into it. With widespread hands to hold her head, he flicked his tongue between her lips, along her teeth.

She opened to him, and he plunged deep.

Savoring her low, soft moan. Wanting more. So much more from her. Of her. In her.

All the color and passion and motion promised by that robe.

He wanted to drown in the sensations, yet he fought back to the surface.

For her.

He'd pulled her closer.

Damned center consoles. What he wouldn't give for an old-fashioned bench seat.

She had both her hands under his jacket, one resting in seeming innocence at his waist, the other at the back of his neck, her fingers sifting through the ends of his hair with a rhythm that should have been soothing.

It wasn't.

His right arm clamped her close. He kissed her cheekbone, her eyelid, her nose, her forehead.

"God, I deserve all the pain I'm feeling for bringing you here."

"Pain?" Her voice's breathy bursts pumped up his ego and libido.

"Oh, yeah. The pain of knowing we can't finish what we've started."

"No." One syllable, two letters, yet it held question, agreement, disappointment, and relief.

"Making out in a car—I haven't done this since I was a kid." Ventures that never felt like this.

"I never have."

"You never—?" He eased her back to look at her.

"I never did—" With her hands otherwise occupied she indicated their entwined bodies by looking down. "—this in a car."

Air whooshed out of him.

He circled his left hand around her neck and drew her to him for a long, hot kiss. He was distracted into another whirl of kisses and caresses.

But he recovered. Eventually. Because the alternative was taking this a whole lot farther a whole lot faster than his gut told him would be good for Vanessa.

When he could, he said, "The boys where you come from must have been blind. Or were you holding everybody a mile off back then, too."

She gave him that impenetrable look, and said as distantly as someone sitting as near to his lap as they could manage, "In high school I focused on my studies. I had gaps to fill."

"Your parents home-schooled you?" Her past might just distract him sufficiently to keep his dignity.

"They taught me to read and write, then lost interest. I was lucky Doug was there a few years. Starlight would wince and complain *Doug* didn't reflect his soul. He'd shrug and keep telling me about Halloween. And math." Handing her a key to heaven, her tone implied. "He'd been an accountant and handled the commune's finances. He taught me."

"You loved math from the start?"

"It's clear. It's logical. It's orderly." She might as well have added, *How could anyone not love it?*

He could see the appeal to a child brought up as Vanessa had been.

"Doug didn't stay. Few did." The line of her mouth eased. "A few months after he left, though, a package arrived for me. The only one I ever received. He sent books, including old accounting textbooks, and a calculator. That was the year I didn't talk. I didn't want any distraction."

His arms tightened for the child enthralled by old accounting books.

For less than a minute, she relaxed in his hold, then stiffened. She'd absorbed as much of his sympathy as she would take.

"So," she said briskly, "when WoodPath left with most of the commune's money, I took over the finances."

"How old were you?"

"Starlight rarely gave the same answer twice about when I'd been born. My best calculation is twelve."

A girl who'd made up her name. A girl who'd made up her birthdate. A girl who'd basically educated herself. "How long did you do the books?

"Books—a ratty notebook with a few columns of numbers. So few people left toward the end—"

"How long, Vanessa?"

"Until my parents died."

There was more. The hairs at the back of his neck were sure of it.

"How'd your parents die?"

"Their truck died on the railroad tracks. A train hit them."

His arms tightened around her. "God, they didn't have time to get out?"

"Witnesses said they had time. Sol kept trying to restart the engine. He and Starlight must have seen the train."

She was way too restrained, way too calm. Even all these years later, some emotion should seep into her voice, her face.

"The police suspected suicide. But that wasn't it. Optimism killed them. Optimism the truck wouldn't break down. Optimism it would start again or the train would stop."

"That's not optimism, that's foolishness."

She lifted a shoulder, dismissing the distinction. Yet, he sensed a raw nerve jangling somewhere beneath all this control.

"Why do you blame yourself?"

Her head jerked, bringing her eyes to his. Almost as fast, she looked away.

Bingo. One jangling nerve hit dead center.

"I should have made sure they got the truck fixed."

It took a beat to work it out. "*You* should have—?"

"They never followed through. I should have made sure. I should—"

"The hell you should have. You were a kid. They were the adults. Sounds like you spent most of your childhood taking care of them. If you hadn't been around they would have died years earlier."

They sat, so close he could have kissed her by dipping his head. He didn't.

She breathed steadily in, then out, four times.

Four times when her breast brushed his arm. Four times when the faint release of her breath brushed his face. Four times when the rhythmic motion of her back raised his shoulder.

Then she burst into tears.

He'd handled more than his share of crying females. None so unexpectedly. None so mortified that he feared she'd bolt. None making him want to tear the world apart.

He used his hand on the back of her head to bring it to his shoulder. Being Vanessa, she resisted. He didn't ease up. After a moment, she emitted a harsh sob and accepted his solace.

Her body shook with the force of her crying. His heart felt as if it were doing the same.

Tears for the loss of her parents. Tears for not having a true childhood. Tears for her misguided guilt. Tears locked away for decades.

He stroked her hair and muttered anything halfway soothing. Mostly her name.

When she began shifting motions that meant she was about to sit up—and move away—he adjusted to keep his arm around her.

"Josh." Her voice was raw.

"Don't bother arguing. You're staying here—as close as I can get you."

He drove the entire way with his right arm around her. At Mrs. Richards', he got around to her car door before she'd opened it. He took her hand and walked her to the front door.

She cleared her throat. *Here it comes.*

"I apologize, Josh."

He consciously contradicted her formal tone with a rough, "What for?"

"For crying all over you, for inappropriately—"

He took her face in his hands, stilling her words and her.

"Don't you apologize for that. Not ever." He kissed her. Her lips parted, and the kiss became more complicated, richer than he'd intended. He drew her into him, enfolding her, stroking into her with his tongue.

In the space of a finger-snap he reached flash point.

With more discipline than he'd known he possessed, he eased his hold, lifted his mouth from hers. But he didn't let her go, not yet.

"I'd be hard-pressed to say which meant more, you telling me about your growing up or being the first guy you made out with in a car."

A flicker of a smile shifted her lips.

"This won't be the last time." He kissed her, keeping a rein on this one, then turned her toward the door and opened it before delivering his parting shot. "We're going to do more talking and more making out—lots more. Soon."

THEY ANNOUNCED WELL-WISHERS had to clear the backstage in two minutes.

"Nervous?"

Topher looked up at Josh's question, his eyes huge and serious behind his glasses. "No. I know all my lines, and Vanessa said people won't really be looking at me. They'll be looking at the character I'm playing."

Interesting.

Did she think that's what she was doing—playing a part—when she became that stiff, distant woman she'd been at the start.

No time to do more than file the thought. His son needed his attention.

"That's a wise thing she told you. I'm proud of you for understanding it. I'm especially proud of you for doing this, Topher. Trying something new."

His son nodded. "Vanessa said she was proud of me, too."

Josh cleared his throat, heading into rougher territory. "You know, Toph, as much as I'm sure Vanessa would like to be here—"

"She said she'll be here."

"I know. And I know she hopes to be. But—"

"She said she'll be here."

He knew from Mrs. Mudge that Vanessa had called twice last week to talk to Topher, also saying hello to Livvy. The calls came when he was at computer lab meetings. There'd been none this week.

He hadn't heard from her.

Not since he'd left her at Mrs. Richards' front door.

It had been a judgment call—risk pushing her into bed when she was vulnerable or risk letting her clamp down the shields again, perhaps permanently. He'd gone with what he'd thought was right for her.

The hell of it was, his son would take the first blow, delivered just as Topher was stepping out of the shadows.

How many times had Josh checked his messages today? Expecting, dreading the one that said she couldn't make it.

But no message, no word at all.

"Sometimes things happen with adults and they can't—"

"She said she'll be here."

"She has a job, doofus," Xena burst out from behind Josh. "Not in New York, but still pretty important and people can't leave jobs like that for stupid kids' stuff."

"Xena."

"It's the truth. Just because she said so doesn't mean she'll be here."

Topher pushed up his glasses as he looked from his sister to his father.

"Dad," Topher said, in his little boy-old man voice, "she'll be here."

JOSH SCANNED THE Community Center auditorium, hoping…

All he saw were the backs of heads. And most of those were masked by people walking, standing, removing coats.

"You should have told him she wouldn't be here," Xena declared.

When had his daughter become such an unstinting voice of doom? *Your rock could shatter.*

Maybe he'd been too quick to dismiss Vanessa's words.

"There's time yet for her to get here." But he didn't believe it.

That's why he didn't call Xena on it when she muttered, "Yeah, right."

Livvy's chatter became emphatic. Her small hand patted his cheek to claim his attention. "Anaterrcup." Livvy pointed. "Anaterrcup."

His eyes must have communicated directly with his pulse, because it picked up before his mind registered seeing the back of Vanessa's head.

"She's here," Xena said from beside him.

What the heck was that in his daughter's voice? Surprise? Yeah. Disappointment? Maybe. Was he letting wild optimism carry him away if he hoped there'd also been respect?

"Yes, she is." He sounded matter-of-fact. Good.

With Xena trailing, he bobbed and weaved from one hello to another, promising to call three people before he reached the row Vanessa sat in.

"Vanessa."

She looked up. The bags under her eyes had multiplied. Her hair had lost a battle with static electricity and she had on a jacket the color of mud.

She smiled, and every bit of him stood up and shouted.

Oh, yeah, he had it bad.

"We have to find seats," Xena said from behind him.

"I thought we'd—"

"Not enough seats," Xena interrupted.

Vanessa sat seven seats in, with one empty seat beside her on this side, none beyond her. He struggled to contain Livvy, intent on launching herself at Vanessa across the space. "Vanessa, want to come look for a seat with us?"

"*Da-ad*," Xena complained. "We have to go. There won't be any seats."

Before he could respond, a lovely older woman stood from a seat between him and Vanessa.

"We'll move down a seat, won't we?" Martha Barrett said.

"Sure," said Dutch Harnett, moving into the empty seat that had separated him from the couple on the aisle.

"That's only two seats," Xena protested.

"I'll hold Livvy," he said, edging past the couple on the aisle, who stood to let him by. "Thank you, Martha, Dutch. Thank you everyone."

He'd reached the seat, but the females on either side of him remained motionless—Vanessa pretending she was a rock sitting in an auditorium seat and Xena sighing in the aisle.

Martha broke that impasse. "Xena, I have photos from the wedding. I'd love to show you Darcie's dress."

Xena expelled a final sigh, put her head down and started into the row. Josh mouthed a thank you to Martha, who smiled sweetly. He'd have to tell Darcie how he and her mother bonded as parents of mule-headed daughters.

But first, he had another mule-headed female to contend with.

"Take Livvy while I get settled."

Vanessa accepted the child with credible aplomb when he plopped Livvy in her lap. Girl and woman smiled at each other.

"I'm glad you made it." He kept his voice low. That, along with Martha's talk should prevent Xena from picking up more than half of this conversation.

Vanessa's eyebrows raised. But almost in slow motion, as if they lacked energy for a fast trip. "I told Topher I'd be here."

"Yeah. But when we didn't hear from you this week—or at all in the case of me…" *We assumed or worried to varying degrees that you were like my ex-wife.* Yeah. Better not to say that.

"Were you expecting me to call? I never said I would."

Blunt was back.

"No. But, yeah, I hoped you'd call. I could say it was solely so I'd know you were going to be here for Topher." He leaned closer. "But I hoped you'd call because I've missed talking to you. I've missed you, period."

Pink tinged her cheeks, and if he wasn't completely delusional, heat came into her eyes.

"You could have called," she said. She had her face down, almost to the top of Livvy's head, so the words were muffled, but he heard.

He took Livvy—leaning closer and longer than necessary. He saw Vanessa's eyes widen, felt the hitch in her breath, experienced the warm scent of her.

"Could I?" The auditorium lights went down, but he was so close he saw the silken gleam of her eyes. "I emailed you the number of every phone I thought I might pass by while you were gone. You didn't even suggest I call the two numbers you gave me—and I quote—for business purposes."

Livvy squirmed, caught between Vanessa's shoulder and his chest, but he didn't back off. Not until he became convinced Vanessa had swallowed hard. She said, "You could have called those numbers. You can call them."

He could have whooped at the shift from *could* to *can*, from past to future.

But that would have disturbed the audience's focus on the stage where the curtain stirred, as if gathering strength. For now, it was enough to smile. And to see, as the curtain slowly opened, shedding a portion of stage light on the audience that she smiled at him.

He sat back, to his younger daughter's relief as she relaxed in his lap and to his elder daughter's satisfaction as she settled back.

He gave all his attention to the stage and his courageous son's debut.

But he made sure he maintained contact between Vanessa's shoulder and his upper arm, side by side.

JOSH INSISTED VANESSA come with him to congratulate Topher.

Amid the chaos of hugs, photo poses and the high-pitched triumph of elementary school thespians, she slowed her pace, effectively putting Josh, still carrying Livvy, and Xena in front of her.

"There he is!" Xena surged ahead. Then stopped abruptly when she reached her brother, still in costume as a gray-haired elder, before giving him a thump on the back.

"Great job, Topher. You were wonderful." Josh encircled his son's shoulders with the arm not holding Livvy, engulfing the boy.

"Thanks, Dad."

Josh stepped back, looking at him. "Aren't you excited?" He frowned, and Topher immediately tensed. "What's—"

Vanessa interrupted. "Perhaps Topher is thinking about the other performances coming up. He might not want to lose his concentration."

Josh's frown lifted. He clasped her hand and tugged her forward.

Startled, she pulled back. Not because she didn't want to join Topher, but from an instinctive desire to hide her hand so blatantly surrounded by his.

Josh didn't relent. Rather than stumble, she went where he wanted, at the same time twisting her fingers to try to free them. He let go. But only when she stood in the circle of his family.

Which was too late, as she could tell from Xena's glower, Topher's concentrated attention, and interested glances from others around them.

"I told them you'd come," Topher said, his slow smile spreading across his face.

"Big deal," Xena muttered. "There were hundreds of people here."

Vanessa' gaze flickered to the unhappy girl. As she looked back at

Topher, she saw Josh wore a thoughtful frown.

"I enjoyed your play very much," she said to Topher, keeping the focus where it belonged.

His smile widened. "Thank you. But I messed up a line near the end. I have to get that right next time."

"If you missed a line, nobody in the audience knew it," Josh said staunchly, though Vanessa had felt him flinch when Topher faltered and heard him expel a breath in relief when the boy picked up his place. "C'mon, let's celebrate."

Topher's head dropped, and his old mumble came. "I want to get to bed early."

Josh's lips parted, as if he'd press the point. Then he slowly nodded. "Okay. We'll celebrate when you want to, Topher."

The boy looked at his father quickly, then ducked his head again. But his words were clear. "Thanks, Dad."

"Costumes! Costumes!" shouted a teacher, circulating through the crowd. "Everything needs to be put away neatly for tomorrow."

"You go change. We'll wait for you at the car."

The teacher arrived with a wig form in hand. "I need that wig, Topher. And you need to get out of costume."

"Yes, ma'am." He carefully drew off the gray-haired wig.

Livvy, who'd been uncharacteristically quiet, clapped her hands, squealed with delight and launched herself at her brother.

"Critrowtik! Critrowtik!"

Topher grinned widely enough to light the entire stage. "I must've been good—Livvy didn't even recognize me."

CHAPTER SIXTEEN

T HE NEXT DAY, Josh asked Malcolm to cover the lunchroom so he could to take his aging car for service at Stenner Autos.

While the mechanic did his magic, Josh headed for the general manager's office. Jennifer looked up from her computer with a hello.

He wasted no time. "Jennifer, you have a daughter. Does it seem to you like I rely on Xena too much?"

"What makes you ask?"

He got the feeling she was buying time. "Someone said it in so many words."

From the grin Jennifer stifled, she suspected who.

"I don't know about *too much*," she said judiciously. "You rely on her a great deal, but she's a very responsible girl."

"Always has been. It's not any different from when Melissa was here." Silence met his statement. "Is it?"

"She seems to worry more now. About Topher and Livvy."

"I know." Topher's growing connection with Vanessa reassured him his son wasn't closed off, but what if she didn't remain in their lives? "It's weird when someone else is more like your child than you are. You don't have that problem with Ashley, with the two of you so close—"

"Bite your tongue. My daughter would go into a hysterics if she heard you say we're close or she's like me." She grew serious. "But I do see how Vanessa and Xena are alike."

"Xena? No, it's Topher. He opens up to Vanessa like I've never seen him do before." He stopped, realizing the truth of his words … *like I've never seen him do before.*

"Oh, you meant personalities," she said. "I meant coping mechanism. That's where Vanessa and Xena are similar. That staunch determination to control everything, so nothing catches them unguarded."

If he'd been a cartoon character he'd have a balloon over his head with a bold "Duh!"

How had he missed it? Not only the similarity, but that Xena felt some of the pressures Vanessa had carried as a child.

He swore to himself—at himself.

All the blame he'd set at the feet of Vanessa's parents, and here came a tide of parental screwing-up lapping around his ankles. Or was it his knees?

Jennifer was going on. "Look at the way Vanessa's taken hold with Fay O'Hearn's difficulties. And now it seems she's found a solution."

Josh frowned. "Yeah? What've you heard?"

"She's found a way for Fay to apply for financial aid without Ellie's cooperation. She called Fay about it from Virginia. But the point is, like Xena, Vanessa takes charge." Her expression combined questioning with concern. "Of course, you know them so much better. Maybe I'm way off."

He managed a quick smile. "No, I think you've hit it, Jennifer. Being alike helps explains why they've butted heads."

She nodded. "And since you asked—yes, I do think Xena's worrying and trying to carry the load more. I mean, you were doing most of the parenting even before—Sorry. I shouldn't—"

"It's okay. I didn't imagine it was a secret in Drago. Xena never got much mothering from Melissa, especially in the year before she left."

Jennifer looked thoughtful. "That's the thing about mothers, Josh. They don't have to be the best mothers to be loved. And to be missed terribly."

"THIS IS WONDERFUL!" Fay O'Hearn threw her arms around Vanessa and squeezed. "You are amazing!"

Vanessa didn't back out of the hug immediately. It was rather nice.

Maybe because she was tired enough that not standing on her own felt good.

She'd worked non-stop to carve out enough time to, first, attend Topher's play, and then to extend her time in Drago.

But when we didn't hear from you this week—or at all the case of me…

Josh had thought she wouldn't keep her word to Topher.

There'd been moments when she'd feared that, too, with all that closing the books and preparing the annual report required.

That was why she hadn't called, even when she'd found herself wanting to hear his voice—because she'd feared the words would slip out: *Sorry, I can't make it. Something came up.*

She stepped back from Fay's hug and set the record straight.

"Janine—my assistant—is the amazing one. She talked to your top three choices' financial aid departments and put together this information about how they decide if a student qualifies for what's called *independent by professional judgment.*"

It was an interesting concept—a mechanism to allow financial aid experts to assess students' situations that fell outside the normal categories.

She slid the folder across the desk recently added to the computer lab's back office. Finishing touches here had taken a backseat while Todd completed the main area for the first delivery of equipment next week. Then began the meticulous set-up and testing process.

"I never dreamed there was a way around needing my mother's information."

"Applying for independent student status is far from a sure thing, Fay. Each financial aid department assesses by its own criteria."

"I understand. But this gives me a chance. I'll apply to every school in the country if I have to."

"I doubt you'll have to do that. What you *do* have to do is get the letters about your home life we talked about. Have you lined those up?"

"I wanted to be sure it was real before I did that. And I wondered—I hoped—would you write one for me?"

Vanessa shook her head. "A letter from me wouldn't carry any weight. It has to be professionals in a position to assess your home life. A therapist or clergy or—"

"Mr. Kincannon?"

"Exactly. Mr. Cottle, too. Officer Barrett would be good. And include the police report." Fay looked dismayed. "You have to be open with these financial counselors, you have to spell it out in the letter you write, and ask the professionals to spell it out, too. It's the only way to get the help you need."

"I just…"

"I know." She met the girl's eyes. "But you have to do it."

Aware of another presence, Vanessa looked up to see Zeke in the doorway.

"Sorry, didn't mean to interrupt," he said. "I can come back later. Or—"

"No, Mr. Zeekowsky." Fay stood, gathering her things. "I've taken more of Ms. Irish's time than I should. Oh—do you know where I might find your wife?"

A smile lit his face, as always, when someone referred to Darcie as his wife. "She should be at the station doing paperwork."

Fay gave Vanessa a meaningful look. "Then I'm heading to the police station. Thank you again, Ms. Irish. Thank you so much."

Zeke watched the girl leave before folding his long body into the chair. "Something going on?"

"Yes."

"Something I need to know about?"

"No."

"Good. Sounds like you've got it handled."

"I hope so." But her mind was on something else. Something that had tugged at her for weeks. And likely had been doing the same to Zeke, judging by this visit. "Zeke, I've been wanting to talk to you. I know I've been leaving more to Beth and Rajeed—"

"Uh-huh," Zeke agreed.

"That will change. I'll be in the office more—"

"Wait. What do you mean in the office more?"

That stopped her. What could it mean except she'd be in the office more?

"I, uh, I'll be hands-on. The way I was before…" Before she'd come to Drago, before she'd met Josh. Before he'd dragged her into his town. His life.

No, that wasn't fair. He'd opened doors and shoved a time or two, but she could have stood firm. She hadn't.

She wasn't sure how she felt about that.

Or him.

She had never before been particularly interested in kissing. But she was with Josh.

Oh, yes, she definitely was.

Beyond kissing…

"Once we get this equipment set up and tested," she picked up with a fair rendition of normalcy, "I can get back to my schedule. I'll be at the office full-time to prepare the SEC filings and annual report."

"Not if I have anything to say about it. That's what you have staff for."

She gaped at him.

"I want Zeke-Tech to be different, Vanessa. Not just for me, not just for the people who move to Drago, but for everybody. Especially you and Quince. I mean, sure, we had to work like crazy to get it off the ground. And we'll never sit in rocking chairs shooting the breeze all day. Although, rocking chairs for the house's side porch aren't a bad idea." He dug in his pockets.

"Zeke, rocking chairs have nothing to do with—"

"Got it." He made a notation in his smart phone. "But they do. Because real people use them a lot. I didn't know that. Or I didn't pay attention. We all need to get out more. You, me, Quince, everybody at Zeke-Tech. So we know what people need. So we know people."

He shoved the phone in his pocket. "I don't want you to go back to the way things were. I want you to spend time away from the office.

I want you to have a good life, enjoy being around people, relax more. And, in the end—" His grin turned a little wolfish. "—that'll be good for Zeke-Tech."

"I don't know if I can." The words were out before she knew they were coming.

He frowned. "That's not logical. You've *been* doing it. And doing great."

"No, I haven't. When I'm here, I think I should be in Virginia. When I'm there, I worry about what's happening here."

"Then Beth and Rajeed should be doing more, not less."

"I don't know if I can let go. I *want* to do the work. It's my job. It's … important to me." She shook her head, trying to clear it.

How important were other things in her life to her?

"Hi, Josh."

She looked up to find another man in the doorway.

This one made her heartbeat stutter.

"Hey, Zeke." He met her eyes. "I've come to take you to dinner."

Zeke stood. "Good plan. It's like a revolving door in here. If you don't get her out she'll stay all night and never get dinner."

"Zeke—"

"We'll talk," he said over his shoulder. "But I won't change my mind."

Left alone, Josh said, "The pleasure of your company is requested at Chez Kincannon for dinner. Topher is eager to rehash his performances, and I said I'd do my best to get you to come. You do have to eat, you know."

"Yes. But…" She looked at her laptop, but found herself thinking of Topher. And maybe of Josh. "Okay."

"Great. What did Zeke mean about it being a revolving door?"

"Fay was here when he arrived. I was giving her some information."

He grunted.

"You've heard about it already."

"Yes."

She considered him. "You're not happy."

"About your finding a way for Fay to get financial aid without her mother's involvement? I think it's great."

"Even though she'll leave Drago to go to college?"

"Even though—and it's only four years. She'll be back. Just wish I'd heard it from you, instead of the Drago grapevine."

"I should have called you? Even though it was Fay's business."

He cocked one eyebrow, which she interpreted as *You might have a point.*

She added, "I don't think she'd mind if I told you now, since she'll be talking to you about it soon."

She explained as she gathered her belongings and put on her coat. At the front door, her mind shifted gears.

"At the next security meeting we need to set a protocol for changing the security code. That should be done frequently, but not at regular intervals and—Why are you smiling?"

He swung around and faced her. "Just thinking about community and computers. Quite a one-two punch." And then he kissed her.

"SHE'LL SCREW IT up."

The eruption came at dinner Saturday night, but Xena had been rumbling like an active volcano all week.

To Josh, it had been one of two pitfalls in an otherwise terrific week.

Vanessa had dinner with them each night except Tuesday, when she had a business meeting with Zeke and Quince.

Topher talked more and more. Livvy wanted Vanessa to put her to bed each night. Xena glowered.

The other drawback hadn't been a surprise, either—no privacy.

They'd had half an hour Monday at Makeout Lookout. Their other visit there, they'd found two cars already ensconced, both of which he recognized as students'. So they left.

He'd stolen a few chaste kisses as Mrs. R's front door, and some not so chaste kisses under the cover of heavy rain and fog last night, parked in front of her house. Lack of privacy and the gear necessary for raw November evenings meant there'd been little beyond kissing ... which Josh tried to view philosophically, when he wasn't cursing celibacy in all its forms.

Today, they'd all gone to Drago High's away football game, then stopped on the way back at his aunt's house for hot cider and cookies. Aunt Beth had taken to Vanessa, which deepened Xena's scowl.

Just now, as they'd finished dinner, he'd told the kids about their bringing cranberry sauce to Darcie and Zeke's Thanksgiving dinner next week.

That's when Xena blew.

He stood and pulled back Xena's chair. "Vanessa, you and Topher and Livvy start dessert. Xena, come upstairs." She didn't move. "Now."

He didn't make it loud, but everyone else jolted.

Xena headed up the stairs with slouching insolence.

He met Vanessa's eyes for an instant. He had no impression of her trying to convey a message, yet he felt supported.

Upstairs, he closed Xena's bedroom door behind him, turned the desk chair to face her as she sat, arms crossed and mouth mulish, on her bed.

"You know I don't allow rudeness, Xena. You've been pushing the limits with Vanessa, and I won't accept any more. Do you understand?"

"It's all her fault. Everything was fine before she came."

"No it wasn't, and you're too smart and too honest to think otherwise. Do you understand?"

She stared at the vining roses on the bedspread selected by Melissa.

"Xena, do you understand?"

"Yes, I understand." She rivaled Topher for a mutter, but she'd said it.

"I know it's been hard since your mother left. It's been hard on all of us."

"Yeah," she said almost eagerly. "You have so much to do, and Topher got so quiet and Livvy—"

"I know you love your brother and sister, Xena. But it's not your job to worry about them. Or to take care of them. That's my job. Your job is to be a kid. To work hard at school, to play hard, and to help around the house. But not to run it. And not to worry about me. That's how it's going to be from now on."

"It's her, isn't it? Are you and she…" He waited, not filling in for her. She blinked hard. "You know … a couple."

"Maybe."

"*Da-ad!* But she's—"

"*Quiet*, Xena."

Only when the stiffness of shock left her face did he go on.

"I want you to think about something, Xena. I like Vanessa, Topher likes Vanessa, Livvy likes Vanessa. We all like her a lot." He stood. "I'm going downstairs now. You have a choice. You can come down, be polite, and be part of the group or you can stay here by yourself while we decide what kind of cranberry sauce to bring to Thanksgiving dinner at Darcie and Zeke's."

He gave her fifteen minutes to stew while they ate ice cream, then he opened the discussion of cranberry sauce.

She lasted another two minutes of lurking on the landing before she came down. She wasn't happy, and she didn't hide it. But she wasn't rude. It was a first step.

CHAPTER SEVENTEEN

Arriving at Mrs. R's to pick up Vanessa the next afternoon, Josh spotted Zeke's car parked in front.

Was she going to have to work on a Sunday?

Disappointment settled low in his gut and stayed there as he approached the front door through spitting sleet and rain. Way more disappointment than missing an afternoon of overseeing homework projects and discussing cranberry recipes together deserved.

To his surprise, Darcie opened the door.

"Here he is," she said, pulling him in. "He'll tell you Zeke and I are fully qualified to look after the kids for an afternoon, won't you, Josh."

Vanessa stood on the bottom step with her coat in one hand and bright red on both cheeks.

"What's going on, Vanessa?" he asked.

But Darcie answered. "It turns out, Mrs. R is spending this afternoon—the *whole* afternoon—at the Drago Christmas Bazaar and then going to dinner at the Mudges. That's what she told Corine, and Corine called me, and we—Zeke and I—thought it would give you and Vanessa a rare chance to be alone. Didn't we, Zeke? To, you know, talk. Work. Or whatever. So, I said Zeke and I will keep an eye on your kids, and from Vanessa's reaction, you'd think we'd never taken care of a kid in our lives."

"Well, I—" Zeke started.

"But I have," Darcie interrupted.

Josh's brain tried to catch up with his hormones, which had gotten the gist of the situation as soon as Darcie mentioned Mrs. R being at the annual Christmas Bazaar.

Time with Vanessa. Alone. In a house. With a bed. Oh, yeah, his hormones had all the pertinent facts lined up.

Just one problem.

"Vanessa?"

She didn't look at him. "There's no reason, Darcie—"

But Darcie wasn't taking any appeals.

She gave Zeke's arm a push and he went out the door, with her right behind. "The two of you stay here and play two-handed solitaire for all I care, but we're going to Josh's house, and we do not want to see you before six o'clock. Got it?"

The closing door punctuated the question.

"Vanessa, I told you—if you don't want anything to happen…"

If there were a Nobel Prize for Integrity In the Face of Raging Hormones, he'd get it hands-down.

With her head down, she muttered. It took a second to untangle the soft words from the roaring of blood in his ears. "I do want it."

"Yeah?"

She raised her head. "Yes. It's strange, but—"

He shucked his coat in the one stride it took to reach her, took her coat from her unresisting hands and dropped that, too. "Nothing strange about it."

He cupped her face and kissed her.

He knew the taste of her by now. He knew the texture and lines of her mouth. And she knew him.

They kept kissing. Mouths open, mouths closed. Hungry, quick, moving kisses. They had each other's rhythm, angles.

That had to explain how they managed to kiss their way up the stairs without becoming another household accident statistic.

They teetered a moment at the top of the stairs when Vanessa wedged off one shoe while Josh was stepping onto the landing.

She grabbed onto his shirt with both hands and held on.

When they regained their balance the shirt was partially bunched up on his back, so he kept the motion going by tugging it over his head and dropping that, too.

He started to take her down to the settee as the closest available surface, then changed direction.

Better a delay of a moment than the crashing disruption of a splintering settee. A bed. Only a few steps away.

She gave a faint protesting sound, but he drew her to the bedroom.

"Bed," he promised.

But once he'd fulfilled that promise—first untangling the condoms he'd carried in half-self-mockery, half-hopefulness since the Homecoming dance from the keys in his pocket, then depositing them on the bedside table, before pitching the two of them haphazardly across the comforter—he discovered a new problem.

"Whoa, whoa, Vanessa. You're shaking—and not in a good way."

"What would be a good way?"

"With excitement. From my touch."

He brushed the top of her shoulder. She tensed. He cupped the back of her head.

"Vanessa." He brought her cheek to his chest. "Tell me. Are you a virgin?"

"No. I dispensed with that mystery. Part of the mystery, anyway. Perhaps for the male—Are you laughing?"

She tried to twist her head, but he held her fast. "No. I'm not laughing. One time? One guy?"

"Two. One would not be an adequate sample. Twice with each. Because once could be an anomaly."

Now he laughed. He definitely laughed. "Ah, Vanessa."

"A sample of one or two or ten thousand is not the point." She sounded flustered.

He rather liked that. Her shaking had stopped.

"Ten thousand would say a lot more about the sampler than the sample. It only takes one when it's right."

She was silent a long time before: "Show me."

"It doesn't work that way—me, alone, showing you. It's the two of us, together. Just like with kissing. You have to admit we're damned good at kissing." She gave a faint sound of agreement, part pride, part pleasure, part shyness. "So, let's start with you helping me get out of all these clothes."

"I've never undressed a man."

But she'd already shifted, applying her attention and her tantalizing fingers to his zipper.

She'd removed his jeans and socks with dispatch, and had a grip on his boxers. Her hands brushed against his erection.

He sucked in, hoping the oxygen also contained a load of restraint. Reversing their positions, he placed a finger to her bottom lip, slowing her, slowing them both.

"You're a quick study. Now, let me catch up."

He stroked down her throat, his fingertips absorbing the leap in her pulse when he reached the top button of her shirt. Her skin jumped and shivered as he proceeded lower.

He laid back one side of the unbuttoned shirt, and bent to her, kissing the soft, white skin below her collarbone.

"I… My clothes—my underclothes—are entirely utilitarian."

"Utilitarian can be beautiful. On you."

The swirl of emotions in her eyes was more familiar now, he caught several of them, nerves and discomfort mixing with desire and eagerness.

He nudged her bra strap.

"And even better off."

He had her bra unhooked and the straps down her bare shoulders before she could do more than emit a small gasp.

Rolling to let him remove shirt and bra, she pulled the comforter over her breasts with would-be casualness. Yes, he'd explore that later.

For now, he was devoted to removing her slacks.

He let the backs of his hands stroke across the smooth, warm skin of her belly as he grappled with the button. And he indulged himself with continued contact as he lowered the zipper with infinite patience.

"I thought—I thought the idea was to get the clothes off fast."

The idea—his idea—was to elicit exactly that hitch in her voice. "The idea is to get the clothes off pleasurably."

"It wasn't pleasurable the way I—?"

"Oh, yeah—and you know it. But there are all kinds of pleasure."

He drew the fabric down her hips. She lifted them cooperatively, and he slowly bared the tops of her thighs, then down and down.

He kissed below her ankle bone, and nearly lost it when she unconsciously let her legs fall open. He forced himself to slow the return trip, with kisses first on one ankle, then the other. Meticulous kisses for each inch of her legs.

His pains—and his pain—were rewarded when she gave a moan of pleasure and frustration.

"What's this?"

She raised her head, looked, then dropped back. "Just a bruise."

He gently stroked the pad of his thumb over the mark across her left shin.

He bent to kiss it, cupped his palm under her calf and raised her leg to kiss it more comfortably, more thoroughly. Then allowed his hand to follow the line of her leg to her knee, lower, to the soft curve of her inner thigh. Lower still, then under the edge of her white panties.

A brush and she moaned, a slow slide into the slick heat and she shuddered.

She was close. He feared he was closer.

He grabbed for a condom. She took advantage of his motion to roll onto him, tugging at his boxers as they went. He kicked them away.

He used his teeth to hold the package while he ripped at it with his free hand.

"Vanessa, I have to…" She wrapped her hands around him. "Wait … wait…"

He begged her, he begged the condom. No way in hell was this thing going to go on. How had he ever in his life gotten one of these on? It was impossible. It was inhuman. It was torture. It was done. At last.

He rolled them once more, yanking at her panties, and blessed them when they tore.

She lifted her hips, her hands on his back, lower, trying to draw him in.

"Wait, wait," he crooned.

He wouldn't hurt her. If he erupted into all-consuming fire right here and now, he wasn't going to hurt her.

Then he was at her opening, sliding slowly against the exquisite resistance, into the unfathomable heat.

She lifted her hips, and he slid deeper. Deeper. He held still with muscle-shaking resolve. She whimpered.

"Wait, wait," he promised her, stroking back her hair.

"I don't want to." She sounded almost as surprised as determined.

She lifted her hips once more, and raised her legs, drawing him down so deep there was no recovery.

He tried to keep it slow. He tried. But their bodies had their own rhythm, their own destination.

A destination rushing up at him with the force and irresistibility of a tornado tearing across open land.

But she wasn't with him.

She hadn't retreated completely from her earlier frenzy, but she hung back. Uncertain. Shaken.

"Let go, honey. Let go."

"I don't ... think I—"

"Don't think, Vanessa. Don't think." He slid a hand between them, tipping the scales.

"Josh... Oh!"

"That's right. Yes. Yes."

And then he saw, felt, heard the whirlwind in her grow, connect with the one he'd been holding at bay, spread and deepen, pulling him in, deeper and faster, and deeper and faster.

Until he was nothing. She was nothing. And they were everything.

Time reasserted itself half-heartedly. He was still mostly on top of her. He should give her air, room.

He didn't move.

"Are you okay?" He kissed the juncture of her throat and shoulder.

"That was the first… I've never… That's why women…" She stopped, apparently to gather breath and thoughts. "You've skewed my sample."

SHE'D FALLEN ASLEEP to the faint rumble of his chuckle.

Now she awoke slowly. Eyes closed, she breathed in, then out.

Aware at some level that the world had changed, that she had changed. But not ready yet to examine any of that. Ready only to lie boneless and unheeding, accepting the warmth and weight that blanketed her.

The warmth and weight of Josh.

Josh.

Awareness flooded back in heat and clutching muscles that sent an after-tremor through her that surprised her perhaps more than all that had gone before.

Forcing muscles to cooperate in a body that felt foreign to her, she jolted out of the bed, picking up her clothes as she made for the bathroom.

She washed herself, somehow not as embarrassed by it as she would have expected to be. She sorted her clothes. Her movement, reflected in the mirror, caught her attention, and she stopped. She saw wild hair, reddened cheeks, swollen lips … and satisfied eyes.

Sucking in a breath through parted lips, she let her clothes drop to the floor. She'd told him she'd wanted this and she had.

She did.

Hands shaking, she pulled on only her robe and knotted the tie.

Josh sat in her bed, pillows stuffed behind him. He looked relaxed and comfortable. And very naked. "Okay?"

"Of course."

"Good, then come back to bed." He held out a hand.

She put hers in it, allowed him to draw her down to the bed, to the nest of pillows.

She'd sat with his arm around her numerous times in the car. It wasn't all that different doing it in bed. Even if he was naked. Even if they had just made love.

"I will be forever grateful to this robe." Josh stroked the material covering her shoulder. "Why did you buy it, Vanessa? Or was it a present? One of the two guys—?"

"No." She hesitated. "I bought it. It... It reminded me of one Mrs. Schmidt had."

He rolled his head on the pillow to look at her. "The principal's wife? The one of the different body type?"

"Yes. But that doesn't matter in a robe." Because she had never expected anybody to see it.

"Do you see the Schmidts?"

"Not since I paid them back. I discovered they'd spent well beyond the state allowance when I lived with them. After Zeke-Tech took off, I was able to repay them."

"You don't spend vacations with them—"

"I don't take vacations."

"—or get invited for holidays?"

"They have invited me," she admitted. "My work doesn't allow me to take off whenever I feel like it."

"You haven't said much about them. Were they harsh or—"

"Never. They were ... very kind."

He hitched up an elbow to look at her. "They took you in, were kind to you, worried about getting you college clothes, but you don't see them? Why?"

His movement brushed the side of her breast. She jolted. From the contact, yes, but even more from what followed, the dart of shivery heat that ricocheted through her.

Muscles long trained to retreat quivered at being held immobile.

No. That was wrong. They quivered from wanting to move forward.

"Do you really want to spend the rest of this afternoon talking? Because I wonder if that first time wasn't an anomaly."

She saw questions in his eyes. But even stronger, she saw desire. "It wasn't."

SHE AWOKE FROM a deeper sleep this time to the soft, hot glide of Josh's mouth on her back.

He began just above her shoulder blades. Thorough, patient, maddening, while she pressed her mouth deeper into the pillow.

He crested the peaks of her shoulder blades, traveled each slope of the valley created by her spine, devoted himself to each bump of that depression, down to its lowest point. Then continued his journey back up.

The pillow absorbed her sounds, but nothing hid the movement of her hips.

"Please, Josh." That whisper had come from her. She'd felt the muscles of her throat create it. Yet she didn't recognize the voice.

"You'll be sore if we make love again."

"Please."

THE SKY HAD lost its last vestiges of gray, deepening to dark. Their afternoon was over.

Josh stretched, both satisfaction and disquiet tugging at him.

Still single father of three, still high school principal, but no longer celibate back into the misty past, and he hoped to God not into the foreseeable future.

CHAPTER EIGHTEEN

THe cranberry sauce debate had raged nightly.

Vanessa kept producing recipes for new and exotic forms of cranberry sauce. Some with walnuts, pecans or pistachios, still more with apples, oranges, blueberries, apricots, pineapple and/or currants. One memorable one with pomegranate. She had quickly withdrawn from contention the concoction that included a hefty portion of port.

Topher maintained that the purest form—cranberries, sugar, and water—would be most historically accurate.

To no one's surprise, Xena held out for her mother's recipe—with apple cider and honey.

Livvy agreed with everyone.

But if things started to wind down, Josh stirred the pot by suggesting they buy a couple cans. Then he'd sit back and enjoy the discussion.

The Monday evening before Thanksgiving had been designated as the Great Cranberry Sauce Cookoff at the Kincannon kitchen.

Each of the three would make a sauce, and then everyone would vote on which one to make Wednesday in sufficient quantity for the next day.

Josh's job had been to buy the cranberries and other necessary ingredients, with lists supplied by each contestant.

Remembering the popcorn, he'd bought extra. The table practically groaned under cranberries, sugar, honey, apple cider, orange juice, walnuts, pecans, oranges, and dried apricots.

"Well," Vanessa said, after a moment's daunted appraisal of the mounded bags of cranberries, "we can each wash and pick over our own, or we can cooperate."

"Cooperate how?" Xena cast a wary look at the berries.

"Form an assembly line. Topher can open the bags, I'll wash, you drain, Xena, and we'll all pick over them. It'll be more efficient."

Topher's hand shot up. "I vote for cooperating."

Although she withheld any enthusiasm, Xena agreed.

But as Josh watched from his seat across the kitchen, where he'd assigned himself the job of keeping Livvy out of the middle of things, he saw true cooperation bloom.

Oh, there were bumps, sure. Especially early on.

"Topher, just tear the bag open and dump it in," Xena ordered at one point. "It'll take forever the way you're doing it."

He continued carefully pouring berries from the open corner of the bag into the colander Vanessa held.

"We might want to use the bags later," he said.

Before Xena could scoff at the idea, which Josh knew would harden her position into intractability, Vanessa spoke. "That's an interesting idea. What are some reasons we might need the bags later? Xena?"

Appealed to directly, his daughter couldn't resist the challenge.

Josh bit the insides of his cheeks to keep from grinning as she reeled off a half dozen uses, while Vanessa solemnly listened to each, including shower caps for dogs.

As they culled unsatisfactory berries, Vanessa led them into a discussion of assembly lines, division of labor, factory workers, use of robots, and—by the time they each had mounds of washed berries heaped on waxed paper on the kitchen table—quality control.

Topher's simple recipe went straight into the microwave while Vanessa and Xena measured and chopped.

There'd been a point when he thought she'd lost Xena. Then she casually mentioned how this all applied to the fashion-industry, and Xena jumped into the discussion with both feet.

Vanessa Irish was no fool.

Except about herself.

She might think she knew little about dealing with people, but she was wrong.

The doorbell interrupted his thoughts. He gave the cranberry cookers a smile, hoisted Livvy onto his hip and headed for the front.

Fay barely waited for the door to open before starting. "I'm sorry to bother you at home, Mr. Kincannon. Oh. And you've got people here.

"My kids and Ms. Irish—all people you know. Come on in."

"I can't. Uncle Al's waiting—" She gestured to the grumbling sedan in the driveway. Josh raised a hand in greeting. "I got a letter today from my first choice school. They want to interview me in person. It's hours away. Aunt Rose and Uncle Al can't take the time off work, and they have just the one car and they need it to get to work, so I don't know how I'll get there and—"

"We'll find you a ride, Fay. When is it?"

"They gave me several options. One's next Monday."

"Tell you what, come into my office tomorrow during study hall, and we'll put out heads together with Mr. Cottle and we'll figure it out. Okay?"

"Oh, yes. That's great. Thank yo—what was that?"

That was a crescendo of excited voices, followed immediately by the dinging of the microwave, then a chorus of dismay.

"I don't know. Maybe I should—"

Simultaneously, Vanessa's raised voice reached him. "It's okay, Josh. Everything's under control. Don't worry."

Josh winced. After quick good-byes, he and Livvy headed for the kitchen.

The microwave door stood wide open. Its insides looked like the special effects of a cheap slasher movie.

Red dripped or pooled on every surface, including the open door. The only exception was a pristine circle in the center of the turntable.

Topher held a clot of paper towels fast approaching saturation point under the open door. Xena knelt on the floor attacking blotches of red there. Vanessa had reached the sink with a large bowl with streaks of gory red down its sides. It appeared to have lost two-thirds of its contents.

Livvy wiggled and squirmed, conveying her desire to get down.

No way. Just what this scene needed—toddler feet.

Vanessa set the bowl in the sink. She had difficulty disengaging her hands from it. As she wiped them on a wet paper towel, she peered into the bowl. "You know, Topher, what's in the bowl looks good. We should taste it."

"Ahem," Josh said from the archway. "If this is the cooking method you all use, I need to make another run to the store for more cranberries."

"Sorry, Dad," Topher said in a small, miserable voice. "I didn't know they'd explode like that."

"None of us did," Vanessa said. "Next time we put on a cover. From that standpoint, this actually is a successful experiment because it happened in the microwave so it was contained. Imagine what it would be like if we hadn't done yours first. If we'd started cooking Xena's and mine on the stove and we had that kind of explosion."

For an instant everyone appeared caught in contemplation of the mess in the microwave expanded to fill the kitchen.

Then a giggle came from the vicinity of the floor.

Everyone looked at Xena. She covered her mouth with the hand not holding red-soaked paper towels, but another giggle escaped.

Livvy, still perched in his arms, picked it up. Then Topher. Vanessa succumbed next.

"You should have seen your face when they started going off, Vanessa," Xena said.

"Well, you said not to open the door because they'd shoot us," Topher responded to his sister.

"And that last one nearly did get you in the ear," Vanessa added.

They were all laughing as they formed another assembly line, this one to clean out the microwave, while Josh did his bit by getting himself and Livvy out of their way.

All still laughing.

FROM HER SPOT as hostess at the end of the long, well-laden Thanksgiving table, Darcie leaned forward and clinked her knife gently against her water goblet. The noise slowly subsided.

"Some people do this before they eat, but since everything smelled so wonderful, we wanted everyone to dig in first. But now, we'd like to go around the table and hear what each of us is most grateful for in the past year. Zeke—" She grinned at him. "—you first."

"You!"

Everyone laughed. No one else said it as succinctly, but others shared their thankfulness for one another—Zeke and Darcie, Jennifer and Trent, Martha and the Chief. Even Mrs. Z said she was thankful Zeke came back and found Darcie.

From the far end of the table, the kids broke the string. Ashley listed being Junior Princess for the Lilac Festival, Xena her birthday sleepover, and Topher—with a shy smile at Vanessa—being in a play.

Then it was Quince's turn, and Vanessa had a sudden recognition of his solitariness. It squeezed at her heart, but he showed no sign of anything but pleasure as he spoke.

"Everyone see that old movie, *White Christmas*? Danny Kaye says to Bing Crosby that he wants Bing to get married and have nine kids, because even if Bing spent only five minutes a day with each of them, it would give Danny forty-five minutes a day of free time. We'll, I'm also thankful that Zeke found Darcie—and that she occupies a lot more of his day than forty-five minutes, so I finally get some free time!"

Under cover of the laughter, Vanessa was aware of Josh looking at her, as his turn approached. She didn't meet his gaze.

"I'm thankful for a lot," he said slowly. "My kids, my community, my friends. And that the circle keeps growing."

That left only her to answer.

"First, I have a question for Zeke. Why did you insist I be onsite for the computer lab?"

He looked surprised. "I missed you."

All the things she'd thought it might be, she'd never thought of that.

She smiled. "Then what I'm most thankful for is that Zeke missed me."

"Here, here!" Everyone applauded. Zeke raised his glass for her to clink hers against. Only as the noise subsided did she meet Josh's eyes.

The heat there should have turned the entire room into ashes.

Under the table, he caught her hand and pressed it.

Another second and she'd stand up and drag him off to the closest bedroom, and damn the reaction.

She retrieved her hand and used it to grab the first serving dish she reached on the table, then stared at it an extra beat before she recalled what it was.

Oh, yes.

"Have more cranberry sauce," she invited Zeke. They'd brought both Topher's and Xena's efforts. Hers had been ... strange. "There's plenty."

From down the table, she heard Xena's giggle.

"CAN YOU BELIEVE this?" Darcie grumbled. "The women are all in the kitchen, cleaning. Because there's a football game on. Hey, I like football, too."

"Believe me, dear, you don't want Dutch in the kitchen when you're trying to clean up," Martha Barrett said. "You get nothing done."

"That's because the two of you are always canoodling," Darcie said.

Martha blushed and smiled, while everyone else chuckled.

"We can put the glasses in the dishwasher," Darcie started.

"Not those!" objected her mother. Mrs. Z tutted in agreement. Darcie rolled her eyes, but didn't protest.

So her mother manned the sink, while Mrs. Z separated out the hand-washables. Darcie put away food, Jennifer loaded plebian items into the dishwasher, and Vanessa dried hand-washed items.

"Anton you don't want in the kitchen, either," Mrs. Z said. "He forgets, and then—" She spread her hands and shrugged her shoulders.

Vanessa nodded. "When we were mostly eating noodles, he kept blowing up dishes and broke a microwave because he'd forget to put water in."

"Okay, so, Zeke's not allowed in the kitchen. But he could take the garbage out. And the rest of them could do this stuff." Darcie waved a towel.

"Some things it's better a woman does," said Mrs. Z. "Raising babies."

Darcie and Jennifer exchanged a look. Vanessa got the impression neither was surprised to hear this sentiment.

Instead, the response came from Martha Barrett. "Are you saying you believe the mother should stay home with her children, Rosa?"

"Yes. You see how sad it is for those babies when Melissa Kincannon goes off to have her career. When you and Anton have babies, you stop being police, yes, Darcie?"

Vanessa dropped her gaze to the pitcher she was polishing despite every last vestige of moisture being long gone.

"It was terrible for them that Melissa left. But that's not the career's fault, Mrs. Z. That's hers. People have careers—men *and* women." Darcie's voice softened. "*If* Zeke and I have babies, I'd take time off. And he'd take time off. Then we'd go back to work."

Holding a glass in her soapy hands, Martha turned from the sink and looked at her daughter, her expression unreadable.

"I think you're very wise, Darcie," Martha said. "Rosa was so fortunate to have such a good marriage. But every woman should be in a position to take care of herself and her children if she needs to."

Mother and daughter exchanged a long look before Martha returned to the sink and Darcie picked up a goblet, her back to the room as she dried it.

"Perhaps, you are right, Martha. I was most fortunate in my Mischar. When he died, I did not know what I should do. Only after the man told me of the insurance, how Mischar planned for me and for Anton, did I know. But even with this, two jobs Anton worked to pay for all his college. If I had a job, even a little, after we came to America, I could have helped Anton."

"Even without that practicality, Mrs. Z, even without what it means to know you can take care of yourself and how that gives you more—" Darcie's gaze flicked to her mother's back. "—choices, I'd still work. I love police work. It's who I am. How can it help a kid to have its mother deny who she is?"

Darcie had put into words a question Vanessa hadn't even known she had.

If she had the answer, maybe she could use it to find answers to more questions. Like whether she fit in to the Kincannon family's future. Whether she wanted to. Whether she could.

But no one responded to Darcie's question, as if they all knew it was impossible to answer.

Vanessa put down the dried pitcher and picked up a wet glass.

"What about you, Jen?" Darcie asked. "You're the only one of us who's had a kid and worked. What do you think?"

"I certainly agree with Martha about every woman being prepared to support herself and her child." Her dry tone reminded Vanessa of hearing that the ex was a deadbeat dad, leaving Jennifer and her daughter in a very difficult financial position. "I'm sure Ashley would tell you my working has been horribly hard on her. But it's been good for her, too."

"How?" The word came out of Vanessa's mouth before she could stop it.

"First, she learned the world doesn't revolve around her. Second, it's been good for her to see me standing on my own two feet. She sees me taking my abilities seriously, valuing myself and my own opinion. Those are good lessons for any kid—girl or boy."

"…AND, FINALLY, THE security code will change on an irregular schedule that Mr. Cottle will keep. Be sure to check with him for updates." Vanessa ticked off the last item on the community committee agenda, and felt anticipation well up. "All that's left is having a terrific opening next week."

As soon as she locked up, she was to call Josh to rendezvous at Mrs. Richards' empty house. With all the Thanksgiving activity yesterday they'd had no opportunity to be alone. But today, Josh's aunt was taking the kids to an outlet mall on the fringes of Chicago to join Black Friday crowds bargain-hunting Christmas shopping.

"Ms. Irish?" Fay stood beside her, while everyone else cleared out. "I wanted to thank you."

"You have thanked me."

The girl shook her head. "Not enough. I can't ever thank you enough. You've made my dreams possible. Without you I wouldn't have a chance at financial aid, and without that I can't go to college, and without a degree I can't teach. I've always wanted to teach—to come back to Drago and teach."

"You might find when you're in college that another career appeals more, and coming back after graduation isn't what you want to do."

"I know you think I should go away, and I don't want to disappoint you—"

"You are *not* disappointing me. And I'm not saying you *should* stay away, Fay, only that you might change your mind. It's good to have options." The girl looked startled at Vanessa's vehemence. Trying to put her at ease, she added. "How did you decide you want to come back here to teach?"

"I was talking with Mr. Kincannon."

Ah. "He talked you into returning to Drago after college."

Head tipped, Fay considered. "He didn't talk much, except to say what you did—that I should be open to changing my mind. But I know I want to come home to Drago."

"You're fortunate to have someone like Mr. Kincannon to talk to."

That produced a smile from the girl.

"You have someone like Mr. Kincannon to talk to, too—Mr. Kincannon."

"YOU'RE NOT THE person I was looking for." Josh slid his fingers into Vanessa's wild hair.

It was about the first thing he'd said that made any sense since she'd opened the front door of Mrs. R's house and led him to her bed more than an hour ago.

Though they'd communicated fine without sensible words.

Vanessa didn't bridle at the comment. She didn't act insulted or upset. One more thing to be thankful about her on this day after Thanksgiving.

She nodded, acknowledging his statement, sighed, then said, "I wasn't looking for anyone at all. I never thought about—Well, not for a long time. It just seemed like something that wouldn't be part of my life. Something I couldn't do."

"What on earth made you think that?"

"The Schmidts."

"They told you—"

"No. No, it wasn't like that. They were kind. And generous. They gave me far more than Starlight and Sol ever did—materially, yes, but also… Attention. Care. Concern. They said … but I couldn't. They seemed to understand."

"Probably thought they were doing you a favor by giving you *space*. When what you needed was someone to batter away at your walls."

"Like you."

She sounded so morose he couldn't help but tighten his arms around her, even as he chuckled. "Exactly like me."

"It's not funny." She pressed a fisted hand against his chest, but her tone had lightened.

"Yes, it is. Neither of us got what we we're looking for—or not looking for in your case. But maybe we both got what we deserve."

"I don't know about *that*."

Desire welled again without warning.

Well, maybe that wasn't quite accurate. How much warning did he need when he was lying naked in bed with this lush, responsive woman?

"Or better than we deserve in my case." He heard the heat in his own voice. She must have heard it, too, because she tipped her head back to look at him, wetting her lips.

That was more than enough.

"And we both got what we need." He rolled her over, covering her soft, silken curves with himself. "Oh, yes, I got what I need. Do you have what you need, Vanessa?"

She opened her legs, making a space for him. The perfect space.

"Yes."

CHAPTER NINETEEN

S TILL IN THAT boneless languor of satisfaction, she reached out for
the sheet and drew it across her torso.

Illogical she knew, yet it let her release a long breath.

From beside her, Josh spoke. "What happened, Vanessa?"

"I don't—" She didn't get out the denial. In a way she was glad.

"You do that a lot—covering yourself up. Covering your breasts."

Perhaps she wasn't as unskilled in the ways of people as she'd
thought.

Because in this moment she knew sidestepping, refusing to answer
would tear at the threads that joined them.

It would be a turning away from him. Even if she didn't mean it
that way. Even if she was simply following a lifetime habit. Even if the
idea of his turning away from her…

She pushed up to a sitting position, taking the sheet with her.

"Two weeks after I started college, a group of male students—they
must have been drinking for a long time…"

The smell seemed to come from their pores, transferring to her
skin and clothes. She had thrown out the clothes, scrubbed her skin.

He sat up abruptly. "God, Vanessa—"

"No, no, it's not what you're thinking. I wasn't raped. I was cutting
across campus from the library at night. One whistled. Then another
called out. I walked faster, but they surrounded me." She was talking
so fast she wasn't sure how he could understand. He encircled her
shoulders. "They were saying—saying things. From all around me. I
tried to keep going, to push past them, but one grabbed at my books."
Carried up, like a shield. "They fell. All over the sidewalk."

She'd had to retrieve them. She'd gone back at dawn to get them. When a jogger came by she'd nearly fainted. But she'd gathered her books and made it back to her dorm room. One had a shoeprint across the pages. Each time she'd used that book she'd seen the shoeprint.

"They grabbed at my shirt, at … me. From all around. The shirt tore. My new shirt. I tried to hold it, but they pulled it off."

"No one helped you?"

"There was no one. I don't think I screamed. I don't think I said anything."

His hands clenched, then slowly released. "How did you get away?"

"One of them grabbed at—" she hesitated, then thought how silly to avoid an ordinary word. "—my bra. The strap, trying to pull it down. I kicked him. In the testicles." Josh kissed the top of her head. "When he fell, he knocked over another one and there was a gap. I ran."

Neither of them said anything.

She felt Josh's breathing, which had become harsher and faster while she'd talked, steady and slow.

She let the memory recede a bit with each rise and fall of Josh's chest.

As the memory returned to where it had come from, she realized that the next time it came it would not have nearly the power it once had.

Josh stirred, stroking her hair.

"The truth is, Vanessa, most males are going to know a desire to touch your breasts because they're breasts. Most will have the decency to keep that desire to themselves. Some will make comments to their buddies or even to you. A few jackasses—including those fueled by alcohol, drugs, or stupidity—will try to act out that desire. They deserve worse than being kicked in the testicles."

His voice changed abruptly. "And I wish I could get my hands on every one of those assholes. I'd—" He broke off with a curse.

Josh spoke again, and something about the way he rested his cheek against the top of her head or the timbre of his voice started the shivery warmth through her. "But those guys aren't me, Vanessa. I want to touch your breasts because they're part of *you*. Because I want to touch all of you."

He shifted their positions, until she had her back against his chest and their legs stretched out.

"I feel your heart beating." He spread his fingers, one dipping under the edge of the sheet.

She forced out a breath, hoping it would relieve the urge to pull the sheet higher.

He kissed her hard and quick, the urge retreated a bit.

Sliding across her flesh, his fingers explored, until one tip brushed her nipple.

She sucked in a breath, felt the dart of shivery heat strike to her core and the rhythm of her heart pick up.

He shifted his gaze from his hand back to her face.

Without moving his hand, he leaned forward and kissed her again, this time slow and deep, taking only a second to murmur, "Amazing."

JOSH STRETCHED GRANDLY, rubbing his leg between hers, both arousing and soothing.

"I wish we could stay in bed for the whole weekend," he said. "But the kids are too old not to be suspicious and too young to leave us alone."

"I have to go back to Virginia in the morning, Josh."

His content evaporated, under the glare of something sharp, dark, familiar.

He sat up, looking at her.

"You're working Thanksgiving weekend?"

She turned away as she reached for her robe. "I know. I'd hoped… But I couldn't do it. I have to go back."

"Training for volunteers starts Monday at the computer lab."

Her voice was calm, reasonable. "Zeke-Tech's trainers are excellent. They don't need me."

"Is that what gets highest priority? Need? Then what about me?"

She blinked.

"I don't—" She'd started to say *I don't know what you mean*, then caught herself. In other circumstances he might have been tempted to smile. Not now. Because her eyes said she truly had no idea what he was getting at. "What about you?"

"I want you in my life, Vanessa. In our lives."

It came out wrong. Harsh. Not the way he meant it.

He should slow this down, not rush her. Better yet stop it all now before—

But she was already answering, her voice steady.

"I have a responsible position. Josh. It's the last week before the annual report goes to press. The Edgarizing should be set, but we have to finalize the 10K. And—"

"Right. I know—*you want to do the work. It's what's important to you. You can't let it go.*" The job. Her damned job. "I heard what you said to Zeke that day, Vanessa. But let me tell you something, you have a lot more in your life now. The way you are with Topher and Livvy. The way you level with Xena. If you'd believe in the woman behind this robe—" He flicked at the lapel. "Don't kid yourself. Drago, my kids, me—you're *part* of us now. We're part of you. And we need you. Before the computer lab opens. And after."

"Josh, I never said—"

Sharper and darker now. "No, you *never*—don't I know it." He got out of her bed. Grabbed his jeans and briefs. Yanked them on. "You never said. You never did. It was me. All me. Pushing and pushing you. To open up. To be with me."

"Yes."

He waited.

But she didn't say more.

That was all she was going to give him? Now, when he needed a hell of a lot more.

She expected him to let it end there?

The dark, sharp thing inside took the reins.

He'd be damned if he'd leave it there.

"I love you, Vanessa."

It was wrong, saying it this way. Saying it now. Being angry when he said it.

All wrong.

What was he doing?

He should shut up.

Stop.

Give her time.

She sucked in a breath, crushing the robe to her throat in clenched fists. "Don't. Josh, don't. I never learned. I can't—"

"Bull. You can. I know you—"

"No, you don't. You *don't* know. The Schmidts? They said they wanted me to be part of their family. They invited me—they keep inviting me. But I couldn't. I can't. I can't go there. I can't see their disappointment that I'm not—I can't—"

He saw her pain, but this time he couldn't console her.

"You can love. I've seen it. What I don't know is if you're willing to take the incalculable risk of admitting that you love. Or if you're still a coward, hiding out."

For an instant she balanced.

Then he saw it.

Saw it in her eyes, even before she pulled the dazzling robe fully around her, closing her off from him. Retreating inside it.

The sound he made scraped at his throat. "We're a pair. You're a coward, and I'm an idiot."

He held up his hands, turning away.

"I swore I wouldn't fall for you. Because you're right. I *don't* know you. I thought I did, but it was just me projecting the same stupid life-will-be-wonderful belief that put my kids through hell already. And I have absolutely no excuse this time around. Because I knew it. I damned well knew it. Hell, you told me flat out—if you *had* to have a relationship, Quince would be *convenient*. And God knows I'm not convenient."

He shoved his feet into his shoes. "At least I didn't make the co-lossal mistake of marrying you. Because I'm not going to set my kids up to go through that again. Not any more than I already have. They need a mother. Not a woman with a career."

And that, wouldn't you know it, was when she spoke up.

"I'm the last person for your kids, but you're wrong about that part, Josh. You're a father—a great father—and you have a career. What are you telling your daughters? That they can't have that, too?"

"After Melissa—"

"Melissa didn't leave because she couldn't pursue her career if she stayed. You told me—she said she didn't feel the way a wife and mother should. That's what made her leave, not her career."

"The end result was the same for my kids. That's all I care about."

In silence sharp and thick, he swung the door open and crossed the threshold, then turned back. She sat straight-backed on the bed, enveloped in the robe.

Their eyes didn't meet.

He said, "Since the computer lab's part of your job and the opening's Friday—"

"I'll be there. Seven o'clock."

CHAPTER TWENTY

"E IGHT-THIRTY," MALCOLM NOTED.

Every face in the computer lab's crowded main room turned to the clock—as if everyone hadn't counted out each minute for the past hour and a half—then to Josh. Probably every face in the overflow areas in the back office and the front entry did, too. But at least he couldn't see them looking at him.

"What do you think, Josh?" Malcolm added for good measure.

"Let's give her a little more time," he said once more.

"Of course." Mrs. R squinted a warning at Malcolm. "We wouldn't be having this opening if it weren't for Vanessa. And you," she added to Josh. "And your generosity, Zeke. Todd's hard work. Warren's done a lot. And—"

"A community effort," Josh interrupted before she named all of Drago.

But his heart wasn't in it.

He itched to swear, shout, break something.

As he had every minute of these interminable days since he'd left her room.

He'd expected today to be hectic. What he hadn't expected was that his duties would include assuring every soul in Drago, including his kids, that Vanessa would be at the opening.

The closest they'd come to communicating all week was cc'ing each other on messages.

As today wore away under a steady drip of "Sure hope to see Vanessa's tonight" and "She'll be coming won't she?" the gnaw in his gut dug deeper.

He kept checking email and phone messages. Half hoping, fully dreading.

Finally, he'd broken down and called her cell, getting only voice mail.

He'd tried her office eventually, too, but a recording reminded him that offices on the East Coast had closed by then.

A tug on his sleeve brought his gaze down to Topher's solemn face.

"She'd be here if she could be," his son said in a low voice.

When Topher gave up, it was time to move on.

Josh looked around, forcing a smile. "Okay, let's start. We have a computer lab to get opened here."

Murmurs of agreement rose. Malcolm, Mrs. R, and others scurried around, as if the arrangements hadn't been ready for blastoff for ninety-three minutes.

No one looked at him.

VANESSA PULLED UP to the computer lab.

Oh, God. A parking space by the door. That had to mean—

But, no. The lights were on.

Please, please, after all this, please…

Unlike the hours of *Please, get me there on time*, then later, *Please get me there before it ends*, she didn't know exactly what she'd hoped for at this point.

Until she'd flung open the door and run halfway into the lab—then she knew what her latest prayer had meant.

Please let Josh be there and let us be able to make everything okay.

A banner welcoming all to the Grand Opening hung across the back of the room. Beneath it, sat a table. The banner drooped on one side. The table was bare, the generous food she knew had certainly been there now packed away.

Josh's face, when turned from where he'd been locking up the back, told her that everything was not okay.

She closed her eyes.

All the rushing and tension and praying flushed out of her, leaving … nothing.

She hadn't fulfilled her promise. She hadn't been here when people had counted on her. The community, Mrs. Richards, Malcolm, Zeke and Darcie, Warren, Topher, Livvy, and even Xena.

Josh.

"It's over." Her statement flat-lined under the overload of the hours since she'd left a week ago.

Hours that followed days that followed weeks that all piled atop the unstable foundation of whatever this was between her and Josh.

Long days had stretched into long nights at Zeke-Tech, going over the work her staff had done, while also delegating future responsibilities, setting up new practices. Condensing into a week what could have taken months.

By this afternoon, as she'd tucked her laptop into its travel case, she'd realized the buoyancy she felt beneath the exhaustion was optimism.

Optimism. A balloon that hadn't deflated into a sigh.

Then the phone call came.

The attorney said he had questions before the annual report went to the printer—ignoring that he was supposed to have delivered it already.

It was her job to take that phone call, her job to cite to the attorney the figures that backed Zeke's CEO letter that he'd read twice before, her job to soothe him that, yes, the figures backed Zeke's use of "superb," her job to go over a "few other issues" with him.

And to not scream at the man.

At Janine's urging, she'd made the follow-up call to the printers to ensure they could deal with this delay as she drove to the airport.

Even so, she'd been cutting it close. Then there was one of those inexplicable traffic jams—no accident, no trooper giving tickets, no roadwork. Simply a slowdown that eventually opened up … but not until she was horribly late.

From the time she parked her car, she ran. To the shuttle, through the terminal, to the gate. She arrived to see her plane pulling away.

She immediately called Janine. There were frequent flights from Dulles to O'Hare, surely she could get on another quickly. Except unseasonal thunderstorms had gripped the East Coast. Flight after flight was canceled. Displaced passengers overwhelmed later flights.

Vanessa felt as if she barely breathed until the plane Janine wrangled her a seat on lifted off—two and a half hours later than her original flight. She could still make it to the opening's start—just—if everything went right.

That was when she realized she'd left her phone on the airline counter.

The pilot's voice came on, announcing O'Hare was backed up as a result of the East Coast emerging from the storm all at once. She begged the use of a fellow passenger's phone. When Josh didn't answer, she left a message.

They circled endlessly over Indiana. The pilot came again: They were landing in Detroit to refuel.

She left Josh a second message from a terminal phone.

Back in the air, the pilot's voice came once more—to the collective groans of the passengers. Except Vanessa. She was too miserable even to groan.

Another holding pattern for O'Hare.

After they landed, it took half an hour for the plane to get a gate. She borrowed another phone, left another message.

But what could she say to him that wouldn't sound like those I'll-be-a-little-late-calls he'd so hated from Melissa?

They deplaned at last, to an airport teeming with travelers frazzled by cancellations and delays. Vanessa jammed her elbow into a man trying to usurp her spot—the last spot—on a shuttle. In her rental car, heading for Drago, she had to consciously ease her foot to keep from pressing the accelerator through the floorboard.

"Yes, it's over," he said.

"Josh, something came up at Zeke-Tech. I—"

"Everything went off without a hitch," he interrupted, his voice cool and calm. "It would have helped if you'd called, so we wouldn't have held off the start in case you were coming. But once we started, it went off without a hitch."

"You didn't—" No, obviously he hadn't gotten her messages. "I'm sorry—I mean, I'm glad it came off without a hitch. I'm sorry I wasn't here."

He smiled, but not a true Josh smile.

He looked at her as if she were a stranger.

No, even when she'd been a stranger he had never looked at her this way—like he *wanted* her to be a stranger.

"We wish you could have been here, too. But we understand the demands of your life. We've always understood this was a small project Zeke added to your important duties. And we appreciate all you've done to make the computer lab happen. It makes sense that now your normal priorities will take hold. And we'll run the lab fine. Just the way we opened it tonight."

Without her.

Oh, yes, his meaning came through loud and clear.

Her failing to be at the opening, despite her promise, was not only to be expected, it wasn't important.

Because she wasn't important.

Not to the lab, not to the people involved with it, not to him.

Those things he'd said the day after Thanksgiving—about her being part of Drago, his family, him—he hadn't really believed them.

Just when she'd started to think maybe he did know her better than she knew herself.

Sometimes it sucked being able to read between the lines.

"Good. That's good."

"Yeah, it is."

She stood in front of him. Not knowing what to say, how to move. Caught in the old, familiar frozen misery.

No, not the old, familiar frozen misery. Because that was a lump of dirt compared to the mountain of this frozen misery.

"Gotta get home to the kids and relieve Mrs. Mudge," he said.

"Of course. I'm sorry to have kept you."

She concentrated on ordering her muscles to turn around, to start herself moving away from him.

SHE HAD EVERY reason to be exhausted and she was. But sleep? No.

Vanessa wrapped her robe tighter and retied the sash. She sat at the desk and opened her laptop. But she didn't turn it on.

She'd done such a good job of clearing her desk at Zeke-Tech that she had nothing pending. And this was not the mental state for starting something new.

She looked around the attic room.

This was the mental state for wrapping up something old.

She felt like the flowers in Mrs. R's garden, blighted by freeze, but without the good grace to let go of the earth until the gardener's firm hand yanked them out.

Methodically, she packed clothes she'd been leaving here. There were new items—a Drago High School sweatshirt, a pair of jeans, a flannel shirt—yet she had room to spare, because she'd gradually returned her business clothes to Virginia. The suitcase was filled, her clothes laid out for the next day.

But items remained. She quietly went down the stairs, relieved all over again that Mrs. Richards had been asleep when she came in.

In the basement, she found what she needed, and returned with a cardboard box.

She didn't let her mind stray from her task: How to pack the program from Topher's play so it wouldn't crease, the finger-painted hand-print from Livvy so it wasn't crumpled, three bright leaves so they didn't crumble.

And then it was done. Nothing left to pack. Nothing left to do.

A tap on the door barely registered before it swung open and Mrs. Richards entered with a tray holding two mugs.

"I made cocoa." Without awaiting an invitation, she put the tray on the desk, and handed a mug to Vanessa. Gesturing to the bed, she ordered. "Sit down now and drink."

Vanessa didn't have the energy to argue. The warmth of the liquid spread across a physical chill she hadn't been aware of until that moment.

"It was a good event," Mrs. Richards finally said. "We were real sorry you had to miss it."

Vanessa's head came up slowly.

Yes, that was sympathy and understanding in the woman's face.

"I am, too." She swallowed more cocoa. Wishing… But wishing accomplished nothing. "I'm leaving in the morning, Mrs. Richards. Of course, I'll pay for the month—"

Her landlady t'ched, dismissing that topic. She scanned the cleared surfaces of the furniture.

Vanessa's gaze followed. The room had returned to how it appeared when she'd arrived. As if she'd never been here.

Just the way Drago would. Except for the computer lab, she supposed. Although that could have been accomplished by any of a hundred people at Zeke-Tech.

Livvy, Topher, and Xena might have benefited in small ways from knowing her. But they were good, smart kids with a great father—they would turn out fine whether they'd ever known her or not.

And Josh?

He would have been better off if he'd never met her.

She had never truly belonged—not in his community, not in his family, and not in his heart.

"You're not leaving anything behind?" Mrs. Richards asked.

Sorrow came so sharp that Vanessa wanted to double over with it.

"No, I'm not leaving anything behind."

JOSH STOPPED ABRUPTLY beside the Lundgrens' garage, staring through the dreary December dawn.

He'd been walking fast enough not to feel the cold. Now it burst through the thin jacket he'd grabbed when this impulse took over.

The kids were up. He'd called Mrs. Mudge and asked her to keep an eye on them for an hour, tops.

Then he'd headed out, not acknowledging where he was going. Perhaps afraid his head would talk his heart out of it.

He'd wrestled with his own words all night long.

We've always understood this was a small project Zeke added to your important duties.

The hell he had.

It makes sense that now your normal priorities will take hold.

No way.

Why hadn't he told her he'd felt gut-punched every second from seven o'clock until she walked in at seven minutes after eleven?

Was still feeling gut-punched every second.

If something prevented her from coming, why hadn't she told him? Why hadn't she insisted that the opening was important to her, that *she* was important to them?

Because she didn't believe any of that, his head had said.

Because he hadn't given her an opportunity to say it, his heart had said.

Now, turning the corner beside Lundgren's garage, he had his answer.

Down the block, lights were on at Mrs. R's against a morning too weak to defeat the night. The widow, a winter jacket over her robe, used her backside to hold the door open as Vanessa exited with a suitcase and a box.

She'd finished her job—her damned job—and she was leaving.

She made another trip, putting her purse and a tote in the front seat.

She paused, then went back to hug the older woman. He could tell from here that Mrs. R was crying. Vanessa wasn't.

She waved once, then drove away.

Out of town.

Out of his life.

CHAPTER TWENTY-ONE

A WEEK.
A week from hell.

Josh had hoped that getting to the weekend would make things better. Not so much.

Errands had been a nightmare, with all three kids cranky and him short-tempered. In the afternoon, he'd come in from shoveling and found them racing through the house screeching at the top of their lungs. He'd outdone them all.

They'd had dinner with his aunt, but Xena had been silent, Topher hadn't eaten, and Livvy was inclined to tears whenever he looked at her.

He'd sent them all to bed as soon as they got home.

He listened a moment to the silence, then walked to the bottom of the stairs. Xena was sitting at the top, chin cupped in her palms.

"Xena—"

"Livvy misses Vanessa. So does Topher."

The words stabbed through his mood. She was putting her own feelings on to her siblings, though the others *did* miss Vanessa.

He climbed partway up, and sat sideways on the stair below her feet.

Xena said, "Livvy's not old enough to have experience with when people go away. Like when the Culbertsons moved to California. Or when Grandpa Mercer went to heaven."

"Or when your mom left?"

She shrugged. "Anyway, Livvy's sad. That's why she's so cranky."

"I know. Livvy misses having Vanessa brush her hair, put her to bed."

Xena gave him a scornful look. "Nah. Mrs. Mudge is much better at that sort of stuff, all the stuff they say women should do. But that isn't the point. Livvy misses Vanessa for Vanessa."

Threads of thought came together, tangled, and exploded into a lightning bolt of realization that left him shaken.

By almost anyone's standards, Melissa had flunked as a mother.

Except to her kids, who weren't handing out grades.

Vanessa had tried to tell him that. Jennifer, too.

The kids loved Melissa—and missed her—for the person she was, not the mother she wasn't.

And they felt the same way about Vanessa.

"Xena, it's time to go to bed, but tomorrow, we're going to talk. All of us."

VANESSA STARED AT the "total" box in the cell where the total went.

How could it have produced a fourth answer in four tries? It made no sense.

She took off her glasses and rubbed her eyes with forefinger and thumb. There went whatever makeup was left from a day's worth of meetings.

Quince had tried to persuade her to join him and three Wall Street executives for dinner.

"C'mon, you've been working non-stop. You deserve a great dinner, and where better than here in New York? We can enjoy the decorations. Get a little Christmas spirit—just over a week to go, you know."

She'd opted for a room service salad, now wilted on the tray.

She cleared the screen and started again.

Her cell, recovered from the airline lost-and-found, rang.

Quince didn't give up.

He'd been after her to take a break even before they came up here to New York, and for the three days of this trip he'd been like a cruise director thwarted by a passenger who wanted to be left in peace.

She answered with "What?"

"Vanessa?"

Her heart swooped, plummeted, rose, then fluttered somewhere in the middle of her throat, all in the space of a breath.

"It's Josh," his voice added.

Oh, she knew. She knew.

"Yes. How are you, Josh?"

"I thought you'd be interested—" He bit it off and started again without answering how he was. "I owe you an apology. I heard the messages you left the day of the opening. I was so busy I skipped them then because I didn't recognize the numbers. I'm sorry. And I wanted to tell you, I've brought the kids to see their mother."

Now her brain was doing the loop-de-loops her heart had gone through.

Their mother? But she was in—

"We got into New York this morning. We're staying for the weekend."

"You're in New York."

"Yeah, I know. I'm surprised, too."

She would tell him she was here.

She could see him, the kids.

They might be blocks apart, certainly no more than a few miles because Melissa lived in Manhattan.

Melissa. The mother they'd come to see.

Not her. They were in the same place only because of happenstance.

"…And tomorrow night we're going skating at Rockefeller Center. I have a feeling it'll be more popular than the museums Melissa had us at today."

But happenstance still meant she could get in a cab and go to him…

"The most amazing thing happened about an hour after we got here, Vanessa. Livvy talked."

She smiled at the phone. "She did?"

"Yeah. Real words."

"That's great."

"Yeah, and it was the simplest thing. Livvy started chattering, and Melissa stopped her and said, 'Use your words,' which we used to tell Livvy so she'd tell us what was wrong instead of crying. Livvy kept on going. Melissa said, 'No, Livvy. Words like everyone else uses.' Livvy looked at her for about a minute, then said, 'Okay.' And that was it. She's been talking like any other kid ever since. Best we can figure is, Livvy interpreted 'use your words' as meaning words she made up, and she sort of got stuck doing that."

He'd been so terribly worried, and Melissa had fixed it.

"I'm glad, Josh. It sounds like a wonderful trip. For all of you."

"It was the right thing to do. You were right about that. You were right about a lot of things. And I … I shouldn't have pretended I didn't expect you to make the opening. I did. I could have tried your phone more. But I … I guess I was afraid." He made a sound that conveyed both amusement and self-derision. "Didn't want to risk hearing you tell me the truth."

"I was afraid, too. Afraid you'd think I was feeding you excuses. I did try to get there," she said softly.

"I know you did." He made that sound again. "We're a pair, huh?"

We're a pair. You're a coward, and I'm an idiot.

That's what he'd said that last day in her room.

When she gave no answer now, he added, "I was also wrong to pretend your being there—or not being there—didn't mean anything. It did. It meant a lot."

He waited.

She could produce no words.

XENA GIGGLED AS her mother pulled her across the ice. It was the most little-girl sound Josh had heard from his daughter in a long time.

Vanessa might have given his heart a good stomping, but about his kids she'd been right all the way down the line.

He suppressed a sigh, acknowledging now that he'd hoped last night's phone call would go very differently.

Especially the ending.

Yup, fool that he was, he'd stuck his neck—and his heart—out again, hoping she'd say she wanted to see him, wanted to come back to Drago or wanted him to come to Virginia or meet anywhere in the middle.

Instead, she had pulled back into silence, where he couldn't reach her.

Xena laughed, joined by Livvy's high-pitched pleasure.

He closed his eyes an instant, absorbing the mingled pleasure at that sound and pain at knowing he'd contributed to not hearing it.

Oh, yeah, the initial fault and maybe even the largest fault, if fault could be carved up like a pie, belonged to Melissa. But he was at fault for relying too much on Xena, and for denying all three kids contact with their mother for the weeks since Melissa first called.

And his fault was all he could remedy.

He looked around and saw Topher standing solid and still on his skates, some distance away from his sisters and mother. Josh glided over to him.

"Hey, there. Don't you want to join in?"

His son looked up, eyes solemn through slightly fogged glasses. "Not yet."

"Something wrong, Topher?"

He shook his head. "I want to watch a while."

Josh looked at his son, watching his mother and sisters with his solemn, contained attention.

The hairs at the back of his neck came to attention, and he heard his own voice, and Vanessa's.

You rush him. Give him time.

Time? How much time? How much more time?

More is counting it by your system. Give him his own time. He has his own way of processing—information and emotions. Not everybody does it the same way.

Being inside himself doesn't mean he wants to get away from you, just that he needs that time with himself.

He heard her so clearly and those hairs at the back of his neck were so persistent that he couldn't stop himself from looking around, examining nearby skaters to see if...

No, of course not.

But that didn't change the trueness, the wisdom, of her words. She had understood his son as he never had.

Give him time, she'd said. And the more he had, the better things had gone.

Being inside himself doesn't mean he wants to get away from you, just that he needs that time with himself.

His feet shifted, translating into a sawing motion that kept him in place as he grasped the implications.

She'd understood because she needed the same thing.

Maybe her leaving Drago hadn't been the complete abandonment it had felt like.

Maybe her silence on the phone when he'd hoped she would say she wanted to see him, wanted to try to work things out hadn't been the rejection it had felt like.

Maybe she was still processing.

Maybe, if he gave her time to stand and watch and consider, eventually she'd join in.

But he had to find a way to let her know he still stood beside her, waiting, hoping.

"Dad? Dad!"

"Yeah, Topher?"

"I think I can skate backwards."

He looked at his son and said, "I know you can."

SHE WELCOMED THE cold. It explained away the stinging in her eyes. It allowed the small comfort of huddling deep into her coat, her arms wrapped around herself.

Vanessa watched the four people who had become so dear to her form a complete unit with someone she didn't know at all.

Someone who had left them. Who had deserted them. Who had walked away when they needed her. Yet here they were now, laughing with her and loving her.

At least Xena and Livvy were. Josh and Topher stood side by side a little distance away. She saw Josh say something to the boy. Saw the brief response. Then another exchange. Josh opened his mouth, then closed it.

That's right, Josh. Stay beside him, but don't crowd him. Let him work this through himself.

He turned slowly, looking around, as if searching the surroundings.

Topher said something to his father. When the boy moved backward, Josh turned to follow the motion, a grin lighting his face.

From this distance she couldn't see details of how it spread his generous mouth, of how it deepened the lines by his eyes. But she could remember.

Topher, followed by Josh, skated to the female Kincannons. With laughter all around, they formed a line, Josh and Melissa on either end, Xena next to Josh, Topher next to Melissa and Livvy in the middle, hands clasped all down the line as they moved forward.

Watching, Vanessa understood Josh's earlier stance so much better.

As an abstraction she'd understood the kids' need to see their mother. But now, seeing them with the woman who had deserted them, accepting her, enjoying her … it made Vanessa want to run down and scoop them up, protect them from any potential hurt.

Livvy's feet kept going out from under her, being held up by her siblings on either side, who in turn were steadied by their parents. With the center of the line flagging, it soon curved, the adults coming closer and closer. If they clasped hands it would be a circle. A closed circle.

Someone who had left them. Who had deserted them. Who had walked away when they needed her.

Oh, God. She'd done that, too.

She'd walked away from them. The four people she loved.

Loved.

She loved Josh and his kids.

Emotion seemed too small a word for what she felt.

Emotion came and went, shrieking to heights then burning away to nothing. What she felt was a certainty. As immutable as three being three.

How had this happened?

She didn't know.

What would she do with this fact that would never budge from her life?

She had no clue.

Melissa Kincannon held a hand out to Josh.

CHAPTER TWENTY-TWO

S NOW MELTING FROM road salt seeped between the seams of expensive boots and iced her feet. Vanessa didn't move.

She'd come here to the Pennsylvania countryside with no plan, no intention. She'd just come.

Guided by a homing instinct she hadn't known she possessed, she'd threaded the car she'd rented in New York through snowbanks to a small motel. Fell into bed and woke only when her body demanded food, water, and a bathroom—not in that order.

She'd sat on the edge of the bed, noting the covers looked as if she hadn't moved once. Then she went to the window and drew back the curtain. Sunlight surged across the west-facing glass like a forest fire.

She'd slept until the middle of the afternoon.

Shock had galvanized her sufficiently to throw on clothes and venture to a fast-food strip. Then she'd driven to this particular spot on a county road that wound up the mountain's side, pulled over, got out, and looked down past bare-limbed trees.

Mounds of snow were all that indicated the one-time formation of the compound. Only two structures were still recognizable as buildings, and their bones appeared as weathered and skeletal as the denuded trees around them.

Maybe that's what you had to do with the past. Wait until the leaves had fallen, until you could see the skeleton beneath the masking greenery.

Or maybe other people recognized the structure right away. Maybe they weren't distracted by fear.

Because wasn't that what it came down to—fear?

So the question became: How to stop being afraid?

Logic said it wasn't a single, giant event, but an ongoing process. Steps steadily added to create a stack so high that standing atop it you could see over the wall of fear. But where did you find that first layer?

How did you start stopping being afraid?

Some people say you should do whatever's hardest for you to do.

Her own voice echoed in her head.

Because it makes you grow ... Stretches the muscles you don't use very much ... It's about becoming a stronger person. Not physically stronger, but more able to do things. Out in the world.

The sun had dropped below the tree line, sweeping gaunt shadows across the snow. A shiver that turned into a shudder rattled through her.

Then came Topher's voice, curious and nonjudgmental.

Do you do it?

VANESSA'S KNOCK WAS firm. But in the instant of hearing the first squeak of the door opening, she nearly bolted.

The woman was as white-haired as Topher's Albert Einstein guise. She was just as thin and perhaps even shorter than Vanessa remembered. And her eyes were as warm and brown as melted chocolate.

They were also wide open and staring.

"Mrs. Schmidt? It's—I'm Vanessa Irish. You and your husband—Mr. Schmidt—" As if the woman didn't know who her husband was. God! She was making a mess of this. Stumbling over herself. Words blurting out. And they wouldn't stop. "—were very kind to me a number of years ago. I know I haven't kept in touch, and I should have called before I came to make sure this was a convenient time. Please just tell me—I'll come back another time, if that's okay with you. Any time you say. Unless you don't want to—I'd understand, because I never—but I did appreciate it. What you did. Everything you did. Both of you. So much. So very much. I wanted to tell you that. I know it's late. I should have said it years ago. I'm not very good at—"

Then the door was full open and the tiny woman was tumbling out as she shouted in a robust voice totally unexpected in that small body, "Bert! Bert! Come quick!"

"Mrs. Schmidt, are you okay? If you want me to leave—"

"Leave? No, no! Oh, Vanessa, no!" She flung her arms around Vanessa.

"What the dickens is the matter, Margaret?" came the male voice she hadn't known she remembered so perfectly. For the first time she realized it was similar to Josh's voice—a bedrock of underlying calm, tinged with ready amusement. "If you didn't go naming the raccoons they wouldn't keep—"

Then he was there, on the other side of the storm door that had slapped closed.

The glass shadowed his expression. She thought … but she couldn't be sure.

"I should have come sooner." Her voice sounded nothing like herself. She could barely make out the words even as she spoke them.

The door swung open, and she was sure.

"Vanessa." And now that remembered voice had the tremble of tears in it. "Dear girl. Dear, dear girl."

He spread his arms wide to wrap them around his wife and Vanessa.

"Oh, Bert!" Muffled against Vanessa's coat, Margaret Schmidt's voice still sounded strong. "Our girl. She's come home."

Vanessa gulped in a shuddering breath, and put her arms around both of them.

"…AND THERE'S THIS envelope for you marked private," Janine said, concluding her litany of updates that had started the moment Vanessa had stumbled into her office at four-thirty Tuesday, some seventy hours since she'd left New York.

She'd spent most of those hours with the Schmidts.

As long as she lived, she would never forget Margaret Schmidt's face when she'd opened the door.

Nor would she forget these past days. Margaret and Bert Schmidt loved her. They *loved* her.

As a girl, she had taken their help, then repaid them every dollar, as if they'd given her a bank loan.

But she had not repaid them a cent of what really mattered. Not until the day before yesterday.

Her words to Fay echoed in her mind. *You have to accept help. And keep accepting it. Until you can pay it back.*

She had to tell the girl she'd been wrong. So wrong.

You had to accept help and keep accepting it, and you could never pay it back, when it came wrapped in love. All you could do was love back.

Vanessa eyed the express carrier's envelope with a lump in one corner. The typewritten form had a return address of the Drago computer lab.

"I can stay to draft answers," Janine said, "but if you don't object I'll wait to finalize them in the morning."

"We'll catch up tomorrow. Go home now."

Janine looked at the stacks of business correspondence, then the envelope with the bold printed "Private" and she left.

As soon as the door closed, Vanessa ripped open the envelope.

A box the size of a Rubik's Cube wrapped in sparkly gold paper with a white ribbon tumbled out. There was no letter, only the box.

It could be from anyone associated with the computer lab. Any of them.

She tugged at the ribbon, slid her thumbnail under one taped flap and pried it loose, refusing to let her hand shake.

The paper revealed a white box. She lifted the lid and there, resting atop the tissue paper that masked the other contents was a note. A half sheet, with handwriting that confirmed the familiarity of the "personal" on the envelope.

Her heart banged at her ribcage, apparently with every intention of escaping.

Dear Vanessa, These carry a message—

He meant the contents. She lifted the tissue paper. Two sturdy keys blinked dully up at her. One was stamped with the name of the security company used for the computer lab. The other with a well-known lock manufacturer. She looked beneath them. Nothing else. She went back to the note.

Dear Vanessa, These carry a message that I want to be absolutely clear. One is the key to the computer lab, which you created. The other is a key to Drago—at least the part of Drago I hope matters most to you. You need to know you can open these doors any time you want. Beyond that, we can figure out anything. Together. Because I do know you. And love you. Josh.

Vanessa felt the weight of the keys in her right palm, the texture of the paper in her left and all that had gone into both of them.

She bolted from her chair.

"Janine! Janine! I take it back. You can't leave. But I promise you the longest Christmas break you've ever had."

"JOSH?" MRS. RICHARDS' voice trembled. "We need you at the computer lab. It's an emergency."

The night of December twenty-third was not the time for an emergency.

He had a wrapping marathon tonight. Tomorrow's schedule was packed right up until Christmas Eve services. He'd be wrapping, along with stuffing stockings, and putting together Livvy's tricycle in the short night between when the kids settled down Christmas Eve and when they woke well before dawn.

And none of it kept him from knowing that Vanessa hadn't responded.

"What's wrong?" But he already had out his list of emergency sitters.

"You have to get here. You just have to!" She hung up.

INSIDE THE UNLOCKED front door, the computer lab was brightly lit, but with no sign of activity.

"Mrs. R?"

Her voice came faintly from the back. Pulling his phone out, he ran, envisioning broken hips, strokes, heart attacks. The office door crashed open.

"Mrs. Richards—are you okay?"

She sat primly at the lone computer desk back here. Her hands suspended over the keyboard as she peered around the chair back at him. "I'm fine, dear. How are you?"

She looked fine. She sounded fine.

"What's the emergency?"

"Just a moment, dear. Let me finish this email. I did tell you—" Her fingers tapped away between words. "—that I've established a loop with correspondents around the world, didn't I?"

"Yes. But the emergen—"

"Wonderful people. I know one must be cautious, as our fine instructors said. I most certainly would not give out personal information. But it's amazing the connections you make, how clearly personalities—"

"If you don't tell me the emergency, I'm leaving, Mrs. R."

She startled up, "Oh, no! Don't, Josh." She looked at the wall clock. "If you could be patient a little longer."

"Patient for what?"

She fluttered her hands.

"Is there an emergency?" Beneath his well-honed tell-me-the-truth stare, she hesitated "Then I'm going home to my kids."

He pivoted. She caught up in the open doorway to the main room. Pretty good for a woman who needed a walker at times. She clung to his arm.

"Wait, Josh. Don't go. Not yet. Sometimes you have to wait a little longer than you'd like, but if you don't you might regret it for the rest of your life."

"Wait for what?"

The front door opened, the blast of frigid air reaching him all the way at this end of the room. Unless something else made his eyes sting and his lungs burn.

Vanessa.

She'd rushed in, made the turn into the central aisle, then saw him and stopped abruptly, one hand trailing a scarf she'd yanked off.

"Not *what*. *Whom*. Waiting for *whom*," Mrs. R murmured. "Well, I need to get home. I'll let myself out the rear door."

She closed the door at his back, nudging him forward.

The length of the main room separated them, the space filled with a silence charged with the static between them. Static that crackled with the heat between them, but that could so easily spark into nothing but pain.

"Josh. I ... I don't—" Panic flared in her eyes.

"Were you behind this, Vanessa? Mrs. R claiming an emergency?" His chest ached with the need for answers to other questions.

"I didn't say emergency, but I did ask her to get you here. I didn't want to call the house. Or go there. Because of the kids. In case—" Her voice caught. He took two involuntary steps toward her. "—this went badly."

"This?"

She sucked in a breath. "I had to talk to you. To tell you... My career's important to me. But I'm not Melissa—"

"I know that, and I'm sorry. That stuff the day after Thanksgiving, I think I was piling everything that Melissa did on to you and that wasn't fair. When you promised, you did your damnedest to keep it. I should have remembered that. And you were right—it wasn't the career, it was Melissa."

"Yes. But I made changes, too, Josh. Zeke wanted me to all along, and it's going to work. I've delegated more and, well, I'm learning I don't have to feel guilty about not working when the work's not there.

And … I went back. To Pennsylvania," she said in a rush. "I saw the commune—what's left. There was something about seeing the place… I think I've let it go. Mostly, anyway."

"That's—"

"Wait." She held off his advance with a gesture. "There's more. I went to see the Schmidts. They … they cried. They cried and hugged me and laughed and said how proud of me they are. They have a whole scrapbook about me, about Zeke-Tech. They insisted I stay with them in my old room. That's what they call it—Vanessa's room. And it was really good. Even though I realize now how I hurt them by staying away. But still, they care about me. They really care about me. And—" She raised her chin, as if daring him—or more likely herself—to argue with what she was about to say. "—I care about them."

"I'm glad. Glad you know that and glad you made that trip, Vanessa."

She took a step forward, still leaving half the room between them.

"I can't claim the credit. I just ended up there. I didn't even know that's where I was heading when I left New York."

"New York?" When was she in New York?

"Yes. I was there for business when you called me. I was … miserable. Especially when I watched you all skating at Rockefeller Center."

His head came up, "You were there. You didn't—"

"Watching all of you with her. With Melissa, who'd walked away. I knew I didn't want to do that—leave you all like that. I wanted to be with you, but my work… I can't give that up. I started driving out of the city, but I didn't know where, and then I found myself—"

"In Pennsylvania." He halved the distance between them. Who knew a woman famed for bluntness could inflict such a tortuous explanation on a man trying to read the bottom line? "If you want to be with us, that's what counts. We need you as you are. I know how much a part of you your work is. And you were right, I wouldn't like anyone telling my girls to give up what was important to them. I'll meet you more than halfway, if you'll consider it. So we can be together."

She frowned, and he nearly came to his knees.

"But that's what I'm trying to tell you, Josh. I do want to be with you—all of you. And I know we can work out something—with my job, with your job, with having the kids raised here—because *I'll* go more than halfway."

He slid his hands into her hair, scattering pins, and kissed her and kissed her.

"I have one question. Even if you bypassed the house because of the kids, why not use the key here. Why involve Mrs. R?"

"You sent me the key, but not the new security code after the mid-month change. So I called Mrs. Richards."

"But she—" He broke off, laughing. "She knew we hadn't changed it. She was probably afraid to tell you we're using the same code."

"Josh," she admonished, "you have to change—"

"The only thing I have to do is this."

He kissed her.

His jacket fell to the floor under her questing hands. It seemed like such a good idea, he gave her coat the same treatment.

He had just enough brain cells left to maneuver her toward the back, through the doorway, then against the wall beside the door, which he closed with one foot.

The door slamming broke her concentration. Not a state of affairs he liked, since her concentration had been focused on unbuttoning his shirt.

"Wait, Josh. If we're both going more than halfway—" She smiled, the heat in her eyes intensifying. "—do you realize what will happen?"

"Oh, yeah. We'll merge in the middle. Wonderful, hot merging."

They kissed again. Long and deep.

Then they got busy at extremely satisfying merging.

Thank you for reading Josh and Vanessa's story!

The expansion of Zeke-Tech into its founder's hometown begins to herald a resurgence in Drago. Which is good and bad news for the recently widowed Anne, whose family farm is far down the tech boom food chain.

When Zeke-Tech exec Quince winds up at Hooper Farm, is the fox now in henhouse? Or do Anne and Quince see a warm front coming on?

Warm Front

Seasons in a Small Town—Winter

Darcie, Jennifer, Zeke, Josh, Quince and friends ask if you'll help spread the word about them and the Seasons in the Small Town series. You have the power to do that in two quick ways:

Recommend the book and the series to your friends and/or the whole wide world on social media. Shouting from rooftops is particularly appreciated.

Review the book. Take a few minutes to write an honest review and it can make a huge difference. As you likely know, it's the single best way for your fellow readers to find books they'll enjoy, too.

To me—as an author and a reader—the goal is always to find a good author-reader match. By sharing your reading experience through recommendations and reviews, you become a vital matchmaker. ☺

For news about upcoming books, as well as other titles and news, join Patricia McLinn's Readers List and receive her twice-monthly free newsletter.
www.patriciamclinn.com/readers-list

The Seasons in a Small Town Series

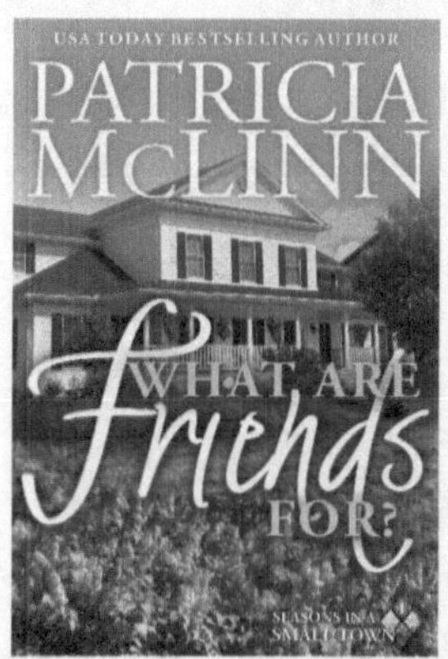

What Are Friends For? (Spring)

Billionaire tech guru Zeke the Geek reluctantly returns to his Illinois hometown as a favor to beauty queen Jennifer and Darcie—the only girl who "got" him.

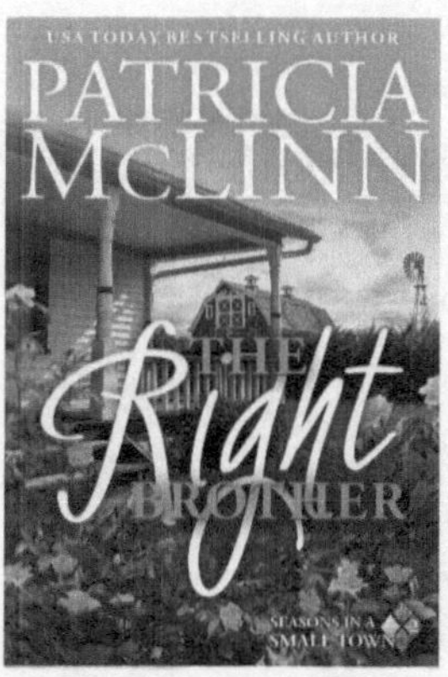

The Right Brother (Summer)

Pretty, popular Jennifer had it made—until her ex-husband left her deep in debt with a child to raise. Enter Trent, who just might right his brother's wrongs.

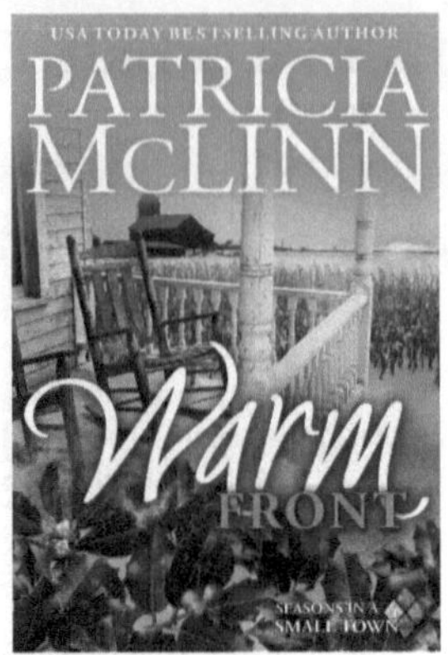

Warm Front (Winter)

Can Annie save not only the farm she loves, but also herself … and
Quince, the new tech executive in town?

What people are saying about the
SEASONS IN A SMALL TOWN series

"You laugh, you angst, you maybe shed a couple tears or two, and at
the end of it you move immediately onto the next book because—
unlike teenage Zeke—you don't want to get away, all you want to do is
go back."

"The town of Drago has insinuated itself into my heart and I can only
hope there is another installment with this small town as its setting."

"Strong characters with enough faults to make them human and real"
yet "The other characters in Drago all add to the story rather than
taking attention from the main action."

"McLinn delivers a fun, engaging, and emotionally complicated
romance."

"Poignant, heart-warming" ... "Funny and heart-wrenching at the same time"... Passionate and sensual without being distasteful or vulgar."

The Right Brother "is excellent in looking at [being female in a world run by men] from both a young teen's actions and her single-parent mom trying to help her daughter not make the same mistakes she had. The romance between the two main characters gradually builds in spite of family problems, outside pressures, and financial decisions. This was a thought-provoking book as well as a good story."

Also by Patricia McLinn

Marry Me Series

Wedding of the Century

The Unexpected Wedding Guest

A Most Unlikely Wedding

Baby Blues and Wedding Bells

The Wedding Series

Prelude to a Wedding

Wedding Party

Grady's Wedding

The Runaway Bride

The Christmas Princess

Hoops (prequel to The Surprise Princess)

The Surprise Princess

Not a Family Man (prequel to The Forgotten Prince)

The Forgotten Prince

Wyoming Wildflowers Series

Bardville, Wyoming Series

A Place Called Home series

Explore a complete list of all Patricia's books
patriciamclinn.com/patricias-books

Or get a printable booklist
patriciamclinn.com/patricias-books/printable-booklist

Patricia's eBookstore (buy digital books online directly from Patricia)
patriciamclinn.com/patricias-books/ebookstore

About the Author

USA Today bestselling author Patricia McLinn spent more than 20 years as an editor at the Washington Post after stints as a sports writer (Rockford, Ill.) and assistant sports editor (Charlotte, N.C.). She received BA and MSJ degrees from Northwestern University.

McLinn is the author of more than 50 published novels, which are cited by readers and reviewers for wit and vivid characterization. Her books include mysteries, romantic suspense, contemporary romance, historical romance and women's fiction. They have topped bestseller lists and won numerous awards.

She has spoken about writing from Melbourne, Australia, to Washington, D.C., including being a guest speaker at the Smithsonian Institution.

Now living in northern Kentucky, McLinn loves to hear from readers through her website, Facebook and Twitter.

Visit with Patricia:

Website: patriciamclinn.com

Facebook: facebook.com/PatriciaMcLinn

Twitter: @PatriciaMcLinn

Pinterest: pinterest.com/patriciamclinn

Instagram: instagram.com/patriciamclinnauthor

ISBN: 978-1-944126-54-4

www.ingramcontent.com/pod-product-compliance
Lightning Source LLC
Chambersburg PA
CBHW050842190726
48286CB00007B/2193